Praise for Suzy

'Layers of intrigue an
brilliant sting in the
Mel Sherratt, author of *Liar Liar*

'Just brilliant! Ridiculously addictive (I DID NOT
put it down) and chock full of twists and turns'
Lisa Hall, author of *The Perfect Couple*

'Suzy K Quinn is a born storyteller'
Erin Kelly, author of *He Said/She Said*

'OMG! What a book! Brilliantly written
and utterly chilling! Just wow!'
Darren O'Sullivan, author of *Our Little Secret*

'Creepy and addictive with a genuine shocker of a twist!'
Roz Watkins, author of *The Devil's Dice*

'A twist so unexpected I had to turn back to the
beginning to see what clues I'd missed! I thought I'd
spotted the magician's sleight of hand, and all the time
I was looking in the wrong direction. Bravo, Suzy K!'
Ruth Dugdall, author of *My Sister and Other Liars*

'A twisty and menacing look at modern
families. Fantastic; I loved it!'
Ali Knight, author of *Before I Find You*

'Deliciously dark; had me gripped from the get-go'
Rebecca Tinnelly, author of *Never Go There*

A note from your author

I still can't believe so many people read my books.
Each and every day I am grateful for you, dear readers.
Thank you so much.
If you want to ask me any questions about the books,
or chat about anything at all, get in touch:

Email: suzykquinn@devoted-ebooks.com
Facebook.com/suzykquinn (You can
friend request me. I like friends.)
Twitter: @suzykquinn
Website: suzykquinn.com

Happy reading,

Suzy xxx

Also by Suzy K Quinn
Don't Tell Teacher

Not My Daughter

Suzy K Quinn

ONE PLACE. MANY STORIES

HQ
An imprint of HarperCollins*Publishers* Ltd
1 London Bridge Street
London SE1 9GF

This paperback edition 2021

21 22 LSC 10 9 8 7 6 5 4 3 2 1
First published in Great Britain by
HQ, an imprint of HarperCollins*Publishers* Ltd 2020

ISBN: 978-0-00-844495-2

This book is set in 10.7/16 pt. Sabon

Printed and bound in the United States of America
by LSC Communications

This book is dedicated to my twin sis, CS Quinn – an amazing author and fantastic human being.

Lorna – Once upon a time …

There was once a woman who had long in vain wished for a child.

— RAPUNZEL

'Lorna Miller?'

I want to stand up, but I can't move.

My sister Dee gives my shoulder an urgent shake.

'Come on, Lorna,' she hisses. 'You're here now. Too late to back out.'

'Ms Miller?' The registrar calls again, looking over the room of couples and their new-born bundles. It's very beige in here. I suppose people don't want too many stimulating colours when they're registering births. It might wake the babies.

My bony legs, bare in denim cut-offs, stick to the fake leather seating. Like they're glued.

It's warm today. Warmer, I'm told, than usual for the UK this time of year. And it's spring here. A time of new beginnings.

Dee loses her patience. 'Miller,' she says, standing. 'Lorna Miller. That's us.'

'You're Lorna Miller?' the registrar asks.

'No,' says Dee, placing a hand on my shaking shoulder. 'She is. I'm her sister.'

Everything feels weird and slow. I'm under warm water and all I can feel is baby Reign's warmth against my chest and the weight of Dee's chubby hand.

Dee's voice becomes urgent. 'Come on, Lorna.' She reaches to take the baby.

'NO.' My arms lock in one tight muscle and the whole room widens its eyes. 'Just … give me a second.'

In one swift 'pulling off a Band-Aid' movement I get to my feet.

The registrar smiles. 'It's okay. Registering a birth isn't an interrogation. Just a bit of form-filling.'

Dee puts an iron-bar arm around my shoulder. I feel like I'm on a rollercoaster – the part where the ride starts and you can't get off.

The registrar leads us into his office. There is a UNISON mug on his desk and a half-eaten Trio bar beside it. Two segments left. Trio bars are a peculiarly British sort of candy; too teeny-tiny to ever be popular in the States. I feel homesick, suddenly, for giant Charleston Chew bars.

'The father couldn't be here today?' the registrar asks. 'Or …'

'There's no father,' says Dee.

My hands make fists around the baby.

There are chairs either side of the desk – sort of like a police interview room. The window overlooks a half-empty parking lot and a green fir tree.

I drop into the chair, feeling baby Reign against my chest, our heartbeats finding each other – hers like a fluttering leaf, mine like a tribal drum.

'So you have your forms with you?' the registrar asks.

'Here.' Dee shoves our envelope to the registrar like it's a biting animal. Her hand drops on my shoulder and I feel she's shaking too.

The registrar opens the folder and flicks through. He makes a clucking sound. 'You've cut this very fine. If you'd left it any later ...'

I nod, but my throat is too tight to reply.

Then the corners of the registrar's mouth drop down. 'You're only seventeen. You have some support here, do you? Your mother?'

'She's in the States,' I say. 'And she's not much of a support wherever she is.'

Dee manages something like a laugh, but her hand is still tight on my shoulder.

There is a pause, then the registrar says, 'You had a home birth?'

I nod, my voice leaving me again.

He squints at the form. 'And your sister ...'

'She ... uh ... witnessed the birth.'

'Yes,' says Dee.

'It was just the two of you at the birth? The father—'

'He's not in the picture,' says Dee.

The registrar hesitates for a moment, and I can tell he wants to ask something else.

This is it. The part where I break down and lose this baby ...

I risk a glance at Dee. She won't meet my eye.

And then it happens.

The registrar writes my name in neat black ink.

Mother: Lorna Miller.

I feel Reign's warm body in my arms and dampness from Dee's palm.

The registrar's pen moves to the next box.

Father: unknown.

It was that easy. Who'd have guessed it would be so easy?

'You're entitled to benefits,' says the registrar. 'Worth looking into. There's no shame in getting benefits. Especially at your age.'

'It wouldn't feel right,' I say. 'I'm not from here originally. I grew up in the States.'

'What about healthcare?' Dee asks. 'My sister ... she had cancer, sir.'

I make urgent eyes – *what are you doing?* Dee makes apologetic *I had to ask* eyes back.

'You'll be entitled to free healthcare,' says the registrar. 'What kind of cancer did you have?'

'Bowel,' I say, just as Dee says, 'Breast.'

We look at each other.

Dee clears her throat. 'Um ... she had both.'

'I'm fine now,' I insist. 'Really. Not worth talking about.'

The registrar glances at me for a moment, then moves to the next box.

'What's the baby's name?' he asks.

There's a long silence. Too long. My mind is wrestling with itself. Trying to pin down thoughts.

I can't call her Reign. It's too distinctive. Why didn't I think of this before?

'Liberty,' I decide. 'Like the Statue of Liberty. Freedom.' And then more words tumble out. 'She'll have a middle name too. Liberty Annalise.'

Dee's hand clenches my shoulder, her nails digging in. 'Are you sure you want that name? *Annalise?* I mean, *really?*'

I nod.

The registrar looks between us. Then he hands me a pen to write the names. Next comes the hard thunk of an official stamp.

As we walk out of the registrar's office, I kiss the baby's soft head over and over again.

Liberty Annalise Miller.

It's official.

Dee won't look at me.

That afternoon, I buy a heavy-duty safe with one-inch-thick steel sides. It costs £150 and takes twenty minutes to carry upstairs.

I put Liberty's birth certificate inside the safe, along with all my medical records and lock it up tight.

The documents are still in there now.

Lorna – Sixteen years later

'Well, well,' said the old woman, peering out with a crafty look. 'Haven't you got a sweet tooth?'

– HANSEL AND GRETEL

W*hy isn't Liberty home?*

I'm in my workshop, legs crossed in paint-stained yoga pants, gluing tiny hairs into a foam-filled werewolf head.

Yoga pants? Leggings, Lorna. *Leggings.* You've been in this country seventeen years now. Butt is bum. A knob isn't always a door handle. And never say 'move your fanny' unless you want to cause offence.

The workshop door is open and I can see our front gate, thick as a fist, the wood warm in the sun.

Warm.

Not hot. It's never *hot* hot in this country.

I grew up under scorching California sun, but I've learned to love these softer British summers. Diet summer. Summer lite.

You know Liberty will be late today. All the students will be talking about their mock-exam results.

These werewolf hairs are a bad job to do while I'm waiting for Liberty. Way too fiddly. But filming starts next week and this guy needs to be ready. It's ironic that I make monsters for movies, given my past. As ironic as my occasional bacon sandwich with Liberty's vegan spread. But life never goes like a fairy tale, right? Maybe these teeth could do with more saliva.

I tap my laptop. The screen shows me the photoshop version of Michael, my nickname for this flesh-ripping, vicious beast. A moment later, the screen turns sleeping black and shows me something even tougher than the werewolf.

Me.

Once upon a time, I was skinny, sickly and quiet.

Not anymore.

My eyes, which my sister used to call cornflower blue, are now steel grey, like the weights I lift. Long hair – once short and naive sandy brown – dyed jet black. Arms no longer bony rods but toned and strong and covered in sleeve tattoos. I'm gym-fit and sturdy. Not the frail cancer survivor I was once upon a time.

Of course, I'm like every other tough-looking woman – soft as a marshmallow in the middle. Someone hurt me once. So I got strong. No choice really. It was either that or fade away.

As I reach for silicon glue, I hear footsteps outside the gate. *Please let this be Liberty …*

But it's not my daughter. I know this because Skywalker, our German Shepherd, watches the gate like a mafia boss, body stiff, ears pricked. Skywalker doesn't do the guard-dog stuff when Liberty comes home; he gets excited, leaping up and down, pawing at wood.

So this must be Nick.

The lock buzzes and my eight-foot wooden gate swings open, making a big, light hole in the safe little world of our house and grounds.

I call out from my workshop, 'Hey, future husband.'

Nick sidesteps through the gate in his gym gear, biceps bulging with hessian bags of shopping.

'Hello, future wife.' Nick bounds into the workshop and kisses my hair. 'I found everything. *Everything* on the list. *Even* cashew nut cheese. I have a good feeling, Lorn. A really good feeling.' Nick has a Yorkshire accent, which makes his boyish optimism sound even more naive.

Should I tell Nick that my teenage daughter might hate him less if he didn't try so hard?

No. Nick is who he is. The man I love. Not with obsessive, fake teenage love. Real, sincere, honest love. It happened slowly, like real feelings should. Not overnight, like …

Michael.

Don't think of him today.

I look around the workshop, mentally naming objects to switch my mind off bad thoughts.

Silicone glue. Silicone paint. Mould. Plaster of Paris. Movie script.

Skywalker trots into the workshop, sniffing the shopping bags.

'Hey, pup.' Nick reaches to pet him, but Skywalker barks and runs off.

I give Nick a sympathetic smile. 'Baby steps, right? Listen, let's start dinner. I need a distraction.'

'She'll be home any minute,' says Nick. 'When I was sixteen—'

'I know. You were hiking alone in the Peak District.' I lift the shopping bags of sourdough bread, tofu and asparagus. 'How did that girl of mine get to like all this fancy food? When I was a teenager, all I ate was hot dogs and noodles.'

'It's great Libs eats mindfully,' says Nick. 'I'm proud of her.'

I bristle at the word 'proud' because I know Liberty would. It's hard, this stepfamily stuff, and somehow Nick always manages to say the wrong thing.

I kiss his cheek. 'Thanks for getting the groceries, honey.'

'Anything to get into Liberty's good books. Do you think she'll get the results she wants today?'

'Oh, sure. I never worry about Liberty in the smarts department. She's so clever.'

Like her father.

I shake the thought away.

'Anyway, they're only mock exams,' I continue. 'No big deal.'

'Well, she's had plenty of time to study,' says Nick.

'Oh, yeah,' I laugh. 'I never let her out.'

I mean this as a joke, but it comes out sort of sinister.

'Don't you think it's time to let Liberty out in the evenings?' Nick asks. 'She's old enough. I was working at her age.'

'We have different parenting styles, Nick. I parent Liberty my way, you parent Darcy yours.'

'We're supposed to be a team. Teams work together. We have two kids between us. We should parent them both together. Like a family. And we *do* parent Darcy together. It's just Liberty—'

'Look, I know the principle is a good one. But the kids are different ages.'

'Why can't I be a dad to Liberty? You're amazing with Darcy. Better than her own mother sometimes …'

'God, don't say that, Nick. Darcy's mom is doing her best. It's a tough job raising a little girl with special needs.'

'Yeah, okay. But you have to admit, Michelle doesn't get Darcy like you do. The special needs thing doesn't fit with her image.' He makes a face. 'You're different. You don't care if Darcy screams her head off in public. And Darcy loves you for that, Lorna. She feels safer here than she does at Michelle's house. If you can parent her, why can't I try with Libs?'

'Liberty's sixteen.'

'Exactly. Sixteen. Don't you think it's time to loosen the reins and let her live a little?'

'Sleeping Beauty had a really bad year when she was sixteen.'

I head into the house with the groceries, throwing a backwards glance at the gate, willing Liberty to buzz herself in.

She doesn't.

I hate this part of the day.

'She'll be back any minute. Okay?' Nick gives my shoulder a reassuring squeeze. 'You worry way too much.'

I nod, but I'm not reassured.

Inside, I dump groceries on the counter and watch the front gate through the kitchen window.

I never thought I'd live in a house like this – a little piece of English history. Growing up in America, my mother called the many different 1950s homes we lived in 'antique'. Around here, most of the homes are four hundred years old.

'Okay, so how do we cook this stuff?' says Nick, looking at the ingredients.

'Um …' I glance at the kitchen window. 'Not sure.'

'Just playing devil's advocate,' says Nick, 'but what if Liberty gets bad grades in these mock exams? What's the plan? I mean, we can't ground her, can we? Since you don't let her out of an evening.'

'Just as long as she tried her best.' I glance at the clock. 'I'm going to give her until 4.30 p.m. Then I'm calling the police.'

Nick laughs. 'They're going to lock you up for wasting police time. You're always overreacting. Liberty will be with her friends, probably writing songs or something. She's okay. Don't you remember being sixteen?'

'Yes, I do,' I say. 'But mostly I try and forget.'

Once upon a time ...

The prince approached her, took her by the hand, and danced with her. Furthermore, he would dance with no one else. He never let go of her hand and said that she, above all others, was his dance partner.

— CINDERELLA

The year was 1996. The band were Crimson. The lead singer was Michael Reyji Ray.

I'd never known a high like it. The heat, the noise, the rush.

A multicoloured sea of arms waved in the air, Celtic armband tattoos and wrists jangling with thin Indian bangles and knotted cotton friendship bracelets.

Michael, Michael, Michael ...

The girls wore light summer dresses with spaghetti straps and DM boots. The boys wore Michael Reyji Ray 'Psycho-Delia' T-shirts, ripped jeans and Vans trainers.

The stadium smelt of beer, incense and CK One perfume.

'There are no strangers here,' Michael boomed into a golden microphone. 'Only friends you haven't met.'

For 13,000 teenagers, Michael Reyji Ray was God that night. We worshipped him.

The world had never felt so real. So awake. I heard the roar of the crowd, felt tribal drum music under my feet, saw colours everywhere. Rainbow flags fluttering on parachute silk.

Michael had short, bleached white hair and wore a black T-shirt, jeans and Ray-Ban sunglasses. His feet were bare, despite the cold night, because, he told us, he wanted to feel the beating heart of the earth.

To me, this statement was beautiful and artistic.

'He thinks he's Jesus,' Dee croaked as Michael spread his arms on stage. She had a cold that night and was a begrudging chaperone.

'Music has power,' Michael boomed. 'And tonight, we're going to change the world.'

'Oh, *wow*.' I grabbed Dee's arm, blinking back tears as we jostled against the cattle bars. 'He is incredible. And he's looking right at me, Dee – do you see it? Tonight is destiny. Michael Reyji Ray saved my life, Dee, I swear to God. It was *his* music that got me through cancer.'

My sister was less than impressed. 'He doesn't even write his own music – the rest of the band are the talent.'

'He writes all the lyrics and they're the amazing part,' I gushed. 'It was destiny I found that first Crimson album, Dee. I swear to you. And now I'm *so* close to him.'

On stage, Michael downed a beer. I took a large gulp from my own bottle.

'Lorna, go easy on that stuff,' said Dee, taking a bite from her hot dog and adding a chewed, 'You're not out of the woods yet.'

'I am,' I insisted. 'It's six months today since they gave me the teen-cancer-girl all-clear. Exactly today. Profound, right? On the very day I see Michael sing live for the first time.'

As the night went on, I danced and screamed like a lunatic, downing beer, singing, holding up a light to the slow songs and putting my arms around complete strangers while my big sister looked on pityingly.

Dee didn't get it. She wasn't a Ray-ite. She didn't get the depth and meaning and poetry of Michael's lyrics. Those of us who did swayed and cheered and sang together.

It was beautiful. I felt like Michael was looking right at me, singing the words to *me*.

Live your life, little one. You're a survivor …

When the concert finished and the crowds emptied, I needed to stay and get near the stage. It felt special – the spot where Michael had stood. I climbed right over the cattle bars at the front, watching the empty stage with big moony eyes.

Eventually a female security guard approached.

'Girls,' said the security guard. 'Time to leave.'

'We should go home,' said Dee from the other side of the cattle bars. 'Lorna, it's cold. I have an excess fifty pounds to keep me warm. You're skinny as a twig right now and still in recovery.'

'*You* go home. Go. I'll catch a cab later. I'm gonna hang out and wait for Michael and the band to leave.'

'I can't let you—'

'Dee, he's in this venue somewhere. I might meet him. *Michael Reyji Ray.*'

'Never meet your idols, Lorna,' said Dee. 'I bet he's even shorter than he looks on stage.'

'I have to try.'

Dee shakes her head. 'Come on, Lorna. I can't stay out late. I'm teaching kids tomorrow.'

'Then go.'

'As if I'd leave my little sister. Come on. We need to get back.'

I pulled my trump card then. 'Dee, meeting Michael Reyji Ray was on my list. The one I wrote in the hospital. Things to do before I die ...'

Dee's face faltered. 'I'm responsible for a whole class of middle graders. I need to sleep—'

'I'm telling you to go. I'll be fine. There are no strangers here, right? Only friends I haven't met. Come on, Dee, I'm sixteen. You moved out of home at sixteen.'

Dee sighed. 'Okay, fine. Fine. But if you're not back by 1 a.m. I'm calling the police.'

'You're the best big sister in the world. Always have been.'

'Okay, okay. Stay out of trouble, little sis, and look after yourself. Take care of your body. Remember how lucky you are to be alive. You're still crazy thin.' She managed a tired smile. 'Even so, you look a darn sight better than I did at your age.'

'Don't be ridiculous. You're the most beautiful person I ever met.' And I meant it. My big sister always looked like an angel to me with her cuddly, curvy body and warm, smiling eyes.

Dee laughed. 'And you're my best little cheerleader. Enjoy yourself. Okay? You deserve a good time after everything you've been through.'

I know Dee still feels guilty about that night. If she'd have stayed with me, Michael might never have happened.

But it's not her fault.

Men like Michael are predators. They're experts at luring you in.

Lorna

Liberty's still not home and I'm starting to panic, pacing back around the kitchen.

The griddle sizzles as Nick lays large, flat mushrooms on hot oil. He watches the pan intensely, glancing between the smoking mushroom and a little black kitchen timer.

'Great job, Nick,' I say, trying not to sound as distracted as I feel. 'Smells delicious. Liberty is going to love this. A plant-based feast.'

'Yeah, it looks good, doesn't it?' says Nick, voice cheerful. 'I'm going to try Darcy on one of these mushrooms tonight. It would be great if she ate a vegetable. This yellow food phase is just going on and on.'

'I'm not sure it's a phrase,' I say. 'I think it's just how Darcy is. You told the nursery that Bella's mother is taking her home tonight, right?'

Nick snorts, still watching the mushroom, spatula poised. 'I was a parent before you came along, Lorna Miller. Don't worry. I told them.'

'I'm giving Liberty one last call,' I decide, taking out my cell phone. *Mobile phone, Lorna, mobile, not a cell phone. You've lived in this country for seventeen years …*

'Lorna.' Nick shakes his head. 'She won't answer. How many times have you called today?'

My flip-flops shuffle on the slate floor. 'Three?'

This is a lie.

'Hold up.' Nick points at the window. 'I think this is her.'

Skywalker is going mad, jumping around at the gate.

'Oh, thank God.' I watch our front gate swing open on its pivot, and my tall, slender daughter appears, army backpack hanging from one shoulder. Her skin is lightly tanned from the sun. Different to my pale skin. I've always been pale. The palest kid in California.

Liberty's wearing a messed-up version of her school uniform, her tie the skinny way around, skirt rolled up and something else: an oversized denim jacket with band patches sewn on it. I've never seen the jacket before, and … what happened to her *hair*?

I feel Nick's arm around my shoulder. 'Whoa. Very rock and roll. It suits her.'

'What has she done to herself?' My voice is shaking.

Liberty's long, chestnut brown hair has been cut to her chin, flicked over in a deep side parting and streaked an uneven blonde, some parts bright white, others orangey.

I put my hand to my own hair. It was short like that once too.

When Liberty comes through the front door, I accost her in the hall beside Nick's 'Steps, Achieve, Goal' pinboard.

'Liberty, what happened to your hair?'

Skywalker barks and barks.

Liberty raises a hand to Skywalker. He sits instantly, tail still and obedient. 'I cut it. And bleached it.'

'Where?'

'At school.'

I watch as Liberty hangs her army backpack and the unidentified denim jacket.

'Where did you get that jacket?'

'A friend.' Liberty clicks her fingers and Skywalker trots to her side.

'Who? Male or female?'

'Does it matter? Gender is fluid these days. Get with the times, Mama.'

'What happened to your duffel coat—'

'Abi has it. We swapped.'

'For a jacket covered in music badges?'

'What's the problem with a couple of band badges? You've got tattoos all over your arms.'

'Liberty, honey. Your hair. Your beautiful hair.'

'It's *my* hair. It's nothing to do with you.'

'Hey Libs.' Nick pops his head out the front door. 'Your mother just worries about you, that's all. We want you to be safe.'

'*You* don't have to worry about me, Nick,' says Liberty. 'Because *you* are not my legal guardian.'

'I'm responsible for you, just like your mother is,' says Nick.

'Not legally,' says Liberty. 'You and my mother aren't married yet. Remember?' Then she mutters under her breath. '*Steroids cause memory loss.*'

Unfortunately, Nick hears. He's mild-mannered about absolutely everything. Except steroid accusations.

'I do *not* take steroids,' he snaps. 'These muscles are born of hard graft.'

'There are helplines you can call.' Liberty tries to dart upstairs, shoulders shaking with laughter.

I grab her arm. 'Hold it right there. Number one, apologize to Nick. Number two, we have to figure out how to fix your hair.'

'Fix it?' Liberty gawps at me. 'There's nothing to fix. And I was just teasing, Nick. That's all.'

Nick goes back into the kitchen and starts cutting tofu, head bent over.

'Apologize to Nick. He's trying his best. He drove to Long Bridge for your vegan stuff today.'

'You're always on his side.'

'I'm on both your sides.'

Liberty flips around her new short hair and kneels to stroke Skywalker's long, salt and pepper body. 'Thank you, Nick,' she says in a tired voice. 'Sorry, Nick.'

'I'm trying my best, Libs,' says Nick. 'All I want to do is be a good ... sort-of dad.'

'Tell us about the mock exams,' I say. 'How'd you do?'

Liberty ignores me and pours vegetarian dog biscuits into Skywalker's bowl. Skywalker sits obediently, as Liberty has trained him to do. Only when she gives him the command does he start eating.

Nick stumbles into the awkward silence. 'Hey, you've done a great job with that dog, Libs. Look at how well trained he is. Just brilliant.'

'What else do I have to do?' says Liberty. 'Mum never lets me out.'

'Yeah, we were talking about that,' says Nick. 'I think it's time your mother let you out more.'

Liberty looks up then, managing a smile. 'Really? You told her that? Did she punch you?'

Nick laughs. 'Just a couple of broken fingers.'

'So tell us about your exams,' I say. 'Don't keep us hanging on.'

'I'll tell you at dinner time,' says Liberty. 'Where's my little buddy? Up in her room reading her number chart?'

'Darcy's still at nursery,' I say. 'One of the other parents is bringing her home.'

'I brought her some patterns from Maths class,' says Liberty, going to her school bag and pulling out sheaves of paper. 'I'll put them in her special drawer.'

When Liberty opens Darcy's personal kitchen drawer – the one with all Darcy's 'important' items in it – she bursts out laughing. 'I love that little girl. She's so funny.' Liberty pulls out a handful of Chinese takeout menus. 'Of course she loves these menus. Every dish is numbered.'

'I'll say one thing about this blended family,' says Nick. 'At least the kids get along.'

'Who wouldn't get along with Darcy?' says Liberty.

'Her birth mother, for a start,' says Nick. 'Not everyone understands someone so particular.'

'Well, I think Darcy's hilarious. I love how straightforward she is. And clever. Worth putting up with you for, Nick.'

Nick laughs uncertainly.

'Liberty, please stop being so hard on Nick,' I say. 'He's one of the good guys.'

'Well yeah, he definitely has his uses,' says Liberty. 'But why not just download a diet and fitness app? That way I don't have to find his hair in the shower.'

'There's a fine line between funny and mean, and you're in danger of crossing it.'

'Okay, okay,' Liberty mutters. 'Sorry, Nick. Sorry, sorry, sorry.'

'Let's get all this food cooked,' I announce. 'Okay? What's this? Jackfruit? What is it, some kind of vegetable?'

'I'll give you a clue,' says Liberty. 'You won't find it in one of your disgusting hot dog cans.'

'Don't mock the afflicted. I can't help my taste in food. I don't know how you got so sophisticated.'

'Maybe I got my sophisticated tastes from my real dad.'

The room falls silent. And then I hear myself say:

'Liberty. Go to your room.'

Once upon a time ...

After my sister left me at the Crimson gig, I followed a tide of fanatical, oddball hangers-on. They swept me out of the stadium and towards the east car park, where the band's tour bus waited on gleaming tarmac.

The girls were obvious groupies, shivering in knee-high boots, Wonderbras and short skirts. The boys were boggle-eyed and acne-ridden under shaggy, Michael Reyji Ray haircuts. They were a fun and sweet crowd, all glossy-eyed and talking about the gig.

I talked music too, but I was there for something more. Something deeper. Love. Wholesome, honest, authentic love. Michael and his music had cured me of cancer. His lyrics spoke to my heart and soul while I was in hospital. The words were written just for me. And I loved him.

It was dark and freezing that night, but excitement kept us warm as we huddled outside the east car-park stadium doors.

I said silent prayers, shivering in my oversized denim jacket – the one I'd decorated with band patches and sharpie silhouettes. Please, God, please. Let Michael grace us with his holiness.

Just after midnight, it happened. The black-painted fire doors flew open and out came Michael Reyji Ray, Paul Graves, Alex Sawalha and a dozen crew members dressed in black 'Crimson' T-shirts.

We all screamed and cried.

Michael walked a little ahead of the other band members, looking thoughtful, hands in greying jeans pockets and walking on bare feet. The way the band and crew had arranged themselves around Michael – he was a king with his subjects.

Michael walked past all the half-dressed girls in short skirts and knee-high boots, his face still apparently deep in concentration.

And then a miracle happened.

Michal noticed the illustrations on my jacket and stopped walking. His eyes followed the long, hard sharpie pen lines and crosshair shading. 'So what do we have here then?' he asked, voice scratchy and deep. 'A little artist. Is this me?'

'I … yes,' I stammered, grinning like an idiot. 'This is you. And this is Sid Vicious. And David Roger Johansen.'

'The New York Dolls?' Michael asked. 'You like them, do you?'

I nodded and nodded. 'I love them. I love punk music.'

'A little American punk princess.' Michael pushed his sunglasses into his hair and took my face in his hands. When his eyes met mine, I felt like I'd been hit with something. He had unwavering, kaleidoscope eyes that saw everything – hopes and dreams, pain and fear. They were the most amazing eyes I'd ever seen and they were looking right at me.

Then Michael put one square, flat palm high on my chest,

right over my beating heart. He held his hand there for a moment, then spoke to me again in his gravelly voice.

'Do you know what?' Then he sang. 'I fee-eel a soul connection.'

The girls beside me swooned on my behalf.

'You'd better come with me.' Michael grabbed my hand, and I felt his calloused guitar-player fingers against my palm.

'Where?'

'To the tour bus.' Michael pulled me across the car park and I stumbled behind him, grinning like an idiot.

'Wait,' I said, looking back at my new-found friends. 'Just me?'

Michael held my hand tighter. 'Just you, Cinderella. I'm taking you to the ball.'

Together, we walked over freezing tarmac to the tour bus.

The ground seemed to lay down under Michael's bare feet. To glow with every step he took.

I kept glancing at Michael and giggling like an idiot. Yes, he was definitely the most handsome man I'd ever seen. A little bit careworn up close. Smaller than he looked on stage. And a lot older than me. But so, so handsome. I was in the company of music royalty. Music royalty was holding my hand.

Lorna

Darcy frowns at her dinner plate. She sits on a yellow booster seat in a cute yellow sundress, yellow sandals dangling. But little-girl embellishments aside, Darcy is the most grown-up, serious four-year-old you could ever meet. Her idea of playtime is numbering all the toys in the room and then doing it again – fifty times.

'It's okay, Darcy,' says Liberty. 'You've had all this food before, right? Except that one. It's called a mushroom. Remember what to do if you're not sure? Just count the pieces.'

Darcy's black hair is tied in a messy ponytail. Liberty did it this morning, and hasn't done a bad job considering Darcy will only tolerate hairstyling for around ten seconds.

She won't let Nick or me touch her head at all in the morning – only her 'big sister Bibbity'. Hair washing must happen after 6 p.m. and only if we're quick. Sometimes, we cut her hair while she's sleeping.

Liberty and I watch across the dinner table, faces tense. Nick looks hopeful, but holds his knife and fork in tight fists. He's taken a risk tonight by putting a mushroom on Darcy's plate. She analyses it with the concentration of a surgeon:

the operation is macaroni and vegan cheese with crunched-up tortilla chips on top and a sliced mushroom on the side. Everything yellow, except for the mushroom – slightly yellowed by frying, but still a grey, white colour.

This procedure is touch and go. Things could go either way.

Darcy's meals have to look and feel similar every time, which means yellow and crunchy. Oven-ready is the go-to safe option.

If Darcy approves the meal, it could be a good evening. If she doesn't, she'll scream the house down and it'll take an hour to make her calm again.

'This is more toe-curling than your YouTube fitness videos, Nick,' says Liberty.

Nick, to his credit, manages an amiable laugh.

Darcy says nothing. She is still concentrating.

Then we get the signal – a full, beautiful smile like the sun coming out. Darcy picks up her fork and carefully loads food.

'One,' she counts.

We all relax.

'Okay.' I pour drinks: Coke for me, Diet Coke for Nick, San Pellegrino sparkling water for Liberty (in a sophisticated stem glass, of course) and Sunny Delight for Darcy.

'So, Liberty, good day?' Nick asks. 'How about those mock-exam results? How'd you do?'

Liberty cuts a mushroom into neat pieces. 'I failed.'

I laugh.

'I'm not joking,' says Liberty, taking a delicate bite of food.

The room goes very still.

I decide to play along. 'You failed drama? The girl who's picked as the lead in every play?'

'Failed it. Maths. English. Science. Fail, fail, fail. U grades. Unclassified.'

'Very funny, Libs.' I cut up food. 'You're the most intellectual teenager I've ever met. You can do a Suduko puzzle while the kettle boils. You're an unbeaten chess champion. You read Dickens and Shakespeare for fun.'

'It's easy to fail when you don't turn up to the exams,' says Liberty.

'You … what?'

'I didn't sit any exams,' says Liberty, sipping sparkling water. 'Except for Music. They predicted me an A-star for that.'

Silence.

Some parents worry about their children getting tattoos or leaving home to join a motorcycle gang. I worry my daughter will be a musician.

Nick looks between Liberty and me, brown eyes startled and unsure. Then he clears his throat. 'Um … at my school sometimes the clever kids pretended to be thick so they wouldn't get picked on. Maybe Libs doesn't want to look too clever.'

'Liberty,' I say. 'What's going on?'

'I'm protesting.'

I swallow. 'Against … against what?'

'I'm not taking my any more exams. Not until you let me meet him.'

I stiffen.

Don't say it. Please don't say it.

'I want to meet my real father.' Liberty looks me dead in the eye.

There they are. Laid right out on the bamboo table top,

making a nasty stain. The words I've been dreading since Liberty could talk.

Under the table, Skywalker makes a sort of snorting, whinny noise. It's like he knows the gates of hell have been opened and Liberty is walking towards them.

'I'm not taking any exams until you let me meet my real father,' says Liberty.

'Why would you want to meet him?' I demand. 'He's a monster. That's not a road we're going down.'

'Well, it's a road *I'm* going down,' says Liberty.

'No, Liberty. Absolutely not.'

We glare at each other.

'Liberty, your mother has her reasons, okay?' says Nick.

Liberty stands and jabs her fork at Nick and me in turn.

'See?' she shouts. 'I get totally ganged up on. I'm sixteen years old. It's time I met my real dad. You should let me decide for myself what he's like. Just because he was bad to you doesn't mean he'll be bad to me.'

Darcy doesn't pay any attention, continuing to count her forkfuls.

'You're young and naive, just like I was,' I say. 'You just have to trust me.'

Suddenly, Darcy stops counting, frowning at a melted piece of cheese stuck on her place.

Liberty goes to helps Darcy cut it free. 'I want to meet him, Mum.'

'You can't meet your father,' I say, voice rising. 'No way. Never. Do you understand me. You can NEVER meet him. Your real father will ruin everything.'

Lorna

I want to meet my father.

For a good few minutes after the 'F' bomb, only Darcy speaks.

'Fork. Food. Eighteen. Fork. Food. Nineteen. Whoops! Start again. Fork. Food. One.'

Liberty is still behind her, helping her free stuck cheese from the plate when necessary.

Skywalker slinks into the kitchen and sits in his basket.

I stare at my plate, not wanting to eat.

When I look up, Nick has worried eyes and Liberty is glaring.

'Okay, listen,' I say. 'The word "father". It has a kind of status, doesn't it? An authority? Like a king. Wise, kind. Fathers are kind men, right? But Liberty, your dad isn't like that. How many times do I have to tell you? We all need to stay away. I've told you over and over again, he is not a good guy.'

'Aunty Dee told me to take your stories with a pinch of salt.'

'Aunty Dee thinks she's protecting you,' I say. 'She used to do that when I was growing up too – tone things down, make them sound nicer. Always the mother figure. She was a great big sister. The best. But sometimes people need to know the truth.'

Liberty snorts. 'And what would you know about the truth?'

'Listen.' My voice hardens. 'Dee was there. She knows all about your dad. She knows full well.' I push my plate of food away.

'Tell me more about him at least,' says Liberty, taking a seat. 'He's half of who I am.'

'I … no,' I say. 'That's not a good idea.'

'If it makes you feel any better, Libs,' says Nick, 'I don't know anything about your dad either. Your mother keeps me in the dark too.'

'He's just a bad guy who I left a long time ago,' I say. 'Can we leave it at that? And I don't want you meeting him, Liberty, because I don't want you getting hurt like I did.'

'Maybe I'm not as weak and pathetic as you were.' Liberty watches me, her eyes flat. 'And I'm sick of listening to all the "Dad is a bad person" stuff without a shred of proof. If you won't let me meet him, I won't retake my exams.'

I cross my arms. 'Fine. If that's what it takes.'

Liberty glares at me. 'I'll ruin my future. You won't let me do that.'

'What kind of future will you have if your father gets a hold of you?'

For the rest of dinner, Liberty is sullen and silent, throwing me the occasional angry glance.

I try to strike up some small talk: 'Do you think robot vacuum cleaners actually *work*?'

Liberty replies, 'They probably don't really clear up the mess at all. Just move it around. Hide it under the carpet.' And eyes me meaningfully.

When we've all finished eating, we all clear and tidy, moving dinner things to the kitchen and loading the dishwasher.

After Darcy meticulously scrapes her plate and loads it, Liberty takes her hand, leads her into the lounge and finds her a YouTube video about a jelly bean factory. She sits with Darcy for a while, explaining the factory mechanisms and jelly bean flavouring process. Then she announces she's heading up to her room.

'I'm going to write a song about controlling parents,' she says.

I sigh. 'Listen, Libs. With your father … some problems can't be solved. Right?'

'Don't be frigging ridiculous,' says Liberty. 'Every problem can be solved. It's just whether you make it a priority or not.'

Frigging is an Americanism she got from me. I have no one else to blame. Ditto when she says crap and Jesus H Christ. And ditto.

'Even kids Darcy's age know hiding from problems isn't healthy,' Liberty adds.

'Okay,' I admit. 'Fine. Usually we face our problems. But when it comes to your father it doesn't work like that. He turns it all around, spins it, makes you look like the crazy one. So can we just drop it?'

'Hey Libs,' says Nick, holding out a chessboard with an eager look on his face. 'Why don't we take our mind off things with a game of chess. Fancy a quick match?'

Liberty offers an eyebrow raise. 'No offence, Nick, but I'll beat you in three minutes.'

'I've been practising,' says Nick. 'I downloaded Chess Tactics Pro.'

'Fine.'

Nick sets up the chessboard, turning the white pieces to face Liberty. 'Here. Ladies first.'

'I like black, remember?' says Liberty, turning the board again. 'The dark, avenging army.'

Nick looks uncertain. 'Um … okay. Right. Okay. I'll go first then.' He looks at the pieces, eyes darting everywhere, then finally moves a pawn.

Liberty checkmates Nick within three minutes, as promised.

'Good job, Libs.' Nick offers his hand to shake. 'I'll keep practising.'

'You're persistent, Nick,' says Liberty. 'I have to give you that.'

'Giving up is not in my vocabulary.'

'Thank goodness,' I say. 'Or you'd have given up on us a long time ago.'

Nick grins at me. 'Never.'

'Okay.' Liberty stands. 'I'm going upstairs to work on my music before I vomit all over the pair of you.' She disappears up the second staircase – the one that leads to her mezzanine landing, bedroom and ensuite. The mezzanine is a yoga space that Liberty and I both used to use, but these days she's more into indoor climbing at my local gym. Chaperoned, of course.

When Liberty disappears, I burst into tears.

'Hey.' Nick jumps to his feet and puts his arms around me. 'Hey, it's all right. It's fine. She'll take her exams. She's just testing you.'

'It's not her exams I'm worried about.'

'So what are you worried about? That she'll go running off to see her dad?'

I nod.

'It's normal that she'd want to, isn't it? I get that you and he didn't get along, but maybe there's a way—'

'No. There's no way she can see him.' I look away from Nick's penetrating stare. 'He can't be part of our life in any way.'

'But clearly Liberty wants to see him. Lorna—'

'It's fine, Nick.' I start doing clap press-ups against the breakfast bar. 'We've been through all this when Liberty was younger. The "I want to see my real dad" phase. It'll pass like it did back then.'

Nick scratches his head in thought. He's the only person I know who literally scratches his head when he's thinking. 'So … you're just going to basically ignore what she wants?'

'Not ignore. Just not give any fuel to it. And like I said, wait until it passes.'

'You never talk about Liberty's father.'

'There's nothing I want to talk about. Liberty's never met him and that's how it's going to stay. Everything is near-perfect here. You have no idea how perfect. Liberty's father would ruin everything.'

We hear the beautiful ebb and flow of acoustic guitar drift over our open-plan living area, floating past the panoramic windows and out into woodland, joining the birds fluttering from tree to tree.

Liberty is musically talented. No doubt about that. I wish she weren't. There would be fewer questions.

I look at the staircase. 'I'll go talk to her. Make sure she's okay.'

'Have a good honest talk with her, Lorna. Get everything out in the open.'

A shiver runs through me.

If I were totally honest with Liberty, I'd lose her forever. I'd lose Nick too. He really has no idea.

'Lorna?' Nick's watching me, and I realize my fists are balled.

'I'm okay. Honestly. It's just … Liberty and I have been through a lot. I'll talk to her and smooth things over.'

Nick pulls me into another big, strong hug. 'Just remember, she's a kid who's dealing with a lot. Sixteen is a tough age. I wouldn't want some weird guy moving into my house, sharing my mum's bedroom.'

'Don't forget your hair in the bathroom.'

We both manage something like a laugh.

'Listen,' says Nick. 'Maybe you've got good reasons for keeping her away from her dad. But let the girl go out with her friends of an evening, at least. If she had more freedom, I think it would help a lot. With everything.'

'You don't understand teenagers,' I say. 'Freedom is the last thing she needs.'

Lorna

Liberty's is a musician's bedroom. No doubt about that. Most teenagers spend their allowance on clothes. Liberty buys electric guitars, tribal drums, electric drum kits and keyboards.

Liberty sort of *knows* music. Picks up instruments and understands how they work. I've never taught her – she taught herself. She has GarageBand on her laptop, surround-sound speakers and a very cool 1960s orange Dansette record player with a cube of vinyl beside it. Van Halen, Suzi Quatro, Joan Jett and Kiss are arranged alphabetically.

'Liberty?' I knock on the bedroom door even though it's already open.

Liberty sits on a rice-filled bean bag, holding one of her acoustic guitars: the red one she bought at a school jumble sale without telling me. She's changed out of her school uniform into tight black jeans and a Runaways T-shirt. Skywalker lays beside her, head on her thigh.

It's still light outside, and the room twinkles with sunshine.

Liberty looks up. 'What?'

'Hey. Sorry. Okay?'

'You always say that,' says Liberty. 'But nothing changes.'

She puts the guitar to one side. 'It's ridiculous. I'm sixteen years old and you won't let me go out in the evenings. *All* my friends go out. And you won't tell me anything about my real father.'

'You don't get it. It's a big, bad world out there. You have no idea how bad.'

'Look, I know you had a hard time with my father—'

'A hard time?' I put a hand to my forehead. 'Oh my goodness, Liberty. You have no idea.'

'Is he something to do with you getting cancer when you were young? Like … bad associations or something?'

'No. I had cancer before your father came along. I was only fifteen when …' I shake my head. 'Never mind. Anyway. I don't want to talk about cancer. Focus on what you want more of, right? Not the bad stuff.'

'Were you scared?'

'What?'

'When you got cancer. You must have been really scared.'

'I don't want to talk about that. It's nothing to do with your father, anyway. I was in remission when we met. I thought he was my happy ending.' I give a hollow laugh. 'Now I know you have to make your own happy endings in life. No one can give them to you.'

'I want to meet him, Mum. I know you had a bad relationship. But I don't believe my real father would hurt me. I just don't.'

I squeeze her hand. 'Honey, you don't know him. And if you did, you wouldn't say that. All teenagers think they're invincible. Until they learn otherwise.'

'I might not be invincible. But I'm not some fragile little doll either.'

'That's exactly what you are, Liberty. And the most dangerous part is you don't even know it.'

'According to you, riding my bike to school is dangerous.'

'I didn't want you taking your bike to school because—'

'Because you heard about a girl getting snatched when she was cycling home from school. Guess what? People get killed in cars every day. Why not stop me riding the bus?'

'We have space around the house to ride.'

'Oh, come on. It's ridiculous. Having a bike and not being able to ride it outside, aged sixteen. Darcy rides her bike to nursery and she's four years old with learning difficulties.'

'It's different with you.'

Liberty rolls her eyes. 'Because my father is such a monster?'

'Exactly right.'

Liberty clears her throat. 'Mum. I have something to tell you.'

'What?'

There's a long pause, during which Liberty looks anywhere but at me. Then she says, 'I know who he is.'

My body goes rigid. 'What?'

Liberty takes her phone from the bedside table. 'This is you. Isn't it?' She passes me the phone.

My mouth turns dry.

I see a skinny, kohl-eyed teenager with chin-length, punky hair and bony body under a Michael Reyji Ray T-shirt. My teenage self is dragging suitcases behind a straggly, dark-haired man in a leather jacket.

The worst thing about the picture is my eyes. They're glazed and lovesick. I've seen the same eyes since in fanatical cult members.

This girl was me, once. A long time ago. But I feel no connection to her. She's like a stranger.

There are more pictures under teenage me: a young Michael Reyji Ray, tanned and handsome. In those days he was in good shape, running around stage all night, slashed-up T-shirts showing off his chest. There's a picture of Michael on stage, and also driving his purple Jaguar F-Type, looking every bit the rock and roll rebel.

Michael is different these days too. I've seen pictures. His face is swollen and craggy under his bleached white hair, chin dusted with black and white stubble. We're both bigger, but I've got fitter, he's got fatter: a toad of a man in black jeans, bright T-shirts and suit jackets.

Liberty watches me closely. 'Michael Reyji Ray is my father,' she says. 'Isn't he? All the dates add up. And ... we have the same face.'

I swallow. 'How did you find this?'

'Someone at school showed me.'

'The girl who gave you the jacket?'

'No. Someone else.'

My mouth is dry. 'Did you read the article?'

Liberty nods.

'What else have you seen?'

'Not much, just ... some old magazine articles. Saying you were sort of obsessed with him. My father.'

'I'm taking this phone.'

'What?'

'Your phone,' I say. 'I don't want you looking at this stuff. It won't lead anywhere good.'

39

Liberty shakes her head like a disappointed parent. 'That's your solution to everything. Censorship. Control. And then you bring in Nick to back you up. Fine. Take my phone. Take it. And while you're at it, lock my door and throw away the key.'

'Listen, you have no idea how good our life is without your father in it. Haven't I warned you enough about him? Haven't I spent your whole life warning you?'

'You know what I think? I think he treated you badly and you need a reason to hate him.'

'That's not true. I mean, yes. He did treat me badly. But I have plenty of genuine reasons for keeping him away.'

'Parent alienation,' says Liberty. 'It's a thing. You should let me make up my own mind.'

I've kept my daughter secure behind high gates. We've stayed hidden for sixteen years. But Michael's still got into our home.

'You can't ever see him,' I say. 'Ever.'

'You can go now.' Liberty picks up her guitar. 'You've made your point. Mother knows best.'

Once upon a time …

When Michael Reyji Ray took my hand on that cold autumn night and led me across the parking lot, it felt as if all my dreams had come true.

As we walked, I risked a glance at the god beside me.

Looking at Michael, even sideways on, was like looking at the sun. He was bright and blinding. Everything was clear as clear. Michael's skin shone. His eyes were glittering stars. All around him was light.

When I was fifteen years old, the doctors found a life-threatening tumour. I'd nearly died. Now at sixteen, I'd gone to heaven. Or at least stumbled upon the meaning of life. His name was Michael Reyji Ray and he was my happily ever after. Our carriage awaited us: a giant black tour bus with wasp-eye wing mirrors and tube-light steps.

The world was brighter than it had ever been and time had slowed so I could take it all in.

'So you like our band, do you?' Michael asked me.

I nodded and nodded. 'I've listened to Crimson's *Big Dreams* album probably a thousand times. You have no idea what that album means to me. It literally saved my life.'

Michael chuckled. 'Well, I am honoured.'

'This is a fairy tale,' I told Michael as he escorted me up the sharp metal tour-bus steps and into rock and roll fantasy land. 'I can't believe this is really happening.'

Everything on the bus was bright, like Michael's presence had lit it up. The leather sofas gleamed, the chrome tables sparkled and spotlights twinkled like shy little stars.

Bottles of Guinness stood on the bar beside magnums of champagne. There were huge meat pies cut into slices, cocktail sausages and loaves of brown bread.

'Who's all the food for?' I asked.

'You. If you want it.'

The bus was empty when we boarded, except for a driver lounging in the front seat, feet on the dashboard. He wore a black-leather eye mask and snored loudly.

Michael flicked the driver's nose playfully and shouted, 'Danny!'

The driver fell about in his seat, sitting upright and ripping the mask from his eyes.

When he saw Michael, he looked momentarily terrified. 'Shit. Shit.'

Michael's eyes were stern as he ruffled Danny's hair. 'Have you been on the beers, Danny boy?'

Danny coughed a smoker's cough. 'Just sleeping. Power nap.'

'Good lad,' said Michael. 'We don't want you dozing at the wheel later on. We have a lot of good people on this bus.'

Danny pulled his mask back on his face.

Michael offered me a seat on a leather sofa and grabbed

two Grolsch beers from a mini-bar fridge. 'You're over eighteen, right?' He winked, popping open a beer and handing it to me.

I nodded quickly.

'I know they don't let you drink until you're twenty-one in this country,' said Michael. 'But this bus is my home town of Dublin. International soil. And in Dublin, you can go to the pub when you're eighteen.'

I nodded and nodded, a big, dumb grin on my face. He thought I was eighteen!

'That is one totally cool jacket you have on there.'

I smiled, too shy to meet his gaze.

'And with a jacket like that you can't drink orange squash, can you?' said Michael. 'You've got to go the whole way. Sex and drugs and rock and roll.'

I kept nodding, swigging from the beer bottle.

'Do you know what?' said Michael. 'You are a very beautiful girl. You're like a little fairy. All tiny and delicate. I can't stand women getting muscly like men. It looks wrong.'

As Michael was laying on the charm, Paul Graves and his wife climbed on the bus. Paul grabbed a magnum of champagne and moved to the back without saying a word.

'Tell me about yourself,' said Michael. 'What brings you out to see a load of old men play music on a cold night?'

'I love your music. I went crazy when I got tickets for tonight. Totally crazy. Everyone knew the gig would sell out.'

Michael watched me intently, his eyes twinkly and black. It didn't feel like a forty-something man picking up a sixteen-year-old. It felt like the biggest rush of my life.

'Hey, will you do something for me?' said Michael.

'Anything,' I gushed, every bit the idiot fan.

'Paul has got a huff on tonight because we cut one of his songs. Hop on down the bus and tell him you were glad we didn't play "Come On Home". Can you do that?'

'You want me to ... what?'

Michael's eyes glittered. 'Just tell him. Tell him you don't like "Come On Home".' He patted my bottom. 'Off you go. Go on, kiddo. I dare you.'

I swallowed and got up. In a daze I wandered down the bus and stood right in front of Paul Graves, who was sitting with his wife. The pair had their heads close together.

I cleared my throat and squeaked: 'I-don't-like-come-on-home. I'm-glad-you-didn't-play-it.'

Paul looked up, eyes slitted and angry. 'What?'

His beautiful blonde wife said, 'Michael must have told her to say it, Paul. The little shit-stirrer.'

I scurried back to Michael, who was laughing. He folded me into his arms and said: 'Well done. Well done. Oh Jesus, the look on his face.'

We talked and talked after that. Or rather, Michael asked questions and I talked. I got enthusiastic about Marvel and manga comics, showed him the Celtic cross tattoo I'd made on my wrist with a needle and black ink and told him about my cancer. Michael learned all about my treatment and my mother and what life had been like growing up.

I told Michael things I hadn't even told my closest friends – stuff about my mom using the San Francisco free-love no-rules culture to justify being a lousy parent, and how unsuitable her life was for children. How if it hadn't been for Dee, we would have been taken away from her.

'My mom wasn't even up-to-date,' I said. 'All that hippy stuff passed through years before Dee and I were born. She clung on to it for dear life.'

I went into huge detail about my cancer too. How embarrassing the treatment was for a teenager just getting to know her body. Having things stuck here and there, being wheeled around without underwear on. So bad. And then having all my hair falling out.

'The tumour was so big they had to cut it in half to get it out,' I told him. 'Do you know what helped me heal?'

'What?' Michael asked, dark eyes big and beautiful and fascinated.

'You, Crimson and *Big Dreams*.' I looked at my hands, feeling awkward. 'You got me through some really bad times. Without your music, I honestly don't think I would have got through the treatment. You gave me a reason to live.'

'We touched something pretty deep when we made that album,' said Michael. 'It was special, that one. And it takes a special person to feel it too.'

I grinned.

Michael encouraged me to talk so much about myself that night, while he sat and listened. As I talked, he touched and twisted the leather bracelets on my arm and the chunky silver chains around my neck.

'You're quite a girl,' he said. 'You've really been through it. We've had a hard life, the pair of us. Harder than most.'

My eyes widened. 'Did you get sick too when you were younger?'

'No. But I had a bad time growing up.'

'Really?' I was fascinated.

Michael nodded. 'My dad was a vicious bastard. Talked with his fists.' He pulled up his black jeans and showed me a long, red scar running over his knee and down his calf. 'I saw the bone poking out of that, once upon a time. But he made me fearless, the old sod. When someone that big pushes you around, you're not afraid of anyone.'

'Your mother—'

'Died, God rest her soul. When I was two. I don't remember her. Probably better that way.'

I think Michael's sadness might have been real. But it's hard to know, looking back. He was so good at fooling people. Maybe he was sad, but sad about something else. Who knows?

'But that's life, isn't it?' Michael continued. 'You should know. You've been through it too.'

As Michael and I talked, crew members and girls filtered onto the bus. Some of the girls I recognized from the stage doors – teenagers, shivering in short dresses and Wonderbras. It seemed kind of sleazy, those young girls with bare legs, sitting with old rock guys. But Michael and I were different. We had a soul connection.

Michael whispered in my ear, 'It's getting a bit noisy. Let's go to the bedroom.' He grabbed a whiskey bottle and a few beers, then led me by the hand into the master bedroom at the back of the bus.

I hesitated at the door, feeling suddenly very sober. The flecks of grey in Michael's stubble and the lines in his face were stark under strip lighting. I suddenly felt my age. A young, naive teenager with a much older man.

'What's up?' Michael asked. 'You look scared stiff.'

I tried to laugh off my nerves and misgivings. 'No. Of course not.'

'What, you don't like the bedroom or something?'

'I love it,' I insisted, nodding at the compact bedroom with cool cube-patterned sheets and plump cream pillows. 'It's nicer than my apartment.'

'Come here then.' Michael pulled me forward, and I stumbled inside.

Michael closed the door behind us, then led me to the bed. 'Are you sure you're not nervous? You seem a little terrified.'

I tried to laugh again as Michael put on music: his own.

'Just a little cold.'

As Michael undressed me, my body grew stiffer. He really was *so* much older. And was it okay to have sex? The hospital said I was fully healed, but was I?

Michael must have noticed I looked frightened, because he said: 'I thought you'd done this before, honey. You really do look scared stiff.'

I faked a smile then, embarrassed. The last thing I wanted was to look inexperienced or naive.

'No,' I said, words steely. 'Not at all.'

'Good,' said Michael. 'We don't want any amateurs here. This isn't amateur night.'

I helped Michael take my clothes off then and he kissed every part of my body from head to toe. At first, he stayed away from any sexual areas deliberately and completely. In short, he knew the moves and I was able to relax. A lot.

I did things that night that I'd never done before. Sex in three different positions. Oral sex, giving and receiving. Truthfully, I would have done anything to impress Michael and show him I definitely *wasn't* nervous. Even though I was.

When the sex finished, Michael and I lay in each other's arms. He stroked my hair and watched me for a long time, then fell asleep and snored. I looked at the walnut dash ceiling, thinking how crazy life was.

Not so long ago, I'd been in a hospital bed, looking at white Styrofoam tiles and thinking they might be the last thing I would ever see.

Now I was in the arms of Michael Reyji Ray. This was my rebirth. A new beginning.

I'd spent my life running with a heavy backpack. Now finally, I could take it off.

Michael and I would get married and live happily ever after, just like a fairy tale.

I was sure of it.

Lorna

Nick and I lay together in bed, my head on his chest.

'Are you still awake?' I ask the ceiling.

'Yes,' says Nick.

'What's the difference between protective and suffocating?' I ask.

Nick snorts. 'Probably only a few inches of padding.'

I laugh too. 'I locked Liberty's phone in the safe.'

'Lorna.' I feel Nick shake his head. 'Why'd you do that?'

'She was using it to find out about her father,' I said.

'And you think taking her phone is going to stop her? Come on. Let her get out there and make her own mistakes.'

We both listen for a moment, hearing Darcy's gentle murmurs. But then they fall silent.

'Phew,' says Nick.

Darcy used to scream the place down at bedtime. But we've got a routine going now, same thing every night. I take her around the house, showing her how I lock everything up, door locks, chains, deadbolts. Then we do a bath (exactly 37 degrees) and count her yellow soft toys, all thirty of them. Now she goes to bed like a dream and sleeps until morning.

Nick and I lie in silence for a moment. Then I blurt it out: 'Liberty knows who her father is.'

'How?' Nick asks. 'You won't tell me or Liberty the first thing about the guy. Not even his name. How could she have found out?'

'She found some stuff on the internet about him. And me.' I shiver against Nick's warm body.

Nick's arms stiffen. 'What stuff on the internet?'

'Photos of me and her father. When we were younger. I don't know if it's enough, but … I'm so scared, Nick.'

'Scared of what?'

'She might try to find her father.' I take a shaky breath. Breathe, breathe.

'I think you have to get a bit real with this,' says Nick. 'How long are you going to be able to keep Liberty away from this guy? If she wants to see him, she will. No matter what you do.'

I ignore him. 'I've just got to keep hammering it home. How dangerous he is. Until she gets the message.'

'How dangerous are we talking, exactly?'

'How dangerous do you want him to be? Dangerous. Isn't that enough?'

'It's not that I don't believe you. It's just …'

'You think there are two sides to the story.'

'I haven't heard either side of the story,' says Nick. 'You've told me nothing. And whenever I ask, you close up. Does your sister know about him?'

'Dee? Yes.'

'You can tell her but not me?'

'I didn't tell her, Nick. She was there. She saw it all.'

'Do you know what I think? I think you're running scared and you should face up to all this. You should at least talk about what happened. You shouldn't run away from it. Face your problems.'

'You can't face Liberty's father. That's not how it works. He twists everything around.'

'So move on and let all the fear go.'

'I can't do that either. If I let my guard down, he'll get in.'

'You know, Lorna, even criminals get visitation with their children. Why don't you set something up? In a safe space.'

I swallow, feeling sick. 'If you knew him like I do, you wouldn't even suggest something like that.'

'So tell me about the guy. Then maybe I *could* know him like you do. Why is everything such a big secret? What did he do that was so bad?'

I roll away from Nick, imagining packing boxes, separating finances ... who will stay in the house? Me or him? It has to be him. Darcy can't go through another house move so soon, not now she's settled. It's not fair. But then again, I chose this area for a reason. A good reason. God – how is this going to work?

I roll back again. 'Listen,' I say. 'If Liberty gets close to her father, he'll turn her against me. That's what he does.'

'I know he hurt you.'

'It wasn't *just* me he hurt.'

'Isn't Liberty old enough to make this choice for herself now? Isn't it her right?'

'No.'

There is a heavy silence.

'What are you so afraid of, Lorna?'

'Her father doesn't have any feelings.'

'That's all?'

I hesitate. 'Trust me. It's enough.'

Once upon a time ...

The night after I slept with Michael, I woke to the sun rising through slatted metal blinds. It was cold on the tour bus, with cloying, damp air. The window was slightly open and morning flowed over my naked body. My mouth was dry and sugary. I wanted to shower and brush my teeth, but I was in heaven. Everything was perfect.

I looked around glossy, fibreglass walls, smiling, smiling. I'd fallen asleep wrapped up in Michael's arms. As I blinked away sleep and felt my nakedness, I rolled around to find Michael's eyes were open too.

'Good morning, my gorgeous girl,' he said. 'Welcome to this beautiful day.'

He had a craggy face that looked even older in the morning light and he smelt of beer and whiskey. There were lines all around his eyes and one huge groove along his forehead. But to me he was beautiful. My handsome prince. My hero. His eyes were intense, mesmerizing pools of light.

'I think I love you,' I told Michael, eyes all big and dumb and earnest. *Jesus*. What an idiot I was.

Michael said: 'Love is a wonderful thing, isn't it? In all its forms.'

'So … where do we go from here?' I asked.

'You can't always have a plan. Right?' Michael pulled me into his arms, holding me against his bare chest.

'We'll see each other again, won't we?'

'The band and I leave for Washington tonight,' said Michael. 'We're doing some photos today, then we hit the road. The big world tour, starting in the US.' He took my hand and drew a road down my palm. 'Washington. Atlanta. Houston. You wanna come with us? Be our lucky mascot?'

'You'd take me with you?' I asked, sitting up. 'On tour?'

Michael laughed, showing white teeth in black stubble. 'You know, it's just travelling on a bus with a load of old men. That's all a tour is. But sure. I'd love to have you along. We'll keep you a little bit quiet, though.'

'Why?'

'Well, my wife can't find out about you, right? Or there'd be trouble.'

I sat bolt upright. 'Your wife?'

'You must know about Diane. You're a fan, aren't you?'

'I knew you got married when you were really young. Your childhood sweetheart. But I thought …' I shook my head. 'I didn't realize … you're still *together*?'

'Together is too strong a word for it. We're friends. Good friends. Not a husband and wife in the true sense. But it would break the poor girl's heart if I put her through a divorce right now. She's just lost her father.'

Happiness drained away like warm bathwater, leaving me cold and exposed.

'I would never have stayed last night if …. I had no idea you were still married.'

'I told you.' Michael lay back then, arms falling away from me. 'Diane and I are just friends these days. But it's your choice, Lorna. If it's not meant to be, it's not meant to be. I'll tell you something though – last night was magic.'

A lump hit my throat when he said my name. 'It was more than magic. Last night was the best night of my life.'

I sure didn't know about playing it cool back then …

'You and I have a soul connection,' said Michael, stroking my hair. 'I felt it the moment I saw you. I believe in that kind of love. Soul love. Not bits of paper, who belongs to who. Boyfriend, girlfriend, husband, wife, all those labels. You love who you love when you love them. But it sounds like the world down here has a hold over you. The planets aren't aligning.'

'I have to go.' I pulled a blanket around my body and searched the shiny floor for my clothes, tears coming.

Michael sat up, watching me. 'Listen, you blew me away last night. Totally blew me away. We had a good time together. Soul mates always meet again. Maybe not in this life but another one.'

As I opened the bedroom door, I saw two other sleeping bodies in the lounge area: girls from outside the stage doors last night. They were naked and partially covered with blankets.

It looked sordid and I felt the cheapness of it all – young girls sleeping with musicians who couldn't care less about them.

Michael came to the door. 'I can see that pretty little brain working. Put all that down. All that stress. That's what gave you cancer.' He put a hand to my chest. 'We're old souls, you and I. We'll meet again somewhere, somehow.'

My chest felt warm with his touch. Like he was imparting some kind of energy.

'I wish you weren't married.'

Michael kissed my head. 'Danny will take you home. Okay? We've got my little Jaguar F-Type tucked under this bus, believe it or not. It's in the hold, right underneath us. How about that? Don't say anything to the press, will you? Don't be that girl.' He pushed the door all the way open. 'Danny,' he shouted down the bus. 'Danny – this girl needs a ride home.'

The driver poked his head out from the cab at the front.

'You'll be safe with Danny,' said Michael, slinging his arm around my shoulder in a pally way. 'I've known this man for years. He'll look after you. Okay, love?'

The term of endearment felt dismissive. Disconnected.

I felt the cold, hard thump of the bedroom door closing behind me.

Lorna

It's 8 a.m.

'Liberty?' I yell up the stairs. 'What's happening up there? It's nearly time for school.'

Liberty still hasn't come down for breakfast. Usually she's up at seven, walking the grounds with Skywalker.

She's angry with me, I'm sure. Sulking.

I wonder how well she slept last night. I only managed a few hours.

This morning, I'm determined to smooth things over.

Last night was not a good night.

I've made Liberty a fresh fruit plate with a side of yoghurt, coconut and quinoa – her favourite.

Nick and Darcy have already eaten breakfast omelettes and left for nursery. Cheddar cheese omelette with crunched-up cornflakes for Darcy; spinach, feta and tomato for Nick.

Omelette is Nick's speciality, and the only thing he can cook well. He makes omelette for himself and Darcy every morning, and sometimes for lunch and dinner too.

'Liberty?'

I carry Liberty's fruit plate to the table and adjust slices of fruit to neaten the display. I've cut the kiwi, mango and strawberries to look like the artist Frida Kahlo, with mango for the face and slivered grapes for eyebrows. Liberty loves Frida, and I love doing fun little things like this for Liberty. Showing my love however I can.

'Sweetheart?' I call. 'Rise and shine. You'll be late.'

Still no answer.

I climb Liberty's staircase, the bare wood smooth and warm under my feet. I am grateful for this house. There was a time I never believed I'd have a life like this. Our own land. A yoga room. Study. Library. And high, high gates all around.

'Liberty?'

I knock on my daughter's door.

'Honey?'

It's unlike Liberty not to answer, but the fight last night was pretty bad.

I push the door open, listening.

There's nothing – no sound, no grumbling, no shower running. Skywalker doesn't come running to greet me.

Liberty's bedroom is dark, but the bed has been made. Liberty always makes her bed the moment she gets up, even when she's not well.

Where is she, then? And where is Skywalker?

I stroke the cotton duvet, feeling for Liberty in the gloom, but find nothing – no soft, warm body.

'Liberty?'

The ensuite door is slightly open, but no light spills out.

Flicking on the bedroom light, I feel uneasy.

I start to rationalize.

She must have gone running in the grounds, maybe she's training Skywalker outside, maybe, maybe …

But things are missing. Liberty's miniature turtle bookmark – the one she keeps on her desk for good luck. Her cherry-red DM boots.

I open her built-in closet, heart racing.

Some clothes are gone and there's a big, gaping hole where her canvas army backpack usually sits.

Suddenly, I am overwhelmed. Immobilized by fear.

'Liberty, please,' I say, voice weak. 'If you're here … it's not funny.'

I go to Liberty's ensuite again. Maybe she's hiding in the dark. Playing a trick on me. But when I pull the light cord, flickering light shows me an empty room. Liberty's bamboo toothbrush has gone. Her hairbrush too.

Oh God. Oh God. Oh God.

Now I'm tearing downstairs, screaming over and over again: 'Liberty! Liberty!'

The chain is off the backdoor. It's never off. I latch it every night. Every single night. It's part of my routine or, as Nick calls it, my OCD.

Why have a chain on the back door? Nobody has a chain on the back door. And when we have that great big gate out there? Isn't this a little bit of overkill?

I imagine someone creeping upstairs in the dead of night. Stealing my beautiful daughter. But Skywalker would have barked. Liberty would have shouted and fought. And none of her things would be missing …

No. That's not what happened.

Liberty crept downstairs – probably early in the morning, after I'd fallen asleep. Skywalker was close at her heels. She carried her army bag stuffed with clothes. The front door would be too noisy, she wouldn't risk it. Instead she headed out the back way, softly slipping the chain from its metal tunnel. She carefully took Skywalker's leash from the hook and clicked it to his collar.

Now she's outside, alone in the dark, heading to the front gate. She knows exactly where she's headed. She's going to see her father ...

I hear myself scream her name. 'LIBERTY!'

Okay.

Calm. Calm.

Breathe in, breathe out.

She could have gone to a friend's house.

Call Liberty's phone, I think. *Just call her.* But then I realize I took her phone last night.

Call the police then. You know the number ...

I grab my own phone from the solar charging station.

I've called the police so many times about Liberty. I am the woman who cried wolf.

'Hello, what is your emergency?'

For a stupid second, I jump at a disembodied voice:

'Oh! Hey. Hello. Police.' And then I add a British, 'Please.'

There's a slight delay as I'm connected.

'Sussex police. Can I take your name?'

'My daughter. She's gone. She's ... she's run away.'

'Can I have your full name and address?'

'She's called Liberty. Liberty Miller. She's tall. Nearly five foot ten. Very thin. Tanned skin. Green eyes and brown hair, but she's cut it short, like chin length, and dyed it blonde. Well, parts of it. Bright blonde. I think she left early this morning.'

I'm crying now, trying to hold it together.

'We need *your* name, madam, before we can take details.'

'My name?' My throat tightens. 'Why? Why do you need my name?'

'It's just the way we do things.'

Of course. Of course they have to take my name. They always take my name. Nothing to worry about.

'Lorna,' I say. And then I add Nick's surname, even though we're not married yet. 'Lorna Armstrong. We live at Iron Bridge Farm, Taunton Wood.'

The policewoman is soothing. 'First things first. Are there any friends your daughter could have gone to?'

'I don't know. I don't know who her friends are. If I did, I'd have Facebook stalked them by now and harassed their phone lines.'

The policewoman hesitates for a moment, and I think she's going to make a comment like most people do. Something about me being overprotective. But instead she says, 'It's good that you care.'

Some people understand. The ones who've seen the bad side of the world.

I give more details, and then the policewoman tells me she'll get someone over ASAP.

'In the meantime, call people you know,' says the police-woman. 'Try not to worry too much. This happens more than you might imagine and they always turn up unharmed. How old is your daughter?'

'Sixteen.'

Another pause.

'And you think she left home of her own free will?'

'Someone could have put her up to it. Tricked her or ... something.'

'But no signs of force? I don't want to scare you; I just want to get things clear. No signs of a ... a scuffle or anything like that?'

'No. She made her bed.' I'm crying again now.

'We'll get a police officer over to you now.'

'There's something else.' I leave the sentence hanging, not sure if I'll manage to finish it.

The policewoman is kind, offering a gentle, 'Yes?'

I grip the phone. 'I think she might have gone to see her father.'

'Oh. Right. Well, that could be a simple answer, couldn't it? Do you ... What's the situation there then?'

'She's never met him before.'

'You have sole custody?'

I hesitate. 'Yes. He's ... not a good guy.' I pause, considering my next words carefully. 'He's famous. It's hard to explain.'

'What's her father's name and address?' the policewoman asks.

'Her father's name?' My throat goes tight again. I know what comes next. I know what happens when I say his name. It's like a witch's curse.

I look up then, seeing my scared face in the sliding-door glass. White skin. Black hair. Blue eyes cornflower coloured again, bright with fear.

'Michael Reyji Ray.'

There's a long pause.

'Michael Reyji Ray?'

'Yes.'

'Michael Reyji Ray is your daughter's father?'

And suddenly the policewoman's tone totally changes – a subtle thing, but I feel it. She's gone from being on my side to thinking I'm crazy.

This is Michael's power. A man she's never met is controlling her.

'Yes.'

'But your daughter's never met him before?'

'No. She's never met him. I don't want her meeting him. He'll use her to get at me.'

Another pause.

'I thought … Michael Reyji Ray is married, isn't he? Has been for years.'

'Yes. Married men can still have children with other women.'

'Have you … do you *stop* your daughter seeing her father, then?'

'Of course I do.'

'So she'd have a good reason for wanting to meet him?'

'He isn't the person you think he is,' I say. 'This kind, environmental, happily married man. It's all just an image.'

'Sometimes when people hurt us—'

'He's a bad person.' I shriek the words.

The police officer's voice becomes more serious. 'Listen. I understand why you're feeling threatened, but let's not start throwing accusations around. You're worried. Your daughter is very young to just be packing a bag and leaving without telling you. But she is legally allowed to do so.'

'Please. You have to get her back.'

'Look, we can't go knocking on Michael Reyji Ray's door, accusing him of taking your daughter away. If she's sixteen and he ... well if he *is* her biological father, she has a right to see him. She has a right to leave home if she wants to. Have you tried calling her?'

I put a hand to my throbbing forehead. 'I took her phone away last night.'

'Oh. Right. Why did you do that then?'

I pause. 'Because ... because she was looking up things about Michael.'

'Listen, we'll send someone over,' says the policewoman. 'But I think you're playing a risky game. If you've stopped your daughter see her father, well, this is the age they rebel, isn't it? And there's no law against that. You can't control them when they get to this age, Ms Armstrong. At some point, you have to let them fly.'

'No.' The word is firmer than I meant it to be. 'She can't fly. It's not safe out there.'

There's a long pause.

'We'll get someone over to you. In the meantime, try to stay calm. I've been in this job a long time. This sounds like something that will blow over. Not as bad as you think.'

'It's absolutely as bad as I think,' I say. 'Every bit as bad.'

Once upon a time …

The day after I slept with Michael Reyji Ray, he was all I could think about. If I'd been obsessed before, that was nothing to how I felt now. It was like being a drug addict, wanting another hit.

Michael Reyji Ray was in my head, like a catchy song.

Danny, Michael's driver, dropped me off outside my shabby brown walk-up apartment, and I climbed three flights of stairs, dropped into bed and stayed there all day.

When the light started to change, Dee came into my room with a bowl of curly noodles. She was soft and round in Minnie Mouse pyjamas – the outfit she always wore around the apartment because she said day clothing cut into her excess weight.

'Do you want some?' Dee asked. 'I've found this great trick. You put the powder on *after* you've drained the water. You can really taste the shrimp flavouring that way. Here. Try some. There's too much here for me.'

I knew this was a lie. Not about the shrimp flavouring. That there was too much food for Dee. I'd known her eat a can of eight hot dogs, plus buns, in one sitting and still have room for dessert.

'I'm too lovesick to eat,' I told her.

'I can't believe my sister slept with Michael Reyji Ray.' Dee sat on my bed, and it squeaked under her weight. 'You *actually* had sex with a real live famous person.'

'I know. It was amazing.'

'You were careful, right? You know what the hospital said about infections.'

'It's fine. I'm telling you, Dee, this was meant to be.'

Dee placed her noodles on the floor. 'Sounds like a dirty old man slept with a teenage fan to me. But it's happened. Can you cross him off your list now?'

'My list said marry Michael Reyji Ray,' I said. 'I haven't married him yet.'

Dee laughed. 'You're too late. He married his childhood sweetheart already. Even I know that, and I can't stand his pretentious Pink Floyd rip-off music.'

'Don't remind me. I thought he and his wife must have split up or something. But they haven't. He asked me to come on tour with him. But … he said I'd have to stay a secret from his wife.'

'Ugh. How gross. Was he into weird rock-star shit?'

'No. He was nice. Good.'

'Maybe you should sell your story. Teach him a lesson for cheating on his wife.'

'Come on. I'd never do that.'

'You look weird,' Dee decided. 'Your eyes are all glazed.'

'I told you. I've really fallen for him. I keep thinking about the tour invitation.'

'Oh, no. Do not be a teenage idiot who runs off on tour with an old, married rock star.'

I gave a romantic sigh. 'It feels like I just passed up destiny.'

'Hey – *Pretty Woman*'s on in half an hour. If you want fantasy land, why don't you watch that with me?'

'I just want to be alone.'

'And no noodles?'

'No thanks.'

Dee left me then, taking her noodles with her and eating as she walked.

I lit two lavender tea lights, watching them burn and flicker on my dressing table.

Breathe in, breathe out. Focus on the breath.

It was sunset outside, all pink and purple and grey. The city winked and glimmered, dusty and brown.

Breathe in, breathe out. Focus.

Breathe in, breathe out and Michael, Michael, Michael.

We were soul mates. He was the reason I'd been kept alive. I'd just walked away from my destiny.

As I tried to clear my mind and find answers, there was a 'bang, bang, bang' on my door.

'Lorna?' Dee's voice sailed through the cardboardy wood.

'I'm meditating,' I called back.

'Um … I think you might want to stop for a minute.' Dee opened the bedroom door and peered around it. 'There's someone here to see you.'

I untwisted my legs. 'Who?' I asked.

'You're not going to believe this.'

'What?'

'It's Michael Reyji Ray.'

'You're kidding me.' My heart began to pound. 'No way. If

this is a joke … this is a joke, isn't it? I didn't tell him where I lived.'

'His driver took you home, right?' said Dee.

'Michael's here? He's really here?' The words were almost a squeal.

'He's really here. But Lorna, don't go doing anything silly now.'

'I … hang on.' I checked my reflection in the mirror, pulling fingers through my hair to give it more volume, then drew on the same kohl eyes I'd worn last night.

'Lorna.' Dee stepped into the bedroom and closed the door. 'If he asks you to go on tour, you won't go, will you?'

My hand hesitated as I drew on kohl. 'Of course not. I'm not running off and leaving you alone.'

'Be careful. I don't have a good feeling about this.'

'You know, he said he and his wife are sort of separated. Good friends, nothing more.'

'Isn't that what they all say? You're not yourself. You've got like … crazy cult-victim eyes.'

'We had this *amazing* connection. We both felt it, I swear to you.'

A seed of denial lies in all of us. Michael was just a gardener. I know that now.

I checked my reflection in the mirror again and threw on the denim jacket with Michael's picture on it.

Okay, okay.

Breathe.

The front door was slightly ajar. Michael's low voice came through the gap: 'Is my punk princess in there?'

Oh my God, oh my God. It really was him. He was here at my apartment.

I ripped open the door, heart pounding, legs weak. And there he was: Michael Reyji Ray on my doorstep.

Michael wore black jeans and a black T-shirt. His hair was dazzling white-blond and his eyes still shone with dark, mesmerizing light.

I started to giggle then and couldn't stop.

Michael managed a smile. 'Something funny?'

'It's weird,' I said. 'Seeing you here outside my apartment, Michael Reyji Ray. In all your rock and roll gear.'

'Danny told me where you lived,' said Michael. 'I couldn't leave without you. You've got in my head. And my heart. The tour bus is ready to go. Come with us. You'll break me if you say no.'

'I can't. I can't just up and leave my sister.'

'What is it?' said Michael. 'You have bills to pay here? I'll pay them.'

'It's not that. Dee has been there for me my whole life. I can't just up and leave her alone.'

Michael pulled a roll of bills from inside his jacket – more money than I'd ever seen in my life. 'Here. Give this to your sister, and you and I can hit the road.'

'I'm taking classes …'

'This is the school of life, princess. You'll learn more on tour than you will in any classroom. Come on. This is the chance of a lifetime.'

I broke into a huge grin and leapt on him, throwing myself into his arms.

I felt like I'd been dipped in gold. Bathed in bright light. My handsome prince had come to get me.

'Is that a yes?' Michael said, laughing.

I nodded against his neck.

Michael whispered in my ear, 'Get your things. Let's get on the bus.'

'I have to talk to my sister,' I said. 'Will you give me a minute?'

Dee appeared behind me then.

'Lorna,' she said. 'What's going on?'

'I was just going to talk to you about—'

'This is your sister?' Michael asked.

'Yes,' I said. 'This is Dee.'

'A pleasure to meet you,' said Michael, reaching out his hand to shake hers. Dee didn't take it.

'Lorna, please don't do what I think you're going to do,' said Dee, arms crossed.

'Listen, I'll take care of your sister here,' said Michael. 'You have my word. And I'll make sure all her rent is covered – whatever you need. I won't leave you in a hole.' He offered the big roll of cash to Dee.

Dee didn't take the money. Instead, she fixed him with hard eyes. 'You're married. Right?'

Michael scratched his nose. 'It's complicated. Diane and I are apart more than we're together. But let's not get into that. Bits of paper and legal crap.'

'Lorna has a life here,' said Dee. 'She has exams coming up. And she's still recovering. Did she tell you she had cancer?'

'She told me all about it,' said Michael. 'The full story. I will take care of her.'

'Lorna, don't do this,' said Dee. 'This is running away from your life. Not towards it. This is escape. Distraction.' She turned on Michael. 'Don't you care that she's studying? That you're taking her away from her education?'

'Sometimes real life is the best education,' said Michael, stroking my arm and looking at me like I was something precious.

'And what's in it for you?' Dee asked, arms still crossed. She knew the answer, of course. Sex on tap with a pliable, stupid teenager. But I have to hand it to Michael. Looking back, he never promised me anything. He was always upfront about who he was and what he was offering. It was me who filled in the blanks.

'I want to go with him,' I told Dee, nodding and nodding.

'Lorna, I do not approve of this. It is not okay with me. This isn't about rent or anything like that. It's about your education and me caring about you. I swear to god, Lorna, if you go with him now, don't come back when it all goes wrong.'

'Fine,' I said. 'Rent my room out.'

Michael turned to me with soft eyes. 'The tour bus is parked right up outside. Shall we get going?'

I laughed in happy shock. 'Your tour bus is outside *right now*?'

Michael put hands on my shoulders. 'We took a detour to come get you. To steal you away in the dead of night.'

'What if she'd said no?' Dee asked.

'Soul mates don't say no,' said Michael with a flicker of a wink. 'Go pack a suitcase, princess. Let's get going.'

As I flung things into a bag – some clothes, books I was

reading for school and all my make-up – Dee stood behind me. 'Please. Please don't do this.'

But when her words had no effect, Dee swung the other way again.

'Fine. Be that way. Leave me all alone. Just don't come crawling back to me when it all goes wrong.'

'It's not going to go wrong,' I promised her. 'This is destiny, Dee. Last night was the most amazing night. I've never felt this way about anyone. It'll be fine. Better than fine. Don't you think after everything I've been through I deserve my happily ever after?'

Dee let me go with a face that told me I'd broken her heart.

As far as I know, she never took Michael's money.

Lorna

I pace the kitchen, phone hot against my ear.

I'm calling the only other mother I know – Helen. And I don't know her that well. She used to bring her daughter, Julianne, here for playdates when Liberty was younger, but Liberty hasn't talked about Julianne in years. I know I'm clutching at straws. I need a Coke for all the straws I'm clutching at.

Liberty's breakfast fruit plate sits on the breakfast table. I've left it there because clearing it away is like admitting Liberty's gone. And that's too painful.

Nick is on his way home. He was on his way to a personal training client when I rang him. Good guy that he is, he turned his car right around and came home, promising his client a month of free sessions.

The police have come and gone. They told me that Liberty is legally allowed to visit her father. There is no reason to suspect that Michael Reyji Ray would hurt anyone. There's nothing on record. It's all fine. Leave her to it.

'Michael Reyji Ray is not a good person,' I said over and over again. I got the familiar looks of disbelief.

Michael Reyji Ray. Environmentalist. Music legend. Happily

*married to his childhood sweetheart. And what a dancer. A bad
guy? You've got to be kidding – I have three of his albums.
And I had the biggest crush on him when I was a teenager …*

I pace by the gate as the phone rings and rings. Eventually
a voice clicks on the line.

'Hello?'

'Hello?' I start gabbling like a maniac. 'Helen? Liberty's
gone. Might Julianne know where she is?'

'Miss Miller?'

I hesitate. '*Julianne?* Is that you? When did you grow up?
You sound just like your mother.'

'Yes, it's me, Miss Miller. Mum left for work already.'

'Do you know where Liberty is, Julianne? She … she wasn't
in her bed when I woke up this morning.'

'I'm very sorry to hear that,' says Julianne.

'You … I mean, you girls were friends once. Has she told
you anything?'

'We were friends about a hundred years ago,' says Julianne,
sounding suddenly prim. 'Liberty changed. She doesn't play
chess or scrabble anymore … and now she's into all that punk
rock music stuff.'

'She talked about someone called Abi. Do you know who
that is?'

'Oh, *her*. Yes, they hang out all the time, singing. Everyone
thinks they're going to be famous.'

'Do you have a number for her?'

'No. I don't even have Liberty's number anymore. Have you
tried calling Liberty? She has a phone, doesn't she?'

'She doesn't have her phone with her. I took it last night.'

'Have you looked on her phone? For friends' phone numbers?'

'Her phone is locked. I don't have the passcode. Where could she *be*?'

'I have no idea, Miss Miller. We don't really hang out anymore. I don't appreciate Liberty's attitude at school, to be honest. She thinks she's better than everyone, just because she's in a band. We don't have an awful lot in common.'

'A band? Liberty's in a band?' Panic. Utter panic.

'Well … yeah. Didn't you know? They think they're going to be like the Beatles or something. Well, not the Beatles. I don't know what sort of music they play.'

'I didn't know she was in a band.' Nausea rises again. And then I start rambling: 'Julianne. I think … maybe Liberty's gone to see her father.'

Julianne hesitates. 'There's someone I could call. One of Liberty's bandmates. Freddy. He's okay. He's in chess club with me. He might know where she is.' I can almost hear her nodding at the phone. 'I'll text you his number.'

Julianne hangs up and I grab an ancient packet of cigarettes from the kitchen drawer and do something I haven't done for years – smoke.

When the text finally comes through, I've smoked a cigarette right down to the butt, coughing after every inhale.

God bless Julianne's reliability. I call the number and a young guy with a cracking, adolescent voice answers.

'Hello?'

'Hi … Freddy? This is Lorna. Liberty's mother.'

'Oh.' A long pause. 'Liberty told me about you.'

He means 'warned' of course. I take the bullet.

'Listen, Freddy. Liberty has gone. She ran away this morning.'

More silence.

'Do you know where she might have gone?'

Freddy doesn't answer, but I hear him breathing.

I try for a softer approach: 'How do you and Liberty know each other anyway? She doesn't tell me about her friends.'

'We're neighbours,' says Freddy, in a voice that conveys both surprise and teenage contempt for the utter stupidity of adults.

'We are?'

'Yes.'

'I can't see the street from our house. I guess … I've never noticed you.'

'I'm the brown guy.'

'So?'

'Well … I stand out around here, is what I'm saying.'

'You're in a band with Liberty?'

A pause. 'Yes.'

'And there's another person in the band? Abi, right?'

'Yes. Abi.'

'Could she be with her?'

'I mean … probably not.'

'How do you know?'

Another long silence.

'Do you know where she is?' I feel a horrible pang as the mother-daughter elastic band of closeness snaps completely. This complete stranger knows more about my daughter's whereabouts than I do. 'Please, Freddy. Please, please tell me if you do. I can't look after her if I don't know where she is.'

More silence.

A horrible chill runs through my stomach.

'Has she gone to see her father, Freddy?' I ask. 'Is that where she's gone?'

A long pause.

'Um ...'

'Please tell me. Please. If you don't, I'll have to send the police around your house and—'

'Yes. Okay, Miss Miller. Okay. Liberty's gone to her father's house. So there's no need to worry. She's been planning the visit for a while.'

'No need to worry!' I scream the words.

One of us hangs up, I'm not sure who. And I'm running to the garage, hunting in my pocket for van keys. It's only when I jump into the driver's seat that I realize I'm about to drive somewhere I swore I'd never go back to. A place where my worst nightmares came true.

This really is happening. Liberty has fallen right into Michael's spiderweb and I'm hurling myself into the sticky silk after her.

Until now, I could have pretended. Maybe Liberty was with friends. Maybe she'd gone jogging around the neighbourhood just to scare the life out of me. Maybe, maybe ...

I swallow down fear and self-loathing as I start the van.

I've always hated being this controlling monster. The woman who watches her daughter's every move. Spies on her. I've tried to keep Liberty safe, but it hasn't worked. I built tall fences but he got her in the end.

I want to collapse against the steering wheel, sobbing,

wailing, but I don't. Instead I accelerate down the drive and through the automatic gates, aerosol cans and silicone body parts jogging around in the back of the van.

There is only one choice here, and it isn't to fall apart.

I need to get my daughter back.

As I roar towards the road, Nick's green MG turns onto the driveway.

I slam on the brakes, seeing Nick's shocked face. Then I wind down my window.

'Nick, can you back up?'

Nick leans his head out of the driver's window. 'You nearly smashed right into me.'

'Please. Can you move? Liberty's gone to see her father.'

'Her father? You're kidding.'

'I spoke to one of her friends. Some guy she's in a band with. She's gone to her father's house.'

'Liberty's in a band? That's cool.'

'Not cool, Nick. Not cool at all. Her father is in the music business.'

Nick frowns. 'Lorna, what's the story with this guy? Don't you think it's time you told me?'

'Nick, please just move. Please.' My eyes flick to the road. 'I'll tell you his name, how about that?'

'Who cares what his name is?'

'He's famous. Okay? Crazy famous. Like, Grammy award-winning millionaire famous. If I tell you who he is, will you move out of my way?'

Nick grips the steering wheel. 'If that's the best I'm going to get right now.'

'Liberty's father is Michael Reyji Ray.'

'Whoa.' Nick stares. 'You're kidding me. Michael Reyji *Ray*?'

'She's gone to his house and I'm going after her.'

'You know where Michael Reyji Ray lives?'

'Yes.'

'Where?'

I hesitate. 'Not far from here. Huntingdon Woods. He owns them.'

'Huntingdon *Woods*? But … that's … like a half-hour drive.'

I nod, eyes looking past him.

'Why, Lorna?'

'Why what?'

'You could have lived anywhere. You're a US citizen. You could have lived in the States. But you chose to live less than thirty miles from the guy, for Christ's sake. Why?'

'It's hard to explain.'

Nick's eyes harden. 'Try.'

'Nick. Right now, I just need to get Liberty out of there. Will you stay here? Someone needs to stay here. In case she comes back.'

Nick's shoulder's sag in resignation. 'I'll stay. But I'm struggling to get it, seriously. Really struggling. We live *so close* to the guy … why not live the other side of London at least?'

'This is her father's world,' I say. 'Don't expect anything to make sense from now on.'

Once upon a time ...

'I feel bad about my sister,' I told Michael as he carried my battered rucksack onto the tour bus.

'Stop thinking so much,' said Michael. 'I'll sort all the rent and bills. Your sister will have the whole place to herself. She'll be okay. Trust me.'

'Okay isn't the same as good.'

'She has her own life to live, just like you have yours.' Michael kissed my hand. 'Welcome to your chariot, my lady. The passion wagon.'

I laughed. 'The passion wagon?'

'We're gonna have some fun times on this bus. Just you wait and see.'

Leaving Dee was a selfish choice. But as a dumb sixteen-year-old cancer survivor who thought herself in love with a rock star, nothing was going to stop me. I climbed right onto that magical, gleaming tour bus, with its fridges of cold beer and lounging rock stars plucking at guitar strings.

This was what heaven looked like, right?

The bus pulled away and I waved goodbye to my sister and sanity.

If only I hadn't walked up those steps. But then again, I wouldn't have Liberty. That's a thought I cling to.

And so we hit the road.

For the first couple of gigs – Washington DC and Atlanta – everything was perfect. I hung out with Michael, the band and crew, being the pretty little tour bunny mascot. Michael gave me tight Crimson T-shirts to wear, and his assistant bought me tiny shorts, tight black jeans and kitten heels.

'You look sexy in those clothes,' he told me. 'Like a super-model.'

The compliments made me miss something important: I was no longer making decisions about my own clothes. Michael was now in charge of my wardrobe.

At night, Michael and I would head to the bus bedroom, crazy in love, naked, staring into each other's eyes, sex all night. Like any good manipulator, Michael made sure he put in a lot of the good stuff up front. He always told me how sexy I was, how beautiful I looked, how madly in love he was, how I was his soul mate, the girl of his dreams. This, to my inexperienced sixteen-year-old self, was what a great sexual relationship looked like.

As the tour bus hopped from state to state, things got wilder. Michael wanted new things. I didn't like all of it, but it was okay because I was still getting what I really wanted – Michael's encouragement and approval.

You're so sexy, Lorna. You're an amazing girl. We're wild, aren't we, the two of us? A pair of rebels. My wife would never do this. We push boundaries. You're doing that just right …

Michael's good opinion meant everything to me, so 'no' was not in my vocabulary.

He would take my palm, find my twisted life line and tell me that was the two of us – knotted together by destiny. And he would listen. To everything. How unsafe I'd felt as a kid. How Dee had taken on the motherhood role, and how there were times when I thought she resented me. How abandoned I felt by the father I'd never met, and how only Dee came to see me in hospital.

'I love you,' we'd say, in unison, and then burst out laughing. Michael talked about all the things we had in common. Our hair colour. Our star sign. Foods we both liked. He put in all that work at the beginning to lodge the hook firmly in my mouth. So when the good stuff stopped coming, I was stuck. Wanting more. Chasing after it.

The European leg of the tour – that's when things started to change. As a matter of fact, I remember the exact moment when Michael showed his bad side for the first time. We were flying to Paris, sitting on huge, cushiony first-class seats and drinking champagne and whiskey shots.

I was reading *The Little Mermaid* by Hans Christian Andersen on that flight – not very grown-up, but one of the few books I had with me. I kept telling Michael how sad the story was.

'It's nothing like the Disney version,' I told him. 'The mermaid dies at the end.'

'What are you reading that rubbish for?' said Michael. 'We live in the here and now. Not fairyland.'

'It's a beautiful story,' I murmured, closing the book. 'She sacrifices herself for the prince.'

'Would you sacrifice yourself for me, my little punk princess?'

'Of course I would.'

'You're all mine. Forever and ever. And you'll never leave me because I'll come find you.' He folded me into his arms.

I felt ecstatic.

'I love you, Michael.'

'I love you too. Listen.' Michael rested a hand on my bare leg. 'We'll be staying in a hotel right in the centre of Paris. A lot of press. We've got to hide you a bit better, okay? The European press are crazy. It's not like in the US.'

'Hide me?' I said. 'Why?'

'Come on. You're not stupid. Diane and I are still married.'

That hit me like a punch in the face. 'But you're separated. And we're together now. The press are going to find out about us eventually. You just said ... I mean, we'll be together forever, won't we?'

'Don't make a drama out of it,' said Michael. 'I told you right at the start, I'd have to keep us quiet. We just have to keep you on the down-low. That's all there is to it.'

'I don't like the idea of sneaking around. Why can't you just tell the press you and your wife have split up? People separate all the time. What's the big deal?'

'You have to be able to handle this, Lorna,' said Michael, topping up my champagne glass. 'Drink this down, there's a girl. When all is said and done, I'm a married man.'

'But if we're together—'

'Diane and I ... it's complicated. I told you from the start I was still married. If you can't handle this stuff, then I'll fly you back home right now.'

'You said you and your wife weren't together. Do you still love her? You must do if you want to hide me away.' Tears came and I tried to get up, but Michael grabbed my arm and pulled me down.

'Jesus, Lorna, calm down. What are you, a drama queen or something? A hysteric? If I wanted one of those, I'd have taken my wife on tour. You wanted to come on the bus. You wanted to be one of the big girls. If you can't handle being a grown-up, go home. This is no place for kids.'

'I don't want to sneak around and hide. If you and your wife are really separated—'

'Christ, Lorna, do you even have a brain?' He tapped my forehead sharply. 'Is everything firing okay in there? One of our biggest songs right now is "Fever Few" and everyone thinks I wrote it about Diane. No one can know we're not together. It would kill our record sales.'

'Did you write it about her?'

'I write a new song every day. I don't know what or why I'm writing the words half the time. It might have been about you, for all I know.'

'You wrote it five years ago.'

'I had a feeling that someone like you was coming along.' He hit me with a mesmerizing stare. 'Listen to me. Diane will be humiliated if photos of you and me come out in the gutter press. Would you put the poor woman through something like that? She's a Catholic girl at heart. Divorce is a sin. She doesn't understand the world like you do.'

'So … what? You're never going to divorce her?'

'Marriage is just a piece of paper. What we have is so

much bigger than that, right? We're soul mates.' Michael took my hands. 'Help me out, okay? And help Diane out – she's already heartbroken, poor girl. Let's not make it any harder for her.'

'I don't like the idea of sneaking around.'

'It won't be for long. But listen, I'm thinking of you too. You don't want the press in your face, writing stories about you, the marriage wrecker.'

'I don't care.'

Michael laughed again. 'So says the naive little idiot who's never had the press come after her. You'll care when they tear you apart. I'm telling you. Trust me on this, Lorna. Come on, now. I love you. You're my soul mate. My little punk princess soul mate. None of this stuff with Diane matters.'

'You mean it? That you love me?'

'Of course.' Michael pulled me into a tight hug. 'Now stop being an idiot. Okay? And do as you're told.' He kissed my head and laughed. 'Or I'll send you back to that sister of yours who never wanted you around.'

I let the hurt be hugged out of me. 'Dee did want me around. She took me in when—'

'She resents you. You told me yourself. Lucky you found me. The one who loves you like no one else ever will. When you're not being a hysterical female.'

'I'm not a hysterical female.'

'Then stop acting like one. You're going to be my merchandising girl for this part of the tour, okay? You'll put on a crew T-shirt and pull the suitcases.'

'You want me to pretend to be your staff member?'

Michael hugged me tighter. 'Oh, yeah. And if you're lucky I'll give you a big bonus tonight when you finish your shift.'

The tour bus pulled up on a wide Parisian street. It was afternoon. Bright and sunny. The buildings were dull in colour but still an artist's dream. The Louvre and the Pompidou Centre ... I felt crazy excitement at the thought of all the creative pilgrimages Michael and I could do here.

Two artists in love and in *Paris*.

But first, I needed to wheel the suitcases.

Just as Michael said, press snapped away as we stepped off the tour bus. Michael pushed on sunglasses and marched into the elegant, thick-carpeted hotel lobby, while I trotted behind like an obedient little puppy. My own rucksack was stuffed into one of the black suitcases, hidden away like my identity. I was getting more lost by the second.

When we reached our penthouse suite, Michael said, 'Put the luggage in the bedroom.' Like I was a bellboy.

'Where's my tip?' I asked.

Michael turned then, hair sweaty from the hot bus, black eyes furious. 'What?'

'My tip. If you're talking to me like the hired help, you should be tipping me.'

'Just put the bloody bags in the bedroom, Lorna, would you?' Michael opened a polished, antique-looking drinks cabinet and poured himself a huge measure of whiskey in a crystal-cut glass. 'Christ, maybe I should take Diane back. If you're going to be giving me all the backchat after we've been travelling for hours.' He knocked it back in three large gulps then vanished into the shower.

For a moment I just stood, gripping the suitcases. Then I pushed them both over.

'Put your own suitcases away,' I said. 'I'm going for a walk.'

Michael's damp head popped out of the shower room. His shoulders were hunched, eyes black. It was a side of him I'd never seen before.

'Do not leave this hotel room, Lorna. Don't you dare leave this room.'

'Why not?'

'Because I said so, that's why.'

'Are you going to apologize?'

'No, I'm not going to fucking apologize. Sit *down*.'

'Do you still love your wife?'

'You leave Diane out of it,' said Michael, voice scarily low. 'You're staying here.'

I hesitated at the door. 'You said you wanted to go back to her.'

'I said Diane never gave me any backchat. You could learn a thing or two about that.'

I felt sick to my stomach. 'Do you still *love her*?'

'Diane was my childhood sweetheart. She'll always have a place in my heart.'

'And what am I?'

'You're my girl right now.'

I left then, slamming the door behind me.

Paris on a sunny afternoon was beautiful, but all I could think about was Michael and Diane. Did he still have feelings for her? Did he want her back? Was it because of me, how I'd acted? If I was sweeter, more compliant, would he love me better? He'd said Diane was his first love. How could I ever compete with that? Would I always be second best? Never as good?

After a few hours I headed back to the hotel.

I felt … nervous.

I only went for a walk, I told myself as I knocked on the penthouse suite door. Big deal.

'Michael?' I called. 'Michael? It's me.'

The door swung inwards with force and there stood Michael, face tight with rage, eyes bloodshot. He wasn't much taller than me, but he seemed to fill the doorframe like a huge, raging demon.

Without saying a word, Michael grabbed my arm and pulled me inside, slamming the door behind us.

'You stupid, dumb little idiot,' he raged, gripping my shoulders, eyes burning. 'Never, ever call at the door like that. The press are everywhere. You do that again and you're gone. I'll fly you back on the next plane.'

He was shaking me. Actually shaking me.

My skinny body went rigid in his arms and I heard myself shouting: 'Stop. *Stop.*'

'You need to do as you're told, Lorna,' said Michael, releasing his grip. 'It's for your own good. I can't have you here if you don't do as you're told.'

'I just went for a walk.'

'You can't ever do that again. Just walk off like that. Ever, ever, ever.'

'I want you to tell me you love me more than your wife,' I said, starting to cry.

Michael didn't answer. Instead, he walked to the drinks cabinet and poured us both large whiskeys.

'Drink this down,' he said. 'You're being hysterical. Didn't I just tell you I can't love a girl who's hysterical? Why do you think I fell out of love with Diane?'

I learned my lesson. For the rest of the European tour, I stayed in hotel suites and on the tour bus, a good girl waiting for Michael to come home. And he didn't always come home now we were in Europe. Some nights I'd lay awake waiting for Michael, and he wouldn't turn up until lunchtime the next day.

'A late one with the boys,' he'd say. 'Christ, Diane would have nagged me like crazy for staying out. Such a relief to be with a cool girl like you.'

So I never complained.

It's crazy to think I visited Paris, Berlin, Madrid, Barcelona and so many other famous cities, but only saw the insides of luxurious hotel suites and the tour bus. Just crazy.

By the end of the tour, Michael didn't bother with the naked nights looking into my eyes anymore. He knew I'd still provide him with sex even if he shook me, screamed at me, kept me in a hotel room all day and stayed out all night.

So I did what every vulnerable, naive teenage girl does in an abusive relationship – waited and waited for the good stuff to return. It would, I was sure, when the tour was finished. Michael was stressed. We'd be staring into each other's eyes again soon, fascinated by each other, soul mates, madly in love.

I convinced myself that Michael really, truly, was my Prince Charming. A rock and roll Prince Charming. A Prince Charming who, right now, could be moody. Sure, he had a temper. But I could handle it.

The course of true love never runs smoothly.

Liberty

I clear my throat and practise saying the words out loud: 'Helloooo. My name is Liberty and I'm your long-lost daughteeeeer.'

This is so weird.

I'm standing outside my real, live biological father's house at 9 a.m. on a school day. There are huge security gates, like we have at home. Only these gates are wrought-iron railings, whereas ours are solid wood. The railing aspect is a plus because I can see through them into the grounds, the fir-tree woodland and strange mansion/castle house on the horizon. The minus is there's no intercom here. Who lives so far from the front gate but has no intercom? *We* have an intercom and our grounds are only an acre.

Skywalker sits by my leg, alert and waiting for instruction.

'How crazy is this?' I tell him. 'My father has built a great big house that looks like a castle. In the middle of the woods. He's got room for ... what? Twenty visitors? Fifty? But no one can buzz to tell him they've come to visit.'

Even though the sky is summer blue, this place has an eternal winter feel to it. If I were to sum it up in a sentence, I'd say: dark Disneyland.

The huge house on the horizon was, for sure, built by someone who wants the world to know they are very grand and important.

I shout through the railings: 'Hellooooo.' But the green, shadowy woods swallow up sound.

Skywalker chews at my denim cut-offs.

'What are you thinking?' I look up at the tall, tall gates. 'Climb?' But this idea is daunting. If I thought our gates at home were high, Michael Reyji Ray's sprawling country mansion has prison-standard security. Ten-foot tall with spikes at the top.

Mum and Michael have something in common: they both want to keep people out.

Skywalker barks and I grab his collar. 'What? What is it?'

Then I see.

Something's moving in those woods. Or rather, some*one* – a person dressed in black, moving between the shadowy trees. It looks like they're wearing a band T-shirt and black jeans.

My hand tightens on Skywalker's collar.

'What are they dragging?' I whisper. 'Scaffold poles or something?'

Skywalker lifts his brown and black nose to look at me, like, 'Don't ask me.'

'Mum will be going insane right now.' I feel a horrible pang in my heart. 'But there's no turning back. We have to do this, Sky. Or there'll be no freedom for any of us.'

I rattle the gates again. 'HELLOOO!'

The person dressed in black doesn't notice us. He or she is engrossed in some activity with silver poles, movements organized and focused.

Suddenly I have a vision: my mother, tearing my bedroom apart, sobbing hysterically, her worst nightmare coming true.

Don't think about her. Don't think about her or you'll chicken out. You have to do this. You have to meet him.

I really have no choice. Things can't go on the way they are. Mum is ruining all our lives.

'Okay, dogface.' I stroke Skywalker's head. 'It looks like climbing is the only option here.'

I put an experimental foot on the railing, seeing if I can get any lift. I like climbing – maybe because a fifty-foot wall is the closest I've ever come to real freedom. But on purpose-built climbing walls, there are ropes and harnesses and no sharp spikes at the top.

As I wedge my DM boot between two railings, I see someone coming out of the main house – a short dot of a man, wearing what looks like a flowing black silk dressing gown. His legs are bare and his hair white-blond above an orangey-brown face.

Could it be?

I hop down, watching as the figure trots into the trees, becomes invisible, then visible again, then appears in the clearing with the band T-shirt person.

I suck in my breath, feeling both sick and excited. 'I think it's him, Skywalker. I think that's my father.'

I've studied Michael Reyji Ray obsessively over the last few months. He is your typical old rock dude, puffy and partied with a weathered face and weight clinging to his waist. But he still dresses young, rocking tweedy Fedora hats over his bald patch, bleaching his hair and always wearing black Ray-Bans. This dressing-gown guy is wearing sunglasses, even in this leafy, shaded forest glade. That's a rock-star move, and no mistake.

Now the man walks to a pile of tarpaulin, pointing, and I get a really clear view. His legs are darkly tanned and his black silk dressing gown billows open to reveal tight red Speedo shorts. Adidas sliders slip around his feet. He wears this casual ensemble like royal robes, strutting as he walks.

It *is* him. Michael Reyji Ray.

This man looks like me. I've seen the pictures. I have his face. Half of me came from him. If he's as bad as my mum says, what does that make me? Half monster?

This is like staring at the cream-covered sponge cakes in our village bakery window. Knowing they're full of cream and eggs, but wanting a slice all the same. Everyone at school eats animal products. Why do I have to be so moral? Everyone else has a father. Why can't I have one?

'Hey,' I call out, rattling the gates. 'Mr Ray. MICHAEL!'

A car horn blares behind me and Skywalker starts barking. I grab him. 'Calm boy. Stay calm.'

I turn to see a black Porsche creeping towards the gate on growling tyres.

Skywalker watches the car with his brown ears pricked. There is a woman inside. She leans out of the driver's window, face tight, lips softly pink and face snow-white. She's attractive in a had-a-lot-of-work-done sort of way, with dark brown hair making a prominent widow's peak on her pale forehead.

'Get away from our gate with that big dog,' she shouts.

Skywalker starts barking.

I pull his collar. 'Shush, doggy.'

'This is private property,' the woman continues. 'If you want to see my husband, buy a concert ticket.'

'I'm not a fan,' I say.

'Then why are you here?'

'Um … there's a good reason.'

'Yes, I have a good reason too,' says the woman. 'I live here. I'm Michael Reyji Ray's wife. And I'm sick of girls thinking my husband is public property.'

'You're his wife?'

I've read about Diane McBrady – the woman Michael married before he met my mother. Her Wikipedia picture shows a dimple-cheeked, cute teenager in wellies and a knitted jumper, holding hands with Michael on an Irish moor. This woman … if she's Diane, the baby face has long gone, replaced by angular lines and plucked-to-death eyebrows. Attractive but definitely not sweet.

'Look, can you just get away from the gate,' the woman demands. 'We have a right to privacy, just like you. How would you like it if I went peering over your front gate?'

'Are you Diane?' I ask.

'Yes, I'm Diane. I told you. Michael's wife.'

'I'm Liberty. Michael's daughter.'

Diane's pink mouth drops open, brown eyes glittering. 'What?'

'I'm Michael's daughter,' I say again.

Diane watches me, unblinking. 'You're … you're Michael's *daughter*? Is that what you said?'

'Yes.' And then I add an idiotic: 'Surprise!' and do jazz hands.

Diane climbs out of the car. She wears tight black jeans, leopard-print boots and a billowing polka-dot blouse. Sort of

95

a punk look. It's a bit dated now, especially on a woman Diane's age. And she's all skin and bones. Like she starves herself. She walks towards me, heels wobbling on gravel.

'You look like him,' says Diane. 'I'll give you that. And you'd be the right age.' She watches me intensely, scanning my face with dark, black-brown eyes. 'Actually, you more than just look like him. You're the spit of him. Jesus. You'd better come inside. What's your name?'

'Liberty.'

Diane swallows. 'Liberty? And … your mother would be Lorna. Is that right?'

'Yes.'

Diane shakes her head. 'Hop in. I'll drive you up to the house.'

I hesitate. Once I'm through those gates there's no turning back. Seriously no turning back.

I feel Skywalker's fur beneath my fingertips. We could just go home. Pretend all this never happened. Say sorry and remain beautiful prisoners.

But no. No, no, no.

Things have to change.

Diane opens the passenger door.

'Is it okay for my dog to come in the car?' I ask.

'Yes, sure,' says Diane, still watching my face. 'I grew up on a farm with pigs and goats and all sorts. I don't mind animals.'

'He's a bit farty sometimes, and he dribbles—'

'He's fine,' says Diane. 'It's okay, love. Come on. Let's take you to the house and get all this sorted out. Jesus in heaven, you … you really do look like him. How old are you?'

'Sixteen.'

'Yes. Yes, you would be.' She stares. 'Well, this is some day. It really is. I think we're all in for quite the event. Hop in.'

I climb into the car, pulling a sprawling Skywalker onto my lap.

Diane throws the car into gear and roars towards the gates. They open like magic and she drives through woodland towards the fake castle.

'Fancy you coming today of all days,' Diane says, staring absentmindedly ahead. 'Life is a funny one.'

'What's today?' I ask.

'Our wedding anniversary,' says Diane, skidding the car to a halt beside a purple Jaguar F-Type and a Chevrolet Corvette Z06 convertible. 'Michael and I have been together twenty years.' She parks at an angle right by the moat bridge, two wheels on grass, as two more people wearing black band T-shirts and jeans scurry past with scaffold poles. The band T-shirts, I realize, I have Michael Reyji Ray's face on the front.

'You see that team of people there?' Diane continues. 'They've come to set up a stage in the woods. Michael will be performing later. You know what he'll sing? "Fever Few".'

'Maybe I should go—'

'No, stay,' says Diane. 'You must have come a long way. Michael will be so happy to see you. Over the moon. He's been waiting sixteen years.'

'But … this is your wedding anniversary,' I say.

Diane raises a neat little eyebrow. 'Yes. It is.'

'Well … I mean, you've been married twenty years.'

'And?'

'And I'm sixteen. So Michael and my mother …'

'Oh, you've figured it out, have you? Yes, your mother threw herself at my husband when we were not long married.'

'If I'd known it was your anniversary today, I would never have—'

'It's okay, love. Look, Lorna's little scheme failed, didn't it? I kept my man. Michael and I are still together all these years later. Until death do us part.'

'But seriously, I shouldn't have come today. It's the wrong time.'

Diane looks tired. 'It's not your fault. What happens on tour stays on tour. Isn't that what they say? Michael is the life I signed up for. Your mother wasn't the only one.'

'But the only one he had a child with.'

Diane gives a harsh laugh. 'As far as we know. Look, it was a long time ago and we survived it. Lorna put us through hell. She tried her best to ruin us. But we came out the other side stronger than ever.'

'My mother is a good person,' I say. 'I don't think she would have intended to have a relationship with a married man or try to … you know … ruin anyone.'

'Relationship?' Diane shakes her head. 'There was no *relationship*. Lorna was just a groupie and a fantasist and … sorry. I shouldn't be saying any of this to you. Look, none of this is your fault. You've only heard your mother's side of things.'

'Not really,' I say. 'My mother's never told me anything. Except what a monster my father is.'

'Yes, Lorna would say that. But what do you think? You

can't think he's all that bad if you've come to see him all on your own.'

'I want to hear his side. It blew my mind when I found out who my father was. I've been reading up about Michael for weeks now, and … you know, all the good things he's done for the environment and his charities. And his music … the lyrics are beautiful. I've always had this picture of my real dad – sort of a cross between a serial killer and a vampire. To find out he's this cool, mega-famous, environmentalist and musician … I mean, wow. And do you want to know something really weird? I'm in a band too.'

'You're in a band?' Diane's brown eyes turn wide and sincere.

'Yes.'

'You know, Michael started Crimson when he was sixteen. Maybe the apple doesn't fall far from the tree.' Diane takes a deep breath. 'Okay. Let's go and talk to Michael.'

I shake my arms out, inhaling and exhaling. 'Right. Yes. I'm ready.'

'Come on.' Diane pats my arm. 'Don't be nervous. He's going to be blown away. Just blown away.'

I climb out of the passenger side, heaving Skywalker out onto dried mud and tree roots.

There are peacocks nearby, strutting through the trees. They watch Skywalker with cocked heads, seemingly unafraid. In fact, it's Skywalker who is afraid, darting back from the birds and barking.

'Skywalker. Heel.'

'There's Michael,' she Diane, pointing at the short man

standing on a now half-built stage. 'Look at him, bossing people around. The lord of the manor.'

In my head, I rehearse the words over and over again:

Hello. My name is Liberty. I'm your daughter.

Hello. My name is Liberty. I'm your daughter.

Once upon a time ...

'You're getting a belly.' Michael knelt down to pinch flesh around my middle.

We were onstage at Wembley Arena – me sitting with legs crossed, looking out at thousands of empty seats flipped up like sad mouths.

Michael was striding between instruments, glaring at me and the set-up, finding fault with everything. Paul's guitars were taking up far too much of the stage. The lighting was pointed at Paul too much. And I was getting fat.

'It's just the way I'm sitting,' I said, rearranging my clothing and pulling at my tight jeans.

'Don't let yourself go, now. I'm not into big, hefty women. You don't want to go turning into your sister now, do you?'

'My sister is beautiful,' I say. 'The most beautiful person I ever met.'

Michael's eyes darkened. 'Okay, okay. Enough of the hero worship. Beware of false idols, isn't that what they say? Because from what I've seen, your sister resents you. She doesn't want you to be happy. Remember how she was when I turned up on the doorstep?'

'Dee doesn't resent me. She just … She had to be a mother to me, is all. At a young age. It's a lot to ask of a kid. She never said she resented anything. That's just me, filling in the blanks.'

'She resents you, Lorna. You know she does. She's jealous. What fat girl doesn't hate her skinny little sister? Still. She won't be jealous soon, will she? Because you're getting fat too.'

'I'm not fat,' I said, hating how desperate I sounded. 'I've lost weight on this tour. Look.' I pulled my jeans from my stomach to show they were looser – which they were.

Michael turned to look at rows and rows of blue seats. 'You know, this place will be full tonight. And then the tour will be over. What will we do with you then? I can't very well send you back to that sister of yours, can I? Maybe I'll keep a hold of you. What do you think?'

I swallowed. I hadn't dared ask what might happen when the tour ended. To tell the truth, I'd been worried Michael was getting sick of me. All he ever wanted me for recently was soulless sex, and even that was less frequent than it had been.

'I don't know,' I said.

Michael's eyes burned. 'You don't know? You don't *know*? I'm asking if I should keep a hold of you and that's your answer? Who do you think you are? You're an arrogant bitch, that's what you are.'

Like an idiot, I started crying. I'd been doing that more recently. Most days, actually. 'I just didn't understand the question,' I sniffled. 'Please. It didn't come out right, that's all.'

'You're nobody, Lorna. Nobody. You don't deserve to be here. I was going to ask you to live with me. Do you get that? I was going to ask you to move in. But now it's all messed up.'

'You want me to move in with you?' I asked, eyes big and incredulous.

'I did. But you can forget that now. You can pack your bags and go back to your *family*.' Then he added a sneery, 'I don't *know*.'

'Please, Michael.' I got onto my knees, hands together, literally begging. 'I didn't mean it like that. Of course I want to move in with you. There's nothing I want more in the world. I love you so much, Michael. *Please*.'

Michael stood up and paced around, toying with me. He bossed around some men in hi-vis jackets. He shouted at the stage manager about the mic. After twenty minutes of torture, he returned, hands on hips, standing over me.

'If you want to live with me, you've got to make me a promise.'

'What?'

'You've got to shut up about my wife. Not one more word about me being married. Things are the way they are with Diane. We're friends. We're separated. But we're not going to divorce anytime soon, and that's just the way it is. You've got to be my cool punk princess who doesn't care about that stuff. Okay?'

'Okay.' I nodded and nodded, relieved at an easy way out of Michael's bad books. He'd ignored me for days before. 'Okay. Of course.' I wiped away tears and managed a smile. 'Will we go to Ireland where you grew up or will we go to the States or …' I hesitated as his expression darkened.

'Don't get too cocky now, Lorna. Stop with the questions. You know I hate a cocky girl. I have a house here in England. It's a work in progress, but it's gonna be a stunner.'

'I thought … don't you live in Ireland?'

'Ireland is my past. England is my future. I'm building a castle. Can you imagine that? King Michael's castle. And a whole forest to go with it. Every girl's dream, right? Like a real princess.'

I jumped up and threw my arms around him. 'I love you, Michael. I love you so much.'

As I was clinging on to Michael for dear life, a woman's voice, husky and deep, boomed through the speakers: 'Michael Reyji Ray. Step away from the girl, Michael Reyji Ray. You are a married man.'

Michael pushed me away so hard I nearly fell over. I'd never seen him look afraid before. But when he saw who was talking into the mic – a messy, bleached-blonde woman – his shoulders sagged with relief.

'Very funny, Cat. You're hilarious.'

The scruffy blonde woman laughed as she untangled her bare legs from trailing cable. 'Relax, Michael. Did you think it was Diane? Or a journalist?' Acres of pale flesh spilt from her barely-there flowery babydoll dress. There was a huge tattoo on her back: *Annalise* in Celtic lettering.

Michael purses his lips. 'Tend your own garden, Cat Cannon. You've got enough of your own problems, haven't you? Without getting into mine.'

'Trying to change the subject?' The woman clicked the mic into its stand and strolled towards us. 'It won't work.' She slung a heavy, pale arm around Michael's shoulder. 'When did you ever get me to shut up?'

'I don't think anyone could ever make you shut up, Cat,' said Michael.

The woman – Cat – gave me a lopsided, red-lipstick smile. 'What's your name, honey?'

I wanted to run. Cat didn't mean to, but she was putting me into a trap. Whatever I said, Michael would be mad at me later. He didn't like me talking to other people.

'Lorna,' I said, head down, glancing at Michael.

'Well, what'd you know? A fellow American. Where are you from?'

'New York.'

'You're not from New York originally. You're too naive. You sound ... I don't know. California somewhere?'

'I grew up in California.'

'Uh huh?' Cat eyed me expectantly, offering slow, encouraging blinks. 'Where?'

I glanced at Michael again. 'Um. Well, my mother moved around a lot. So ... uh ... we lived all over. San Francisco. Las Vegas for a while. Los Angeles. All over. We sort of moved whenever the rent was due.'

Cat laughed. 'You know, my mother was a train wreck too. I don't even call her Mom anymore. I call her Nancy.'

I looked at her then, almost smiling. 'You too?'

'Uh huh. It's hard, isn't it? It hurts. When they don't love you.'

We shared a moment. A moment I knew I'd pay for later, when Michael flew into a jealous rage. He hated me connecting with anyone, even for a few seconds.

'So you know what Michael wants, right?' said Cat, leaning close enough for me to smell alcohol and pot. 'Skinny little yes girls who do as they're told. The younger and skinnier and more vulnerable the better. I've seen the pattern. Run, run as fast as you can. I can say it. No one else dares.'

She tried to wink, but ended up blinking instead.

I watched Michael, expecting to see his evil twin appear: the black-eyed, hunched-shouldered guy who flung me across rooms. But he just said: 'Cat, I hear your daughter is getting friendly with one of the sound guys. Better check she's not getting herself in any trouble, right?'

Cat rolled her eyes. 'Christ. That's all I need. A teen pregnancy.' She went back to the mic.

'ANNALISE! COME HERE THIS INSTANT, YOUNG LADY!'

From the back of the arena, a sandy-haired girl appeared wearing a flowery babydoll dress and DM boots. Her outfit was similar to Cat's and she was pale like her mother, but her face was entirely her own: widely spaced blue eyes, messy brown brows and a square jaw.

'What?' the girl asked.

Annalise was younger than me and skinnier. She had the frail, vulnerable kid thing going on and I felt wary. I knew Michael liked that dynamic. It made him feel big and strong.

I hated Annalise on sight, with her bad goth eyeliner and plum-coloured lipstick. Who did she think she was, a teenage rock star?

Cat shouted: 'Are you back there flirting with the sound guys?'

'I was doing my *school work*,' said Annalise. Then she noticed Michael and her voice turned breathy. '*Michael*. How are you? Are you rehearsing?' She tried flicking hair around in a sexy way, looking for all the world like a little girl tottering in her mother's high heels.

Michael turned on his deep rock-star voice. 'Annalise. Are you being a good girl for your mother?'

Annalise gave a half smile then, affecting a jolting, flirtatious walk towards the stage. 'Have you met my mother? She doesn't want me to be good. She doesn't even want me to do my homework.'

Michael chuckled, and the sound hit my stomach like a kilo weight. He was being sexy too.

'You don't strike me as a rebel, Annalise,' he said. 'A little English rose is what you are, with that cut-glass accent. You're nothing like your mother after all that time in British boarding school. But you've got a bit of spark to you. For certain.'

Annalise giggled like a kid at a sleepover. How old was she, anyway? Twelve?

'What are we going to do with you, Annalise?' Michael asked, sitting cross-legged on the edge of the stage. 'I know you like performing. But you don't fit in a rock and roll circus.'

Annalise came right up to the stage then, hands gripping the rubber edge, looking up at Michael with glazed, lovesick eyes. 'I fit with you.' Then she noticed me watching and added, 'Onstage, I mean.'

'So we need to make that happen,' said Michael. 'It's about time I listened to your songs. Right?'

I marched up to Michael, putting my hands on his shoulders, and glared at Annalise.

Michael turned his head to me, irritated, pushing my hands away. 'What do you want, Lorna?'

'Just showing you I love you.' I kissed his cheek.

Michael ignored me. 'So how about it,' he asked Annalise. 'You want to play me some of your songs after the show tonight?'

Annalise's smile widened and her square jaw looked even more pronounced. She sort of squealed, then tried to look cool. 'Hey, that's great.'

I almost cringed for her.

'What kind of music do you like, my little English rose?' Michael asked.

A sound escaped my throat. Something like a 'Ha!' but it bit my vocal cords. I glared at Annalise, trying to send killer laser beams from my eyes.

Back off.

'Well, not my mom's stuff,' said Annalise. 'I like kind of Alanis Morrisette. And Shampoo.'

I really did cringe then. 'Shampoo?' I said, voice mocking. 'Two blonde teenyboppers singing about trouble. How *cool.*'

Annalise took my hit with an irritated blink, then pulled some cooler music tastes out of the bag. 'And I like the Vaselines too. And the New York Dolls.'

'Get out of here,' said Michael. 'Lorna loves the New York Dolls.'

'I'm a *real* fan,' I said. 'Do you know their first album, Annalise? The second track … do you know that one?' I knew she wouldn't. I was hitting out at her. Making her feel some of the pain I was feeling.

'I'm not into CDs,' said Annalise airily. 'Most of the time,

I see bands live. It's better listening to music that way.' She smiled at Michael, and I felt my face turn boiling hot.

'Indeed it is,' said Michael, holding Annalise's gaze. 'Live is always better. And live is how I want to hear you, Annalise. So you'll sing for me after the show?'

'Of course, Michael,' said Annalise, big, wide eyes all over him. It was sickening, and my hands found Michael's shoulders again.

'I'll listen to your stuff right after your mother and I sing to 90,000 people tonight,' said Michael, pushing my hands away again. Then he shouted out: 'Right, Cat?'

'Sure,' said Cat. 'Wait. What's happening?'

'Annalise is going to sing me some of her songs,' said Michael, dropping the sexy rock-star baritone. 'That's all. Okay?'

'Don't get too friendly with my daughter, Michael Reyji Ray,' said Cat. 'She's fifteen and you're an old pervert. So don't even think about it.'

'I'm a happily married man.'

'Like hell you are.'

Cat stumbled down from the stage then and attempted to link Annalise's arm. Annalise shook her off but still followed her backstage.

I turned on Michael.

'You're a happily married man? So what am I?'

Michael slapped me cleanly around the face. There were staff all around. People setting up equipment. Doing sound checks. They must have noticed, but no one said a word.

'I just asked you to move in with me,' Michael snarled.

'Count your blessings. I don't need a hard time today, Lorna. I have a show to do.'

The message was clear. Don't get above yourself. Cat Cannon is famous. She has value, so she can talk to me however she likes. You can't.

Liberty

Hey. I'm Liberty. I'm your daughter.

Seeing Michael Reyji Ray up close, this famous musician with my face … it's strange and scary and exciting all at once. Michael looks like me. I was prepared for that. But the energy around him – that, I wasn't excepting. He's sort of like a planet. He has a gravitational pull. I wonder if I have that energy.

You'll like him when you meet him, Liberty. And then he'll turn you against me …

For some reason, my legs don't want to move.

Michael stands on a partially constructed stage, strutting back and forth over a boardwalk of platforms with little nests of silver struts piled around.

'Great, guys,' Michael says, his voice smooth and clear. 'It's coming along great.' His silk dressing gown is wrapped tight around him, and Ray-Bans cover his eyes. Up close, his bleached-blond hair has salt and pepper roots.

'How are you feeling?' Diane asks me.

'Um …'

'A little bit daunted, are you?'

'Yes.'

'Just remember he's a normal man with a heart and skin and bones like the rest of them,' says Diane. 'I knew him when he was a schoolboy in short trousers. He's not Jesus. The rest of the world would do well to remember that at times, I can tell you.'

My father.

This man is my actual father.

I'm half him.

Michael turns as we approach.

'Diane?' He glances at Skywalker. 'You didn't go and get a rescue dog without telling me, did you? We said we'd go together.'

Up close, Michael's tanned face looks friendly. There are smile lines. His voice is kind.

'We're not getting a dog,' says Diane. 'Forget the dog. Look who's *with* the dog.'

Michael smiles, nods at me, but barely looks up. 'Oh. Right. You're here for the internship, are you? Welcome to Michael Towers. Don't let Diane boss you around too much. She can nag for England, this woman.'

I clear my throat. 'Um … my name is Liberty. I'm your daughter.'

When I rehearsed the words in my head, they sounded profound. Now they just sound like a weird thing to say to someone I've just met.

Michael looks up then. He looks up so sharply that his neck clicks. 'You're … What did you say?'

'I'm your daughter.'

A pause.

'My ... *what*?' Michael's eyebrows lift above his sunglasses.

'On today of all days, right?' says Diane. 'You said she'd find her way home eventually, and here she is.'

'Oh holy Jesus.' Michael lets out another blurt of laughter. 'Oh Jesus. You're ... Oh, wow.' He clambers down from the stage, mouth twitching into something like a smile. 'I can't believe it. I didn't know ... I mean I never imagined you'd just *show up* here ...' He turns to Diane for clarification.

'She was right outside,' says Diane. 'I found her by the gates.'

'You look like me. Doesn't she, Diane? She looks just bloody like me.'

'There's certainly a resemblance.'

'So ... what did you say your name was? Liberty?'

'Liberty.'

'I called you Reign. Reign Janis Ray. God.' Michael looks up at the sky and throws his hands together. Tears glisten on his cheeks. 'Thank you. Thank you. You were born right here on these grounds. Did you know that?'

'I ... No.'

Michael nods, voice fading to a whisper. 'The best and worst day of my life. To be given something so precious. And then have it taken away. Listen, I know you'll have been told all sorts of stories. But the woman you grew up with isn't what she seems, Liberty. She isn't what she seems.'

'That's ... uh, sort of why I came here,' I say. 'To hear your side. But Diane said today is your wedding anniversary. Maybe it's not the best day for all this.'

'It's fine,' says Diane, eyes soft and warm. 'Our wedding anniversary is day one. That's what we always call it. A fresh start. We let go of everything on this day. That's how we survived your mother. So what better day for you to come? A new beginning.'

'Diane is an incredible woman,' says Michael, eyes clouding. 'My better half, as they say. I've put her through a lot. But she's always stuck by me.'

'For better or for worse, Michael Ray.'

'Wowsers.' Michael places chubby hands on my shoulders. 'I can't believe you're here. This is a dream come true. Listen, are you tired? Hungry? Have you … did you fly from somewhere to get here?'

'I didn't fly from anywhere,' I say. 'I took the bus.'

'From where?'

'Taunton Wood.'

Michael turns to Diane, hands falling from my shoulders. 'Jesus Christ. She didn't …'

'It's so *near* to us. Practically down the road.'

'Do you live on a lot of land there, by any chance?' Michael asks. 'A big patch to yourselves? I can't imagine Lorna wanting to live cheek by jowl with other people. Not with everything she's trying to hide.'

'Yeah, we have some land. I mean, nothing like what you have. But yes.'

'Funny to think of Lorna living in the British countryside,' says Michael. 'What has she got? One of those old-fashioned houses with the quirky English names. Back O' Beyond or Forty Winks. Who'd have thought that would be her scene?'

'We live on an old farm. It's called Iron Bridge.'

'I bet it's like Fort Knox.'

'You can say that again. Mum has more security than you do.'

'That woman,' says Diane. 'Just when you think she won't stoop any lower—' She notices me then and her pink lips snap shut.

'Lorna never could let go,' says Michael. 'It makes sense, when you think about it. We should have guessed.'

Diane shivers, despite the warm day. 'For her to be so near, she must have been watching us this whole time. It gives me the creeps.'

'It's okay,' says Michael. 'It's all going to be okay. We're starting again, right? Liberty and I have the rest of our lives from this moment on.'

'Lorna told Liberty you're some kind of monster, Michael,' says Diane, shaking her head. 'Tried to poison her mind, like she did with everyone else. Liberty – don't you listen to a word of it. I've been with this man for twenty years. He's got the biggest heart of anyone I know. Too big sometimes. He lets people take advantage. Don't get me wrong, he's far from perfect. I've had cause to hit him with my handbag on more than one occasion. But the *shit* that woman says about him ... and Lorna is still at the Nazi propaganda, Michael. All these years later.'

'I don't believe everything I hear,' I insist. 'Not even from my mother. I can make up my own mind.'

Michael claps me on the shoulder. 'Still, must have felt like you were walking into the lion's den, coming here today. Am I right? A big scary monster ready to eat you up.'

'Something had to change. Life is unbearable at home.'

Michael takes off his sunglasses, and I see his face is soaked with tears. 'I'm sorry to hear that. God. I'm so glad you came, Liberty. I can't tell you how happy. I've been waiting sixteen years. Hey, listen. Come into the house. I've got something to show you.'

'Show me what?'

'Well, that would ruin the surprise, wouldn't it?' Michael bites his lips. 'You've been so close this whole time? This *whole* time?'

I nod.

'And you didn't know I lived in the same county?'

'I didn't even know who you were until a few weeks ago.'

'That must have been quite the surprise.'

'A big one.'

'Your mother is good at keeping secrets.' Michael puts an arm around my shoulder, steering me through the trees. 'And she certainly knows how to the twist the knife too, keeping you so close by. I turned San Francisco upside down. LA. New York. London too. But you were right here. Hiding in plain sight.' He takes in a deep breath. 'But hey. You're here now and that's all that matters. Listen. Are you ready to see something special?'

'Sure.'

'It's inside the house. Come on, I'll show you. You're gonna love this. Just you wait and see.'

Lorna

'MICHAEL, GIVE ME BACK MY DAUGHTER!'

Can throats bleed? If they can, I should be swallowing blood right now. Rivers of it.

My eyes scan the awful, frightening woods – trees I ran through with a baby in my arms.

Where is she? Inside Michael's castle? In one of the turrets? MY turret? Or … my stomach drops … the little cottage in the woods?

Bad memories tumble with blind fury as I rattle the gates, black metal paint flakes scratching my palms.

The fir trees … the smell of earth … those golden twisty turret towers.

There was a girl here once. A skinny, weak, pathetic girl. A girl who cried and pleaded and never fought back. Why didn't I? Why didn't I kill Michael when I had the chance?

I remember my sister coming to these gates. Begging me to come home. Pain and fear pulling at her soft, plump face.

I'll never leave you, Lorna. I'll always be there for you. No matter what …

Dee never did leave me. She was the only thing in my life

that was real back then. My mother, my friend and my hero. A real hero, not just the image of one.

More memories come, thick and fast.

Me at the window of that turret room, waiting, waiting for my prince to come home. Michael, chasing me through the woods. And Annalise ... no, don't go there. Don't even think about her right now.

Coming here is like a lid coming off a bubbling pan. That crazy person – the maniac who ran from this house with a baby in her arms. She's waking up again. I want to stuff her down, but I'm not sure I can.

Tears fall.

'MICHAEL,' I scream. 'PLEASE. Give me back my—'

My words fall away as I see Diane through the trees. She's walking carefully, lips pulled tight. Her eyes are fixed on the ground, but I know she's seen me.

My hands freeze on the cold metal.

Diane is dressed in punk rock leopard-print boots and black jeans, skinny as a broomstick, stuck in a time when Michael loved me best. Her brown hair is cut into neat ends and tucked behind her ears, just like mine used to be. Is she trying to look the way I used to? Or is she just doing what I did – moulding myself into something Michael likes?

As Diane reaches the gate, her head flicks up. 'Hello, Lorna.'

'I shouldn't have done it, Diane.' I know my eyes are wild and crazy. 'I told myself a bunch of lies about Michael. I was such an idiot and I'm sorry. I'm so sorry. I just want her back. Give my daughter back and I swear to God I'll leave you both alone.'

'She's come to see her father. The man you stole from her life.'

'Please. Don't let him take her away from me. I love her.'

'You're not capable of loving anyone.' Diane's voice is cold. 'All you do is tell lies and make a mess. Try to break up happy marriages. Hide an innocent child from her own father. Thank God Liberty had some sense about her and wanted to find out the truth for herself. I can't imagine the courage it must have taken her to come here. After all the evil stories you must have poured into her.'

Liberty's name feels like a bullet in my stomach.

I grit my teeth. 'Michael's the one who tells lies, Diane. Open your eyes.'

'Don't start that again.' Diane's voice rises to a shout. 'Don't you dare. After everything you've done to him, to try and blacken his name—'

'I didn't try to blacken his name. How can you not know what he is?'

'Michael isn't perfect. But he's a kind, loving husband. I've known him since I was a child. He's always done right by me—'

'Even when he was sleeping with me?'

Diane's face tightens. 'You bitch. You cheap groupie bitch. Throwing yourself at married men.'

'I never threw myself at him,' I say. 'He pulled up outside my apartment in a tour bus and whisked me away with him.'

'These are stories, Lorna. Your fairy stories.'

'And he told me you two were separated. And that you were too weak and pathetic to deal with a divorce. You want to know what else he said?'

Diane's eyes burn on mine. 'Go ahead, Lorna. Give it your best shot.'

'He said you married too young. That you were just a teenage infatuation, someone who played hard to get and wouldn't have sex unless you were married. He said I was the real thing. True love. The best sex he ever had. And he said he couldn't divorce you because you'd kill yourself. That's what he said.'

'You should be ashamed of yourself,' says Diane. 'They save the hottest part of hell for women like you.'

'Do you think I'd have been with Michael if I hadn't thought you were separated?'

'Yes,' says Diane. 'That's exactly what I think. I think you were obsessed with my husband and looking to get him any way you could. Listen, I know you were ill. That your mind isn't quite right. That you were looking for a happily ever after.'

'Of course that's what you think,' I say. 'You want to believe the Michael fairy tale, just like I did. The truth is too painful. But were you there? Were you in the bedroom with us when he told me I was his one and all?'

'Get the hell off of our property,' says Diane. 'You're a bitter, twisted, jealous groupie who tried to get my husband put in jail. Honest to God, look at you with all those tattoos. What are you … a Hells Angel or something?'

'No, I've done my time in hell,' I say. 'When I lived here.'

'You never lived here, Lorna. That's another of your many fantasies. And you don't care about Liberty. You're here because you've lost power over her. Have the decency to go home and let Liberty get to know her father.'

Diane whisks around and totters back towards the house.

'GIVE ME MY DAUGHTER,' I scream. 'GIVE HER BACK TO ME.'

Diane doesn't turn around.

'YOU KNOW WHAT HE DID TO THOSE GIRLS. YOU MUST KNOW.'

Diane stumbles and catches herself on a tree. But then she carries on walking.

Once upon a time ...

When the European tour finished, Michael and I drove through the English countryside in a rented limousine. I remember green fields, yellow autumn corn, red leaves on trees.

'This house will be spectacular when it's all done,' said Michael. 'A real king's castle. I'm having them build turrets and all sorts. You'll have your own tower, like a princess.'

Michael drank vigorously from the limousine bar during that drive – straight whiskey. I joined in the rock and roll party by having a rum and Coke. It wasn't even lunchtime, but we were rock stars. It was fun. Exciting. That's who we were and what we did.

Michael and I were getting along a little better since the tour ended. He seemed to want a lot of sex all of a sudden, and I was desperate to be with him.

I wore leopard-print leggings, a red vest held together by safety pins and spiked-up hair. Sexy punk rock chick, just like Michael wanted. And I was skinny, like he wanted too. Skinnier than I'd ever been thanks to his comments about my weight.

Michael dressed all in black.

I remember joking about bed linen and hanging pictures, because of course I wasn't that kind of girl – the home-making kind. That's what a wife would do. What Diane had done. But I was too cool for all of that.

I also remember asking if I could call my sister when we reached the house.

'What do you want to call her for?' Michael asked. 'You have me now.'

'Just to tell her I'm okay. Dee worries about me. Especially since the cancer—'

'Well, she shouldn't. I'm taking care of you now. She should stop interfering in your life, Lorna. It's not normal.'

'She doesn't interfere. I've only called her once since I came away with you, and Dee can't call me. She's my sister, Michael.'

'Are you a grown-up or a little girl? We're in a real adult relationship here. Or are you still a child, needing a mammy to look after you. Which is it?'

'I'm a grown-up.'

'So what do you need to call your sister for? You know she's crazy jealous, don't you? I don't want you having anything to do with her. She's toxic.'

'She's my sister, Michael. She's been there for me my whole life. She worries—'

'Can you stop going on about this, Lorna? The phone line isn't set up for international calls anyway. You'll have to write her a letter.'

Eventually, the limo drove down a long, tree-lined lane, then stopped outside a dark wood of Christmas trees and cobwebby branches. There were huge, wrought-iron gates with dragons chasing around in the metalwork. I thought the whole place looked haunted.

'Here we are,' said Michael. 'Our country love nest.'

'Where's the house?' I asked.

'It's there through the trees,' said Michael. 'There's a lot of building work going on right now. See the scaffolding?'

I saw glittering metal scaffold rods and piles of bricks, but no house. But when the gates opened and the limo wound through the trees, I finally saw the shell of an English country mansion, some walls half built and the beginnings of weird concrete turrets at the sides.

The house was perfectly Michael: a blended bunch of egos. Country gent, Tudor lord, medieval king and modern millionaire celebrity.

I managed: 'It'll be big when it's finished.'

'Oh, yeah.' Michael nodded approvingly. 'The biggest house in the south-east, as a matter of fact. Acres of land around it. I've bought up all of Huntingdon Wood. The whole lot. Your bedroom is in that turret there.' Michael pointed.

'My bedroom? Won't we share a bedroom?'

'Don't you want your own space? We've been cooped up on a tour bus for months on end.'

'No, I want to be with you. Like a normal couple.'

'Normal is boring. Forget about normal.'

'Michael—'

'Come on, Lorna. Not today.'

I downed the last of my rum and Coke.

'Whose is that quad bike?' I asked, seeing a red all-terrain vehicle sitting near the moat wall. 'Yours?'

'Oh. Yeah. That's a new toy. To go racing around the woods on. They're vast, these grounds.'

'Can I ride it one day?'

'Not on your own. I'll take you.'

Of course not on my own. Giving me even the tiniest bit of power was too dangerous. Keys to a vehicle? No way.

As we pulled up by the moat bridge, Michael sat up tall in his seat. His arm came across to hold me in place, even though I was strapped in.

'Stay here, Lorna. Okay?'

I followed his gaze. There was a beautiful woman outside the house, wearing classic country attire – a box-quilt body-warmer, green wellington boots and a blouse tucked into plain blue jeans. She was older than me. Probably in her thirties. Her arms were crossed.

'Who's that?' I asked.

Michael's arm was like an iron bar. 'Wait here, okay? Don't move, okay?'

'What? Why—'

'Just stay in the car, Lorna.'

Michael climbed out of the limo, closing the door quickly behind him. I watched him give the woman a long, swaying hug. She was short and skinny, like me, and fitted Michael's body perfectly, her head leaning on his shoulder. After a few minutes, Michael came back to the car.

'Lorna,' he whispered. 'Diane's here. She's taking our separation very hard. To tell you the truth, I think she's losing her mind. You just wait here in the car until I sort everything out.'

Michael slammed the door before I could protest. The

driver got out too and he, Michael and Diane went into the house.

Hours passed. With a mother like mine, I was used to being tossed aside, forgotten and uncared. But then lunchtime came and went and my humiliation and discomfort grew. If Michael loved me, how could he treat me like this? Leave me out here all day, forgotten?

Finally, Michael came trotting out of the house and opened the limo door.

'Come with me, Lorna.' He clicked his fingers at me, looking back at the house. 'Come on.'

'What's going on, Michael? Why is Diane still here? Can't you tell her to leave?'

'I can't bloody tell her to leave.' Michael glanced back at the house again. 'I told you. She's losing it. Hurry up now, we need to get you into the house without her seeing. Unless you want to stay in the car all night.'

'I'm not sneaking around—'

'Yes, you bloody well are.' Michael pushed a hurried hand through his hair. 'Diane's flipped out. She'd scratch you to bits if she saw you. Let's just get you inside, up to your room.'

'I'm not doing that, sneaking inside, hiding from your wife. Just tell her to leave.'

'I never thought of you as a cruel person,' said Michael, dropping his hand to my shoulder. 'Come on. Diane is having a hard time. We don't want to make it worse, right? Just help me out on this one. In a year's time it'll all be fine. But right now, she's struggling. Listen, I'll take you in the house and we'll go right upstairs. Diane's in the kitchen. She won't see you. Sound okay?'

'No. It sounds sneaky and awful.'

'Lorna.' Michael's voice dropped to danger level. 'Not today, okay? Don't mess me around today. It's been bad enough Diane turning up out of the blue. Would you just behave yourself? She's my wife, Lorna.' Michael gave me hard eyes. 'My wife.'

I got the message. I was the interloper here, not her.

'Do you still love her?'

Michael whipped round furiously. 'DROP IT. You're supposed to be a cool girl. Well, prove it.' He grabbed my wrist and pulled me towards the house. 'Don't make a sound. Not a sound.'

As Michael pulled me along, I looked over at that big, lonely house – the place that was supposed to be my new home. Diane was lady of this castle. I was the courtesan, sneaking in the back door.

Inside the house, there were dust sheets and building materials everywhere. It looked like someone was trying to construct three different houses: a glossy Italian marble Versace palace, a modern bachelor's pad in graphite and a British stately home with antiques and oil paintings.

'How long will Diane be here for?' I whispered when we reached the first-floor landing.

'Would you just be quiet?'

'I was just asking—'

'Lorna, shut up. I'm stressed enough as it is. If you keep this up, you and I are finished. I mean it. Show some respect.'

I followed Michael to a smashed-out archway propped up with scaffold. It led to a wooden spiral staircase held up by more metal poles.

'This is your bedroom.' Michael pushed me into a round room with bare plaster on the ceiling and a mattress on the floor. 'I had them do it out in your style so you'd feel right at home. Not that you deserve it right now, the way you're acting.'

The room was small and smelt of paint. Two walls were patchy with careless black paint strokes. A paint can and petrified brush sat in the corner, like someone was coming back to finish the job.

'What's my style? Train wreck?'

'Hey.' Michael took both my hands and gave me his signature whirlpool eye stare. 'There are new things for you in the wardrobe.' He opened a wonky cupboard, also painted a patchy black. Inside were packages of underwear – fishnet tights, suspender belts, red lace bras, all stacked up.

'So, what? I wait here and dress in underwear while you entertain your wife downstairs?'

'You're not a girl who likes to upset people, right? Diane's been through enough. She dreamed of a simple married life and it's all come tumbling down. Have a heart. Stay here. Just stay put, okay. You're my number-one girl.'

'Michael—'

Michael put a heavy hand on my shoulder. 'Listen. When you're staying at my house, you follow my rules. I'm lord of the manor here. There can only be one lord, okay? And you're the princess. I lead, you follow. Everything is better that way. Count your blessings.'

'And if I don't?'

Michael did that angry, shoulder-hunching thing. 'Then get out of here, Lorna. Go back to your crap little life. And don't expect anything from me, ever again.'

Michael left then, slamming the door.

I went to the window, tears forming. I would leave. I'd walk right out the door and through the woods and …

It took about three seconds to understand the practical reality: I was in the middle of nowhere with no car, no friends and no money. But more than that – I didn't know how to be without Michael. Whenever he left me alone, I felt empty. Lost. Sad. My life now was spent waiting for him.

Back then, I was certain I would never be happy without Michael in my life. He was the only thing that made the sadness go away. I didn't realize that, like any drug, Michael caused both the sadness and the happiness.

I sank to the black-painted floorboards and cried into my knees.

Somehow, I would have to make this relationship work. We had to get things back on track. Find the love again. Make things like how they were in those first few weeks.

Michael was my happily ever after.

Liberty

Okay. This house is even weirder up close. I mean, what is it? It looks like a picture Darcy would draw. Turrets stuck on here, a stained-glass guitar window added there, now let's paint the whole thing white and gold and put fake flowers by the door.

'So … you have something to show me inside?' I ask, hand on Skywalker's collar.

'Do I ever, daughter of mine.' Michael gives me a soft, teary smile. 'Do I ever. Come this way.'

We head around a moat, where there's a collection of quad bikes parked under a corrugated shelter and a butchering table with a headless rabbit on it. There are wooden bows and arrows lying around too, and a hefty-looking crossbow.

'Ignore that,' said Michael. 'Just a bit of population control courtesy of my groundskeeper. We've got a rabbit problem.'

We pass a guitar-shaped swimming pool and reach bi-folding doors leading to a huge kitchen.

'You get a workout at this house, I can tell you,' says Michael. 'A lot of square footage. A lot of land. What I want to show you is this way – come on into the kitchen.'

Skywalker barks and barks.

'Your doggy here doesn't like new places?' Michael asks.

'No,' I say. 'He gets nervous.'

'What about you?' Michael asks.

'Oh. You know. Not usually, but …'

Michael frowns. 'I shouldn't have walked you past all that hunting stuff.'

'It's okay. I get it. I grew up in the countryside. I don't like hunting but I know it happens.'

'And you're okay to come inside the house? You don't think I'm going to chop your head off, like one of those bunnies?'

I try to laugh then. 'No. Honestly, I'm fine.'

'You know, you don't have to come inside at all, Liberty. We can go to a café or something. Neutral ground. Have a chat and a catch-up. But I really, really do want to show you this thing in here, that's all.'

I take a deep breath. 'I'm okay. Honestly. Show me.'

We're about to cross the threshold when Diane appears, stumbling on kitten heels. I never get how women can walk on shoes like that.

Diane's face is haggard and tense. 'MICHAEL.'

Crinkles appear outside Michael's sunglasses. 'Jesus, Diane. What is it? Are you okay?'

Diane puts hands on her thighs, out of breath. 'She's … Lorna is at the gate.'

'Jesus.' Michael closes his eyes for a moment. 'Well, it was inevitable she'd show up, wasn't it? Only a matter of time.'

'My mother's here?' I ask.

'Yes.' Diane nods. 'She's outside.'

'Don't let her in.' My voice is harder than I mean it to be. 'She can't come in here.'

'God, no.' Diane gives a high laugh. 'I've called the police.'

Michael looks at the house. 'Maybe I should go talk to her.'

Diane shakes her head. 'No. You shouldn't go anywhere near the gate. You know how Lorna twists things. You go out there, and she'll claim you tried to shoot her or stab her or something. You stay here until the police come.'

'You really think my mother would do something like that?' I say. 'Make something up?'

'She's done it before,' says Diane. 'Many, many times. She's tried to ruin us. You never know what she's capable of. God, I'm shaking.' She holds her hands out, and I see trembling red fingernails. 'I gave her a piece of my mind, Michael. I couldn't help myself. She was saying all sorts of things. So much nonsense. I couldn't stand it.'

'Lorna always had an interesting relationship with the truth.' Michael gives Diane a knowing look. 'And no doubt she'll be telling people we're keeping Liberty prisoner here.'

'Prisoner?' Diane gives another harsh laugh. 'Yes, I imagine that will be the next lie. We've heard that one before. About Cat's daughter.'

My stomach creeps at the thought of my mother waiting at the gates. I know she'll be crazy upset and I hate myself for doing this to her. But it's the only way. Time to move forward, no turning back.

'Can someone just tell her I'm not here?' I say. 'That she's made a mistake?'

'We can't lie to her,' says Diane. 'We're not those people.

We don't do things the way Lorna does. Look, the police will sort it out, okay? You two shouldn't be disturbed. She should have the decency to let you catch up after all this time.'

I fiddle with my silver Gemini ring. 'Will they arrest her? I don't want her to be arrested.'

'It's okay, Liberty. The police know the history. They know your mother has … some mental issues. They'll be fair and kind. God, I need a drink. Come on.' Michael ruffles Skywalker's head. 'Tell this fellow he needn't be afraid. Let's go inside and I'll show you the thing I've been saving for you all these years.'

I kneel to rub Skywalker's face. 'It's okay, boy. Nothing to be frightened of. Come on. My dad's just going to show me something. Okay?' I stand and click for him. 'Heel boy. Let's go.'

Still Skywalker won't move. I grab his collar and pull. 'Come on, Sky. It's okay. Really. It's just a kitchen.'

Skywalker whines as I pull him onto the marble tiles, his claws clicking as he steadies himself.

'I'm going back out to the gate,' says Diane. 'To see if I can persuade Lorna to leave before the police get here.'

My stomach crumples like a piece of paper. 'Tell her I'm okay,' I say. 'Would you? That I've chosen to be here. And that I'll be home soon.'

'I'm not sure you should speak to Lorna again, Diane,' says Michael, eyes swimming with concern. 'You know how she twists things.'

'I'm wound up, Michael,' says Diane. 'I want that woman off our property.' She glances at me. 'Sorry, love. Look, I know it's your mother. But we've suffered a long time. A very long time. I just want her gone.'

I swallow. 'As long as she leaves. That's the main thing.'

'She will, love. One way or another. The police are on their way. Go on in with Michael now. Let him show you this thing of his, whatever it is.'

'This way.' Michael waves me towards a pantry, opening the door. 'In here. You go first – I'm a tubby little fellow these days; I'll squeeze in after you.'

Skywalker barks, and I hesitate at the door.

Michael laughs. 'Calm down, doggy. It's just our larder. Listen. I'll go first, okay? So your doggy doesn't get separation anxiety.' He walks inside the pantry. There's a lot of convenience food on the shelves – crisps, sugary drinks, biscuits, sweets and packet cakes.

Skywalker sits by my heel, looking up at me with big brown eyes.

'My word, there's a lot of junk food in here,' says Michael, picking his way to a freezer at the back. 'A bit embarrassing, you seeing my bad eating habits. And I can't blame Diane. She's part of the my-body-is-my-temple crowd. Hardly eats a thing.'

'My stepdad is into healthy living,' I say. 'He won't shut up about protein.'

Michael laughs. 'Is he a good fella though, your stepdad?'

'Probably.'

Michael opens the huge, humming chest freezer at the back of the pantry. It's an old, energy-inefficient 1980s model – the decade that hated the environment.

'Right.' Michael smiles as lemony light spills out of the

freezer lid. 'You've got to come inside and see this, Liberty. It'll be worth it, I promise you.'

'This is the thing you want to show me?' I ask. 'In the freezer?'

'Yep.' Michael gestures me forward. 'Come on in.'

Skywalker growls.

'Your dog is still nervous?' Michael laughs. 'He can't be scared of a freezer.'

'Come on, Sky.' I step forward, my hand held tight on Skywalker's collar. 'Let's go see.'

Lorna

'LIBERTY!' I'm screaming, really screaming, through the railings, boots wedged on twirling wrought-iron dragons. 'LIBERTY!'

'Get down from the bloody gate, Lorna.' Diane appears through the trees again. 'Before you hurt yourself. What do you think? You've got a few muscles, and now you can scale a ten-foot fence?'

I drop to the ground. 'I'm stronger in every way these days, Diane,' I say. 'Now I don't keep myself as thin as a twig for Michael.'

Most women fill out a little in middle age, but Diane hasn't. She has skinny limbs like a teenager. Too thin. Brown hair. White skin. Michael definitely has a type: pale, frail and vulnerable. I often think, if the cancer hadn't made me so thin and weak-looking, Michael wouldn't have been interested.

'Have you no shame?' Diane puts hands on boy's hips in tight jeans. 'Do you know what today is? Our wedding anniversary.'

'Send Liberty out and I'll leave.'

'As if I'd take your word for anything.' Diane sounds tired.

'We both know it's meaningless. How can I trust a liar? Look, just leave, okay? Haven't you hurt us enough already?'

'Give me my daughter.'

'She's here to see her father,' says Diane. 'They're catching up on the years you stole from them. Can't you give him that, at least? Can't you have the decency to let them get to know each other?'

'Get to know each other? He's brainwashing her, the way he's brainwashing you. Haven't you figured it out by now, Diane? Nothing he says is true. None of it is real.'

'It's you who tells lies.' Diane's lips pull tight. 'I'm sorry Michael wasn't kind to you. But Jesus, had you no common sense, woman? If you will sniff around after a married man, what do you expect?'

'I was an idiot. I'm not saying I wasn't. But Michael picked me up, not the other way around.'

'What man's head wouldn't turn when a semi-naked teenager hangs around a stage door like a prostitute?'

'I wasn't semi-naked.'

'Look, Michael did wrong,' Diane continues. 'Fame went to his head. He thought he could sleep with who he wanted on tour and no one would get attached. What happens on tour stays on tour. Musicians aren't saints. Everyone knows that. But he isn't the reason you had a mental breakdown. We hope you find peace and the help you need.'

'Please. Please, Diane. I'm begging you. Give my daughter back. Don't take her from me – you know what Michael's doing. He's turning her against me to get revenge for those press articles.'

'She's with her father right now,' says Diane curtly. 'And I dare say he's telling her all the things you've left out of the story. The truth. Something you wouldn't understand if it came up and bit you on the behind. Just go home. Okay? Liberty will come back to you when she's good and ready. *If* she's good and ready, after all the lies you've told her. She can stay here just as long as she needs.'

'You need a reality pill, Diane,' I snap. 'We're both his victims. You just don't see it. He's using you. You're good for his image.'

'I'm not a *victim*,' Diane shouts. 'Michael and I are still going strong after twenty years, in spite of girls like you throwing yourselves at him. What did you expect when you picked up a married rock star outside of a concert? Happily ever after?'

The truth is, that's exactly what I expected – stupid little teenage idiot that I was.

'I'm asking you to leave our property,' says Diane. 'I have an anniversary party to organize.' She gives an odd smile, then turns back to the house.

'Please, Diane—'

'Excuse me, madam.'

I feel a tap on my shoulder.

Two police officers stand behind me. One has shiny brown hair pinned into a bun, large sun spots on her cheeks and carrying a good twelve pounds of flesh around her stomach. She looks overheated and holds her cap in short, fat fingers.

The other, a male, reminds me of a milk bottle: tall, pale and skinny with an impeccable uniform. And way too young to be doing this job.

'What?' I demand.

'You're on private property,' says the policewoman.

'I have a right to be here,' I say. 'My daughter is here. Behind those gates. She's only sixteen.'

'Mrs Ray told us the full story,' says the policewoman. 'You're on private property, so if you could come with us, please, Miss Miller.'

'How do you know my name?'

'Mrs Ray filled us in.'

'Get my daughter out of there and I'll go with you.'

'Miss Miller. If you don't come with us now, you'll be charged with trespass. We know … we know you've had problems.'

'You've got your facts mixed up.' I turn back to the gate, wedging my foot back into the railings. 'Michael isn't what you think he is. He's a monster.'

'*Miss Miller!*' The policewoman shouts. 'Come with us now, before you get yourself into any more trouble. This is Mr Ray's private property and you have no right to make a nuisance of yourself.'

'You don't understand,' I say, finding another foothold on the gate and pulling myself up. 'If you did, you'd be telling Michael to open the gates and let my daughter out.'

'We understand the situation.' The female police officer looks up at me. 'You've been … very keen on Mr Ray and his music for a long time. And you just want to get close to him.'

The skinny policeman adds: 'The word is stalking.'

I look down. 'This is a set-up. I don't care if you arrest me for breaking and entering – I'm speaking to my daughter.'

'We *will* arrest you *right now* for attempted breaking and entering,' says the policeman.

'So don't do anything silly, okay?' says the policewoman. 'Listen. We know you've had some issues in the past.'

'I'm not leaving here without my daughter.'

'Let's give Mr Ray the respect and space he needs. He's entitled to enjoy his home without fans mobbing the gates.'

'He's allowed his privacy,' chimes the male police officer, coming forward to grab my arm.

Fury rises to the surface. 'Michael isn't a good person. He's fooling you. All of you. It's what he does.'

'Get away from the gate right now, Miss Miller,' says the policeman, tugging at me. '*Right now*. I'm this close to arresting you.'

'Arrest *me*?' I cling tight to the bars. 'What a bunch of bullshit. Do you know what happened behind these gates? Do you have any idea what Michael's capable of?'

'Come down now, Miss Miller. Or we'll be forced to remove you.'

I try to climb but feel hands grab my ankles and wrists.

'You're his puppets,' I yell as my fingers are peeled from the bars. When my boot accidentally hits the policeman in the face, he loses his temper.

'*Get down now!*'

'Keep it calm, PC Holmes,' says the policewoman. 'Let's all stay nice and calm, shall we?'

Eventually they pry me off the gate and drag me flailing and shouting to the police car. I'm proud to say it takes them at least twenty minutes. I'm nothing like the skinny little girl who cried her eyes out over Prince Michael all those years ago.

Not anymore.

Once upon a time …

Welcome to your new life at Michael's mansion, Lorna. Lady of the house. Queen of the castle.

I cried all afternoon in that turret bedroom, lying on the single mattress, looking up at an unpainted ceiling of raw pink plaster. I wanted to go home. I wanted my sister. I wanted to eat. But more than any of those things, I wanted Michael to come up here and tell me he loved me.

As dusk fell, I was too hungry to cry anymore. So I used the black paint and stiff brush to draw a silhouette of Johnny Rotten over the fireplace.

Michael was still downstairs with his wife, Diane. Did he love her? Were they still having sex?

As I put the finishing touches to Johnny Rotten's eyebrows, the smell of steak and fries drifted up the stairs.

That was it. The absolute limit. I hadn't eaten all day and I was starving. Michael hadn't bothered to feed me. This had been a regular thing on tour – probably because Michael thought I should stay skinny – but tonight was different. He and his wife were eating dinner *together*, while I was stuck up here, hungry, looking at streaky painted walls.

Diane would be making big eyes at my man, playing the sympathy card. 'Don't leave me, Michael, we're married. Give us another chance. Please.'

What if she succeeded?

I worked myself into a jealous fury, imagining my territory being invaded by this woman. Diane and Michael had known each other since childhood. She was beautiful and so skinny. Michael liked skinny. And they were still married. What if Michael was too weak to say no? What if they ended up getting back together?

Something snapped and I just lost it.

I stormed down the staircase, tripped and climbed over building materials, and marched through a hallway into a partially built kitchen extension.

Michael and Diane were in the kitchen, sitting on plastic chairs and eating a steak dinner from china plates in the midst of building chaos. There was a rose sticking out of a coffee cup and a bottle of champagne on a workman's bench. Tealight candles glittered on top of an oven still in its wrapping.

Diane looked stunning, her pale skin gleaming, eyes glittering. Her blouse was a little bit open and I could see the top of a white lace bra.

'What's going on, Michael?' I demanded.

Diane shrieked and leapt out of her seat, plate smashing on the concrete floor.

Michael stayed calm, putting his plate on the floor and standing. 'How did you get in?'

'You brought me in. Tell her the truth, Michael.'

'You shouldn't be here, love,' said Michael. 'This is my

home. You need to leave.' He took my arm, fingers digging, and pulled me out of the kitchen.

'What are you doing?' I said, trying and failing to pull my arm free. 'You're having dinner with her while I'm upstairs? She wants you back, don't you realize that? Tell her the *truth*, Michael. It's time she knew about us.'

Diane took deep breaths. 'Who the hell is this, Michael? What is she doing in our house?'

'It's okay, Diane,' said Michael. 'She's just a girl from the shows. A fan. Let me get her out of here.'

'Get *me* out of here?' I struggled against his grip. 'It's her who shouldn't be here. She needs to get over you and move on. She's had her time. It's my time now.'

Diane's eyes widened just the right amount to show she thought I was crazy. Then Michael manhandled me through the house and out the front door. I struggled, but Michael always had superhuman strength when he was angry, and I ended up stumbling behind him.

'What do you think you're playing at?' Michael raged, pulling me away from the house and under dark, cold, hostile trees. 'I told you to stay in your room. Now you've started all kinds of trouble. I feel like strangling you, I swear to God.'

I'd never seen Michael so angry, and for a brief moment I imagined him throttling me and dumping my body out in the roaming woods. He certainly looked like he wanted to.

My stomach pulled into a tight ball. 'You left me upstairs all day.'

'You're pathetic,' said Michael. 'Like a child.'

And he was right.

'It looked romantic,' I said, my voice high and frightened.

Michael still had tight hold of my arm and began dragging me further into the woods. I couldn't see the house anymore and the dark anonymity, coupled with Michael's mood, terrified me. I'd been scared of Michael before, but nothing like this. I'd never felt this blackness from him.

'If you'd have stayed put there wouldn't have been a problem,' Michael raged. 'You're jealous. You saw what you wanted to see. I was making things right with Diane. Calming her down. You have to know how to handle her – she can really lose it.'

'You told her I was a fan. She thinks I'm crazy.'

'You've made a big mess, Lorna. A really big mess. What did you expect me to do? I have to clear it up somehow.' Sweat glistened on his forehead under a full moon.

'I want to go back to the house, Michael, please.' I pulled at him. 'Where are you taking me?'

Michael met my eyes, all intense and staring. 'You know I care about you. Right? But you can't go back to the house now. You're gonna have to sleep out here tonight.'

'Where?'

'Here. See?' He pointed at shadows through the trees. 'You're gonna sleep out here in the cottage. Diane's gonna stay over and—'

'No way.' I pulled back. 'She's staying the night? Absolutely no way. If you do this, Michael …'

'What? You'll leave? Where will you go? Back to your sister who can't stand you?'

'She can stand me. I'll … I'll …'

'Hitchhike your way back to America? Go then. Go on. I'm not stopping you. Good riddance.'

I burst into tears. 'Do you mean that? You don't love me anymore?'

'Sometimes I wonder. Just … don't get smart, Lorna. I'm trying to fix this. It's all your fault. Help me out, for God's sake. I don't want Diane to flip out again.'

I could see the form of the cottage now, bulky and brown, under the waving branches of giant fir trees. It was a tumbledown place; little holes in the roof and metal boards on the windows. There was a metal door too, with a huge open padlock hanging off it.

'Please, Michael.' I shook my head, eyeing over the dark spots where roof tiles had skidded apart. 'I can't stay out here. It looks like a horror movie. What is this place, anyway?'

'It's the old farm cottage that came with the land,' said Michael. 'A beautiful little place. You know, the builders camped here while they were laying the foundations for the mansion. You'll be fine. Stop being such a princess.'

'Michael, please don't make me—'

'Listen.' Michael lowered his voice. 'Diane has pills with her. A whole bag full of pills. If we hadn't have showed up this morning, she would have taken then. She was this close.' He held up thumb and finger pinched together.

That changed things. Michael always knew how to pull my strings.

'Okay,' I said. 'I didn't know she was … okay. Okay, I get it.'

Michael nodded, placing a fatherly hand on my shoulder. 'Now you understand why I have to play things a bit carefully.

Baby steps. The candles and roses – all a bit of acting, but you're grown-up enough to handle that, Lorna. I know you are. I wouldn't be with you otherwise. Think of it like this. I've got a sick child to look after.'

I looked over the spooky, boarded-up cottage. 'It's scary out here.'

'You'll be fine.' Michael led me into the building. 'I'll come out later with some blankets and food.'

The cottage was bare inside except for a mattress and bucket on the floor. The whole place smelt funny, like metal. One wall had angry axe marks in it.

'I'll come see you later,' Michael whispered. 'I'll sneak out. Like Romeo and Juliet. Okay?'

'Not okay.'

'Watch yourself, Lorna. Don't be spoiled or I'll lock you in.'

I didn't want to sit on the mattress, so I huddled up in the corner, hungry, cold and wide awake, listening to the night go on forever.

I guessed it was gone midnight when Michael came back, but I couldn't be sure – time drags when you're cold and uncomfortable.

Along with owl hoots and fox barks, I heard crunching footsteps and guessed they belonged to Michael. They were stumbling and out of rhythm.

'Michael?' I called out.

Suddenly the door flung open and I screamed and shrank back.

A heavy hand clamped on my mouth and I smelt whiskey. 'Be quiet. Don't make so much noise.'

I looked up into Michael's bleary, bloodshot eyes. He climbed right on top of me, eyes glazed, then tugged at my jeans.

'Michael.' I turned my head and tried to push him away. 'Stop. You're drunk.'

But he didn't. Instead, he pulled and yanked at my jeans until I was naked from the waist down, then climbed on top of me and banged away, bang, bang, bang.

He was a drunken dead weight and strong, but once he started I didn't try to stop him. He was my boyfriend. We'd had sex many times before.

The sex wasn't quick, and when Michael finally finished, he rolled off, stumbled out and slammed the metal door behind him.

I huddled back to my corner, heart pounding, confused, scared, not knowing what to do, say or think. It was cold – I knew that much. Michael hadn't brought blankets. But it was too scary and dark out there to consider leaving the cottage. And even if I did make it to the house, who knew what Michael would do when he saw me?

I thought of Dee, and wondered what she was doing now. Working, probably. Looking after a bunch of middle graders. Tears came. If she knew her little sister was here, cold and alone in this abandoned cottage, she'd come and get me. I knew she would. She always fixed everything.

When I was little and Mom told me we couldn't afford this or that, I'd say, 'Dee Dee will get it for us.' I thought my big sister, with her paper route and spare cash, had magical powers. She could always fix things my mother couldn't. But even if

Dee came to fetch me, I'd still be trapped. Because the cottage wasn't the trap. My mind was the trap. That was something I'd have to fix all by myself.

Eventually, I fell asleep.

In the morning, I woke to sunlight and soft knocking at the cottage door.

I sat up tall, heart racing.

'Lorna?' It was Michael's voice, gravelly and deep.

When I didn't answer, the door flew open and Michael entered the cottage with a red rose in a skinny vase. He wore jeans and a T-shirt and was showered and shaven.

'Why didn't you come back into the house?' Michael asked, eyes full of concern.

'What?'

'I told you to wait out here for an hour while I got rid of Diane, then come back inside. Why didn't you?'

'You never told me to come back inside. You said to stay out here. That you'd bring me blankets.'

'I didn't say that, honey. I said give me an hour to get rid of Diane, then come back in. Remember? I told you to listen for her car leaving.' He put down the tray and gave me his big eyes. 'Look, I'm sorry about yesterday. Forgive me. Let's get back on track.'

'Last night ...' I began.

'Yeah, sorry I didn't come get you,' said Michael. 'I thought you'd be sulking so I left you to it. Then I had a few too many drinks and crashed out. Talking to Diane tires me out. She just goes around in circles.'

'No. You did come out here.'

Michael looked genuinely confused. 'No, honey, I fell asleep in the house.'

'You came here,' I insisted.

'Sweetheart, you must have been dreaming. Was it a good dream?'

'No. It was a bad dream. A nightmare, actually. You were just disgusting.'

'I hate to tell you this, sweetheart, but I think you're getting confused between sleep and real life,' said Michael. 'You know how you make up stories sometimes. I passed out all night. I came nowhere near this cottage. You know how your mind can be. You're not always in the real world, are you? After your mother neglecting you like that. And then the cancer. The treatment played havoc with you, didn't it?'

It's true, I thought. *I'm not stable. I'm losing my mind. It was some weird dream. He fell asleep in the house and I made up the rest.*

'Well, you still left me alone all night,' I said.

'Sweetheart, I'm so sorry. I passed out. Swear to God.'

'It was scary out here. And cold.'

'Let me make it up to you. I can hardly help falling unconscious through tiredness, can I? Forgive me. Let's not hold on to this. Listen, Diane's gone now. She left last night. Let's get everything back on track and I'll make sure you're the girl who gets steak today, okay?'

'Diane left last night?'

'Yeah.' Michael rubbed his nose and forehead. 'She's not good. Not good at all. Still talking about suicide and all sorts. It scared me, to be honest. Here I am living with another woman, and she's telling me she'd break into a million pieces if I ever left her.' He kissed my head. 'But my little Lorna wants me to tell Diane the truth, and the truth it shall be.'

'You know, maybe you should hold off telling her about me,' I said. 'Until Diane's better. I don't want to be the cause of anything bad happening. And if she's so fragile …'

'But, princess, you don't like all the sneaking around. Right?'

'I don't. But … I don't want Diane to hurt herself. It's fine. Like you say, a bit of acting might be needed. We know what we have.'

Michael gave me his earnest eyes then. 'You are pretty much the perfect woman, do you know that? The perfect, understanding, considerate woman. And I am madly in love with you.'

I grinned reluctantly then, sun coming out from behind a cloud.

'So what do you want to do today?' Michael asked. 'I need to make this up to you. We have the whole day together. Do you want to go out on the quad bike?'

'You'd let me ride your bike?'

'On one condition,' said Michael, kissing my neck. 'You take your clothes off while you're doing it.'

I laughed. 'I'll do anything to ride that bike around.'

Michael made it sound like a fun game, but naked bike riding was just another control thing. If I was naked, I couldn't go far. Like always, Michael made sure he had an invisible leash around my neck.

Michael took me back into the house and made me steak for breakfast, just like he promised. Then he gave me a ruby ring for my little finger and made beautiful love to me in his bed. Michael wasn't anything like the man I'd imagined the night before. That man, I decided, was definitely some warped dream born of my creepy surroundings. This was my Michael – gentle and caring. It felt like when we first met and it was perfect.

After that, Michael took me into the woods and let me drive his bike around in my underwear. He brought a shotgun with him and pretended to aim it at me as I drove, saying he was practising his hunting skills.

'It's not loaded, is it?' I called out, laughing and ducking as I drove past him.

After finding Diane at the house and the awful disconnected sex I'd dreamed the night before, I clung to Michael's loving and attentive mood. Yesterday, I'd felt like a total interloper. Diane had the greater claim. Childhood sweetheart. Married. But today I was his princess. The love of his life.

Still, my brain hurt.

It was getting harder and harder to make the pieces fit together. The things Michael was saying didn't match the things he was doing.

I knew it but chose not to see it.

I hate myself for that now. I hate myself for so many things I can never change.

Liberty

Skywalker barks and barks at the doorway. Poor little dude, he doesn't like it when there's someone between us.

'What am I looking at?' I ask Michael, peering into the chugging chest freezer. It glimmers with sugary delights – cherry and chocolate ice cream, Black Forest gateaux, a box of macarons in pastel colours, all bathed in acid-yellow freezer light.

Michael pulls out a clear bag of sliced cake. 'This.'

'Cake?'

'Not just any cake. It's birthday cake. Can you guess whose?'

'Whose?'

'Yours, Liberty.'

'This is my birthday cake? But it's not my birthday.'

'I know. There's are sixteen pieces in there. I held a little birthday party every year for you. Every single year. Sang you happy birthday, lit some candles. Thought about what you looked like and prayed and prayed we'd find you. Then I cut you cake and stored it in the freezer. I was so certain that one day you'd walk back into my life.' Tears fall down Michael's craggy cheeks. 'And on that day, I wanted to show you I'd never forgotten you. Give you something of the life you'd missed out on. It was my way of doing something positive, you know? I couldn't freeze time and stop you growing up without me. But I could freeze the cake.'

'Wow.' My lips feel swollen. Hot tears sting around my eyelashes.

'I love you to infinity. You're my darling daughter. I turned the world upside down looking.'

'I can't believe this is the first time I'm meeting you,' I say, words cracking in my throat. 'That my mother kept me away. She hates you so much.'

'Lorna doesn't hate me, Liberty,' says Michael. 'She loves me. That's what all of this is about. She can't stand that I stayed with Diane. Taking you was her revenge.' Michael's phone bleeps and he frowns at it. 'Oh, look at that. Talk about timing. The first of the guests are at the gates.'

'I hope my mother has gone,' I say. 'It would be so embarrassing if she's still out there. While your guests are arriving. God.' I put my head in my hands. 'SO embarrassing.'

'Don't you worry about any of that,' says Michael. 'Diane will have sorted it.'

'My mother will be going out of her mind, knowing I'm here.'

'Can't say I blame Lorna for worrying,' says Michael. 'There's a lot she's kept hidden from you. If I were her, I'd be crawling over hot coals to keep it all quiet.'

'What has she kept hidden?'

'We'll talk about this some other time, Liberty. The guests are arriving. You don't want to get into this with people turning up.'

'I do,' I say, taking a kitchen stool. 'Mum has always been secretive. Not just about you. About lots of things. Medical reports. My birth certificate. All sorts of things. I know there's more to this than just you supposedly being a bad guy.'

'Yeah, you're a smart girl,' says Michael, taking a stool. His phone bleeps again. 'Okay. This is Danny, my driver. He's just let the first round of guests through the gate. Which means your mother has gone.'

'Then you'd better tell me quickly.'

Michael laughs. 'Okay. Well, I can tell you one thing. A good friend of mine will be here soon. Have you heard of Cat Cannon?'

I nod slowly. 'The singer.'

'And I take it, by the look on your face, that your mother has told you about Cat Cannon? And her daughter?'

'No, but … I read articles about them. Cat Cannon supported one of your tours. And her daughter went missing shortly afterwards.' I pause. 'Her name was Annalise, right? The daughter?'

Michael nods.

'My middle name is Annalise.'

'That's your middle name? Really?'

I nod.

'I suppose it makes sense. Your mother would have something of a guilty conscience.'

'Meaning?'

'Forget I said that. That's unsubstantiated. Listen – this I can tell you for sure. Those newspaper stories. The ones that accuse me of God knows what. They were your mother trying to ruin me. But she didn't ruin me. All she ended up doing was tearing Cat's heart out. Annalise might still be alive, for all anyone knows. Lucky for me, Cat saw through it all in the end. But it was touch and go. She hated me for a long time.'

'So you're still friends with Cat Cannon?'

'Oh, yeah. She'll be here any minute.'

'But … it wasn't just my mother throwing around accusations. Cat accused you of kidnapping her daughter too. I read the articles.'

'She wasn't in her right mind,' says Michael. 'And forgiveness is the mark of a strong person. It was a long time ago. Water under the bridge. Lorna was in Cat's ear at her lowest moment, telling her all kinds of crazy shit. God, your mother caused some pain, I can tell you. And I'll tell you something else. If anyone knows what happened to Annalise, it's Lorna. Your mother saw that young girl as a rival. She wanted to be rid of her like she wanted rid of Diane. It wouldn't surprise me if … Oh, forget it. Let's not go down that road.'

I swallow. 'You think my mother knows what happened to Annalise?'

'I don't know.' Michael rubs at his forehead and eyes. 'But I do believe Lorna knows a lot more than she's letting on. Now isn't the right time for all of this. We're getting this party together and it's a celebration, you coming home. Hey – you're into music, aren't you? You said you were in a band. You know, there'll be a lot of industry bigwigs here today—'

'My mother does that,' I say. 'Changes the subject.'

'Well, look, it's some pretty dark and heavy stuff we're getting into,' says Michael, standing. 'I'm just saying … let's park it for now and enjoy this magical moment. Father and daughter reunited. The party's starting and there are a lot of people I want you to meet.'

'But I want to talk about it *now*,' I say. 'That's what I'm here for.'

Michael's eyes turn serious. 'We will talk, Liberty. When the time is right. But you've only just got here. I tell you the truth now, and you're likely to think I'm as crazy as Lorna. You need to get to know me first, at least a little bit. Meet my friends. See who I really am. Now, listen. About this band of yours. What's it called?'

'Skywalker.' The word is reluctantly said as I take a kitchen stool. 'After my dog. We're sort of punk, new age meets rock and roll. A bit of everything.'

'Sounds brilliant. Now, as your old man who also happens to be a rock star, I would like to meet this band of yours and see what I can do for you. How about that? You know, I've got a music studio out there in the woods. There's a little cottage out there – I converted the place. It used to be the old farm cottage. How about you bring your band here and we record some of your stuff?'

I swing my DMs under the counter. 'I mean … that sounds great. But how do you know we're worth recording?'

Michael laughs. 'You're my daughter. Of course you're worth recording. You'll be ace. It runs in the family.'

'I don't know if I'm good. I just know I love performing and writing music.'

'The music industry is a tough business,' says Michael. 'But if you really want your band to go places, I'll help you all the way. Listen, stay for the party today. There'll be music guys here. My producer. A couple of agents. Some real heavy dudes in the industry. I'll introduce you around and start the wheels turning. Sound good?'

'That's like every teenager's dream. Really? You'd do that?'

'Of course. Anything for my little girl. So what do you do? Sing? Play guitar? What?'

'I'm the singer. Well, singer-songwriter. And yes, I play guitar. Any instrument I can get my hands on really.'

'Of course you do.' Michael ruffles my bleached hair. 'You've got the old Reyji Ray lyrical blood in your veins. Well, I'll introduce you around today and see if we can start making some connections.'

I'm nodding and nodding. 'Yes. Wow, yes definitely. Cool.'

'And you write your own songs, do you?'

'Totally. It's what keeps me sane. When I'm stuck in my bedroom, writing songs is like my freedom. It's like the only thing that's mine. Everything else Mum controls.'

'Your mother is scared, Liberty,' says Michael. 'Scared of losing you. She has good reason. And I will tell you all about it. I promise. Later.' He takes my hand. 'You've got your real dad back now. And if you want to get into the rock and roll business, I'll help you every step of the way.' Michael cocks his head. 'Hold up. I think I hear Diane.'

I sit up straight. 'I hope my mother didn't give her a hard time.'

Michael shakes his head. 'Your mother has gone. Probably Diane was the one who got rid of her. One way or another. I know it sounds harsh, but if you knew what Lorna had put us through—'

'Then you'd understand.' Diane strides into the kitchen, boots clicking on the floor. She rests a hand on my shoulder. 'Your mother has gone now, sweetheart. I ... Look, the police took her. It had to come to that. She wouldn't have gone otherwise.'

'It's okay.' I feel my chest rise and fall. 'I know what she's like. I live with her. She wouldn't have gone without a fight. She goes crazy if I'm home ten minutes late.'

Diane nods. 'Now, listen, Michael. The guests are arriving.'

'I know. Danny phoned.'

'So.' Diane tries for a smile. 'Time to put Lorna behind us and enjoy this party.' She nods and smiles, then bursts into tears.

'Hey.' Michael leaps up and hugs her. 'Hey, it's okay. She's gone now.'

When Diane emerges from the hug, her kohl eyes and black mascara are smudged.

'Sorry,' she says. 'It's just got me all shaken up, you know? I've waited all these years to have it out with her. I thought I'd feel better but all I feel is upset. She's so delusional. You can't make a dent, you know? She believes her own rubbish. But she's gone now. Look at me, getting all emotional.'

Michael looks deeply into her eyes. 'What an old softy you are. I know, I know. It was tough, but it was a long time ago, sweetheart. And everything is looking up now.'

'Is it?' Diane's eyes dart around. 'Because there's a can of worms here, Michael. That woman is back in our lives again. Stalking us. And all the chaos that comes with her—'

'I won't let that happen,' says Michael. 'The police know

about her now. It's fine. Okay? It's all fine. They'll handle everything.'

I shuffle in my seat. 'The police didn't arrest her, did they?'

Michael and Diane exchange glances.

'I doubt it, love,' says Diane. 'Unless … well, unless she resisted them.'

'Let's change the subject again,' says Michael. 'I know how you love people doing that, Liberty.' He raises a playful eyebrow. 'Guess what, Diane? Liberty's going to stay for the party.'

'Great.' Diane smiles at me, eyes soft. 'I'm pleased.' Then her eyes falter. 'Oh, for goodness sake. Maybe I'm being too kind, but you'd better call your mother. Tell her you're okay. Maybe she'll feel better if she hears it from you.'

'No way,' I say. 'She'll think Michael's brainwashed me. That's what she always says about him. Stay away from that man, Liberty. He'll mess with your head. You won't know your own thoughts. He'll warp your mind.'

'I hate to put it this way,' says Michael, 'but Lorna's mind was warped when I met her. She had so many problems. Her own mother was a piece of work. Wanted to go out galivanting rather than look after her kids. Then Lorna had cancer at such a young age. It would mess anyone up. I was like this Jesus figure to her. She thought I could turn water into wine. Make everything better. But I couldn't.'

'God.' Diane shakes her head. 'That woman. She'll rot in hell for what she did to you, Michael.'

'It's in the past now, Diane,' says Michael. 'And Liberty will know the truth about her soon enough. Now then, guests are

159

arriving soon and—' He cocks his head to one side, listening. 'Anyone hear what I hear?'

I listen too.

There's a sort of swooshing, rattling noise overhead, and the bi-folding doors vibrate a little in their frames.

Diane is nodding. 'Trouble.'

'What's that noise?' I ask.

'The devil in a pretty dress,' says Diane, giving Michael a hard look. 'Miss Catherine Cannon.'

Lorna

Most people would feel embarrassed being driven home in the back of a police car. But right now, I couldn't care less. Who do I know around here anyway? Only Nick. My big sister is thousands of miles away. The only thought on my mind is getting back to Michael's house, climbing those gates and pulling my daughter out of there.

In the end, the police had to handcuff me. I still tried to open the police car from inside, but it didn't work – there were child locks.

We're cruising past the village post office. Heads turn. It's unusual to see a police car around here.

'You think you're on the side of truth and justice,' I tell the police officers. 'But you're just a bunch of pawns being moved around by a chess player.' I glare out of the window. 'He's got us all playing his game. Again.'

The police remain silent. I'm sure they've heard worse insults in their time.

'My van.' I sit upright. 'I left my workshop van outside his property. You have to drive me back.'

The policewoman turns around. 'You'd be trespassing,

madam. The road to Mr Ray's house is private property. We'll have a police officer bring your van home. Just leave us the keys.'

'That van belongs to me. You have to let me get it.'

The policewoman puts up a hand to stop her colleague replying. 'If you're not happy with us driving your van, send a friend for it. Maybe your partner? I'd recommend you staying away from Mr Ray's house right now.'

'Mr Ray is not his real name,' I say. 'It's all fake. Everything about him is fake.'

'I'd be careful if I were you,' says the policewoman. 'Mr Ray can file for a restraining order if you cause too much of a nuisance. You don't want something like that on your record.'

My eyes squeeze together. 'He saw me coming a mile off today. Of course he did. You've been primed. That's what he's done. He's prepped you. Had you ready and waiting for me.'

'Mr Ray didn't contact us,' says the policewoman. 'His wife did.'

'He put her up to it.' I turn to the window again.

'I think you need to go home and have a nice rest.'

I won't rest until I get my daughter back.

The police car drives further down the village high street, past the small supermarket, past the playground. A woman chasing a toddler down the street turns as we passes. I recognize her; she's a teaching assistant from Liberty's old primary school. When she sees me in the police car, her mouth falls open. I raise my hand and wave. She stares like I'm a lunatic. But who cares? Like I say, it's not as though I have a social life around here.

'Do you have a friend who can pick up your van?' asks the policewoman.

'No,' I say. 'I don't do friends anymore. You never know who has a Michael Reyji Ray album hidden in their collection. And you can't ask to see people's music library – you look like a weirdo.'

The policewoman glances at her colleague. 'Where are you from originally, Miss Miller?'

'San Francisco.'

'I have a cousin near there,' says the policewoman.

'In California?'

'New York.'

'That's about a thousand miles away from San Francisco, but okay.' I stare out of the window again.

There's a long pause, and then the policewoman says: 'So … you're from the States originally?'

'Yes.' My eyes fix on the little cottages lining our village high street.

'What made you settle in the UK?'

'Michael. He flew me here.'

'You never wanted to go back home then? After you had your daughter?'

'It … wasn't convenient.'

'Don't you have family out there?'

'A big sister.'

'Do you get along?'

'Of course we get along.' I hope the police can't see tears coming. 'She's the best sister anyone could ever ask for. She brought me up. She looked after me when I was sick.'

'But you've chosen to live away from her. Here. In this country. Near Mr Ray.'

I hesitate. 'It just worked out that way. Moving here. I knew the area.'

'You haven't seen Mr Ray since you've moved here?'

I look out of the window. 'No.'

The car slides to a stop outside our house.

'There's a lot of security around your house, isn't there?' The policewoman opens my car door. 'Big gates.' Her eyes wander over our expansive fencing. 'You know, this isn't America. There's no gun crime around here. Nobody needs security like this. Well, unless you're a celebrity like Mr Ray. You might enjoy life more if you opened up your house to the street. Became part of the community.'

'You haven't got a clue.'

I walk away and fingerprint buzz myself through the tall wooden gate. Once the gate is slammed behind me, my body sags against the wood, jaw tight, fists clenched. The moment I hear the police car drive away, I let out a furious scream, punching the wooden gate over and over again.

'Lorna.' Nick jogs out of the house in his tight T-shirt, hair clipped and neat, face tight with worry. He sweeps me into his arms. 'What happened?'

'Liberty's there. She's at Michael's house. The police drove me home.'

'The police? What, they arrested you?'

'Not exactly. But Michael has them in his pocket. I should have known. It's just like before.' I put knuckles to my mouth. 'He has her, Nick. He has her.'

164

'Hey. Hey, let's keep things calm. Liberty … is she physically okay?'

'I have no idea. They wouldn't let me see her.'

'But if the police … they know Liberty is with him, right? With her dad?'

'I told them Liberty was there. But whether they believe me is a different story. I'm not even sure they believe Michael is Liberty's father.' I look at my bleeding knuckles. 'He's so clever, Nick.'

Nick steps back and puts steadying hands on my shoulders. 'Come on, let's just keep it calm. Liberty will be okay. You don't know anything bad has happened to her—'

'He's warping her mind,' I say. 'That's what he's doing. Right now. Psychological abuse is worse than physical abuse. Did you ever hear that? It causes more damage.'

'Liberty is a bright kid, Lorn. She has her head screwed on. Have faith in her. No one's going to twist her mind. She loves you. You're her mother.'

I flinch. 'Nick, I need your car keys.'

'Why?'

'Because I'm going back to Michael's house.'

'I don't think that's a good idea, Lorna. If the police just drove you home … you're going to get yourself arrested. Why don't I go? Try and reason with the man?'

I laugh.

Nick looks offended. 'I have three celebrity clients, Lorna. I know how to deal with ego.'

'If you went to Michael's house, you'd end up having a beer with him and a game of pool. You'd come out telling me what a good guy he is and how I've got it all wrong.'

'Give me some credit,' says Nick. 'You're my fiancée. I'm on your side. And I'm on Liberty's side too.'

'Really?'

'Of course I am.' Nick crosses his arms, fists automatically going to pump out his biceps. 'Come on, Lorna. I'm big enough to overlook a bit of teenage anger. Of course I'm on her side. Poor kid must be confused as hell right now.'

'I need your car keys.'

'Come inside. I'll make you a cup of tea—'

'Caffeine is a stimulant. If you want to calm me down, offer me Jack Daniels.'

'Just come inside—'

'Nick, I'm not going to sit around drinking tea while my daughter is with a monster.'

'So what are you going to do? Drive right back there and get yourself arrested? You're not going to help Liberty from a prison cell. Let's make some calls and find someone who can help us.'

'Like who?'

'I don't know. A good solicitor.'

'Michael would run rings around a solicitor. My sister. I need Dee. She was with me when it all happened. She knows the truth. She saved me. She knows about Annalise.'

'Who's Annalise?'

I can't meet his eye.

'Lorna?'

'Annalise was Cat Cannon's daughter,' I say. 'You've heard of Cat Cannon, right?'

'Cat Cannon …' Nick's eyes shuffle through memory files

until he finds the right one. 'The heroin-addict singer with lipstick all over her face? Who fell on her backside on *The Tonight Show*?'

'She's clean now. From what I hear.'

'I didn't know she had a daughter.'

'Yeah. She did.'

'Wait a minute – Annalise ... that's Liberty's middle name.'

'Yes.'

'So what happened to this girl? This Annalise person?'

'Officially, nothing. She's a missing person.'

'And unofficially?'

'Can we talk about something else, Nick? I've gone to too many dark places today. We need to call Dee.'

'You're sure you don't want me to go to this man's house?' Nick asks. 'See if I can get Libs to come home?'

'No one should go to Michael's house yet,' I say. 'You're right, Nick. We'd just get arrested. This is a chess game, right? Michael's good at chess. He'll be expecting that move.'

'So ...'

I sigh. 'We'll do what you said. Drink tea. Stimulating tea. And work out a move he doesn't expect.'

Liberty

Through glass doors, we watch a black helicopter tip and tilt over the huge lawn beyond Michael's swimming pool.

'The extravagance of it,' says Diane, lips set in distaste. 'Catherine Cannon always has to make an entrance. She can't come through the gates like everyone else.'

'She's one of a kind,' says Michael. 'And I'd have it no other way.'

The helicopter settles, giving the kitchen doors one last rattle.

'Listen, Liberty,' says Michael. 'You're a smart girl. You know Cat was on the scene back when I knew Lorna, right?'

'Um ... well, yeah. You were on tour together, weren't you?'

'We were. And you also know that Lorna accused me of some awful things.'

'Yes.' I meet his eye. 'So did Cat.'

'Look, I know you'll have questions.' Michael's dark eyes turn sad and pleading. 'Cat's been through hell and back, love. Please don't ask her about the past. Not today. I'll answer everything when the time is right, but this is Diane's day too.'

We watch as a woman with messy blonde hair hops out of the helicopter. Cat looks so much smaller than I'd imagined her. In pictures, she's full-on big hair, red lips and personality. In real life, she's tiny.

'Did she have her assistant flown in too this time?' says Diane. 'Or has she sacked the latest one like all the others?'

'Give her a break,' says Michael. 'Sure, Cat gets through her assistants. But she's a unique personality. Not everyone is going to fit. And she doesn't need an assistant for a party.'

'I think it's criminal the way she disposes of staff at the drop of a hat,' says Diane. 'You've had the same driver and assistant for over twenty years, Michael. You're good to them.'

'Come on now, Diane. Cat's good to her assistants too. She always gives them a big whack of settlement money.'

'How kind of her,' says Diane. 'Mouth-shut money.'

We watch as Cat totters around the swimming pool, waving and laughing. She wears a black ballgown split at the front with bizarre ruffles at the neck, pearls and spike heels that are not getting on well with the grass.

'Does Cat know about me?' I ask.

'No, love. We'll keep you quiet today. No sense going there when Cat's still so fragile.' Michael puts his arms around mine and Diane's shoulders. 'Okay, girls. Come on, let's move on from the bad stuff, okay?'

Cat is nearing the glass doors now, sticking a playful finger up at Michael, still laughing.

Michael waves back. 'Listen, Liberty. When I tell you what happened the day you were born, everything changes. Right? Everything. A bomb goes off. I wouldn't mind getting to know you before we light that fuse, okay?' He goes to open the kitchen doors. 'Ready to meet a rock and roll legend?'

'More like a rock and roll mess,' Diane mutters. Then she glances at me. 'God, I hope these doors are soundproofed.'

Michael pulls open the bi-folding doors. 'Cat Cannon,' he shouts. 'How was the chopper?'

Cat totters over slab paving, then throws herself into Michael's arms. 'Hey Micky Ray. It's good to see you. Another year, another anniversary. And both of us still alive. The helicopter was great. Loved it. Felt like royalty. I'm still the only guest you do that for, right?'

'You're the only one,' says Michael. 'I know you too well, Cat. You can't arrive without making an entrance. Can I get you something to drink?'

Cat extracts herself from the hug. 'Got any green tea?'

'Green tea?' Michael laughs. 'How times change.'

'Buddha happened. Namaste.' She puts her hands together and bows.

'Diane, do we have any green tea?' Michael asks.

'I'll take a look,' says Diane stiffly.

'HEY!' Cat grabs Diane's wrist and pulls her into an awkward hug. 'Hello, hello, hello. DIANE. Sorry. Forgot you again, didn't I? How are you doing?'

Diane manages a soft smile. 'It's okay. People always forget me when Michael's around.'

Cat releases Diane, then notices me then. 'Who's *this*?' She stares. 'Jesus, you look … just like Michael.'

'She's a long-lost relative,' says Michael, beaming. 'A niece.' He puts an arm around my shoulder. 'This is young Liberty.

It was a surprise, her turning up out of the blue. But I'm glad she's here today.'

Cat's big blue eyes widen even further. 'A niece? I thought none of your brothers had kids.'

'Like I say. Liberty here was a surprise.'

Cat blinks. 'Okay. I get it. None of my business. Right?'

Michael claps her on the back. 'Ask me no questions and I'll tell you no lies.'

Cat looks me over, her eyes loose and worried. 'How old are you?'

'Sixteen.'

'Come on, Cat Cannon,' says Michael. 'Let's go mingle. The party's about to get started.'

'Of course the party's starting, Michael,' says Cat. 'I just got here.' She turns to look back at me. 'Sixteen, huh? That's a hell of an age.'

Michael laughs. 'It certainly is.'

Lorna

The international dialling tone rings like a distress signal.

'Booooop. Boooop. Heeeeelp. Heeeeeelp.'

Come on Dee. Pick up. Pick up …

I know she will. She always picks up for me.

There's a click as the line connects. 'Lorna?'

Hearing Dee's voice floods me with relief. My warm, loving big sister. The only constant, my whole life. The one I can always rely on.

'What's up?' Dee asks. 'I'm on my way to work.'

I start crying like an idiot. 'Liberty,' I jabber. 'She's found out who her father is. She's *gone*, Dee.'

A pause.

'Okay. I'll be on the next flight out.'

Liberty

I know this party isn't a *real* music festival. But I'm pretending like it is.

Out here in Michael's woods, for the first time ever I feel like I'm living a real teenage life – dancing in bare feet and denim cut-offs, covered in mud and rainbow make-up, singing along, arms around a big bunch of strangers.

I've taken my shoes off to feel the earth, as instructed by Michael during his first performance just after lunch. Other bands played during the afternoon, and now Michael is back on stage again.

The party is in full swing and the woodland clearing is packed with people, dancing, swaying their arms. Almost everyone here has bare feet, and we stand on summer-warmed earth together, swigging from cider bottles and listening to the air crackle with live music. Well, okay – I'm swigging organic apple juice, but close enough.

On stage, Michael's croaky voice demands to know if we're having a good time.

'YES!' everyone shouts back. And I hear myself shout too.

'Everything is connected,' says Michael. 'Do you feel it?

We're connected by love and music and freedom. This is our own little world and we don't need anyone else.'

Everyone looks happy, except for Diane – who is walking through the crowd towards me, eyes concerned.

'Have you had enough to eat, Liberty?' she asks. 'The chef just put out a load of veggie hot dogs. Are you helping yourself?'

'I am. Thanks.'

There are hundreds of people in Michael's woods now, all talking and dancing and drinking. Guests have been arriving all afternoon and now this place is mobbed. I'm surrounded by more leather jackets than I've ever seen before. What's the collective noun for a group of people in leather jackets? A throng? A black?

'Look at my husband, up there on stage,' says Diane, shaking her head. 'Man of the moment. He always has to be in the limelight.'

Cat Cannon weaves up onto the stage too and grabs a mic, throwing her arm around Michael's shoulder. 'This guy, is like the GREATEST guy in the world. The greatest front man EVER.'

Diane frowns. 'Jesus. No wonder that woman was a heroin addict. She needs calming down.'

On stage, Michael laughs and takes the mic back. 'We're one big family today,' he booms. 'Love is all there is and love is who we are. Everyone here …' he points to the crowd. 'Do you feel it? Do you feel the love here?'

A collective 'Wooo!' passes through the crowd. I feel my fist raise in the air.

'Woo!'

Cat stumbles down from the stage then and lights a cigarette. She notices me and stares for a moment, a frown creasing her pale skin. Then a man in a leather jacket leans to whisper something and she throws her head back and laughs, turning away.

Diane shakes her head. 'This isn't my scene, you know? Hedonism. All the dirt and noise. I'll be relieved when everyone goes home.'

I notice Diane is one of the few people still wearing shoes – heels, actually, that spike little holes into the baked mud clearing. I guess she isn't feeling love in the bare earth, like everyone else is.

'Do you want *me* to go home?' I ask.

'Oh, no, love.' Diane's eyes widen. 'I just meant … you know, Michael and I have different tastes when it comes to celebrations. I'd rather just be at home, having a meal with a few friends. But that man of mine likes to make a big romantic public spectacle every year, so here we are. Love isn't love unless he's booming it through a microphone apparently. But listen to me, complaining like an old woman. Michael's enjoying himself. And you are too, by the sounds of things.'

'I'm loving it,' I say. 'I've always wanted to go to a music festival. This feels kind of like that.' I raise my voice as the live music starts up again. 'A big festival in the woods.'

'Are you sure I can't get you anything else to eat?' Diane shouts back. 'You've had some lunch, haven't you?'

The music dies down a little and I nod. 'Three veggie burgers and a veggie hot dog.'

'Well, now it's supper time,' says Diane. 'How about some

bread? I've just put some in the outdoor oven. The chefs are still working away. They've got three grills going over there now. Two of them veggie only, so you needn't worry—'

'I'm okay,' I say. 'All I want to do is talk to Michael.'

'Oh, that's almost impossible at one of these things,' Diane laughs. 'Look at him. Peacocking around on stage. He's in his element here. But I promise you, love, he'll find time at some point. Michael is a man of his word, whatever Lorna might have to say on the subject. He is a show-off. Don't be under any illusions there. Show him a stage and he can't stay away. But he's a man of his word.'

We watch as Michael sings a few notes into the mic, throwing his head back and spreading one hand wide. Cat is back on stage too now, strumming at a red electric guitar.

'You'd never guess this was our anniversary, would you?' says Diane mildly. 'More like the Michael and Cat show.'

'Do you mind?' I ask.

'Not often,' says Diane with a wry smile. 'Hardly ever, actually. It's just how it is. True love is selfless.'

'Yeah,' I say. 'I know that one. I have a little sister. Well, stepsister. Darcy. She has autism. So life sort of revolves around her. It has to. Darcy gets really upset if we don't stick to a routine or do things a certain way. I can't even wear hats because it freaks her out. But it's fine. Because I love her and I know it's what she needs. Love makes it okay. You know, putting up with the bad parts.'

'What a beautiful thing to say.' Diane smiles. 'You're a special girl, Liberty. Lorna did something right. Raising someone like you.'

On stage, the music fizzles out and I see Michael slapping the backs of the musicians.

'I'm not all that special,' I say, watching as Michael hops down from the stage and weaves through the crowd, shaking hands and patting shoulders. 'Plenty of people make themselves second best because they love someone.'

Diane nods and nods. 'Yes. Yes, they do. And it's okay, isn't it? Like you say, we accept it.'

Michael comes bounding up to us. 'Everything okay with my girls? I could see you from the stage, the pair of you looking ever so serious. What's going on here then? Nothing bad, I hope?'

'We were just having a nice girls' chat,' says Diane, squeezing my hand. 'And *this* girl is getting desperate to talk to you, Michael Reyji Ray. So I'm going to leave the pair of you to it.' She winks at me. 'I'll go mingle. Back in a sec.'

'How are you liking the party so far?' Michael asks.

'I'm having a great time,' I say. 'It's awesome. Like being inside the pages of *NME*.'

'Yeah, I've collected some good people around me over the years,' says Michael. 'And let me tell you something, young Liberty. You are nothing without other people. Absolutely nothing. You can have all the talent in the world, but if no one wants to help you or work with you, you're finished.'

'It's an amazing party,' I say, looking at the crowd. The air is buzzing, even without the music, and the collective feeling here is one big good mood. Rainbow flags fly from the branches, musicians arrange themselves on stage and food sizzles on grills at the edge of the clearing.

All around us are eager faces, many clearly desperate to speak with the great man.

'But you want to talk,' says Michael. 'Right? As in *talk* talk. I can see it in your face. Why don't we find a little quiet spot, the two of us? Come on. We'll get away from this noise.' Michael points to three tree stumps arranged like a table and chairs in a small clearing. 'Let's have a father-daughter catch-up. Step into my office. Do you play chess at all?'

He pats a shaded chess grid carved on the largest tree stump.

'Is this a chessboard?' I ask.

'Yeah. Not very rock and roll, I know, but I just love the game. I've carved all the pieces too. I'll show you.'

Michael reaches into a hollow part of the tree stump and pulls out a waterproof bag – the kind you put survival gear into. He opens it and shows me crudely carved wooden chess pieces.

'My groundskeeper and I spent weeks whittling these,' says Michael. 'His wife died, so ... you know. He likes to keep himself busy. I tell him to spend as much time here as he likes with us. He's not keen on being at home.'

Music boom, boom, booms from the woodland stage and I hear Cat's croaky, cigarette-ravaged voice singing 'My Way'.

'I love chess,' I say. 'I was captain of the school chess team. But then I got into music.'

'No kidding? Like father, like daughter. A logical mind under the chaos and creativity. Hey, you must be a bit good if you were captain of your team.'

'Well ... yeah.' I manage a smile. 'I mean, I never lost. Not to players my own age.'

'I should have known a daughter of mine would be a chess

champion,' says Michael. 'Well, that sounds like a challenge to me. Let's set up the pieces.'

I examine a roughly carved bishop. 'If we're playing, we won't be talking about anything meaningful.' I look up then, right into his dark eyes.

'You're giving me credit for more intelligence than I have,' Michael laughs. 'I'm not plotting some great distraction. I just wanted to play a chess game with my little girl.'

'If I win, will you stop beating around the bush and tell me what you know?'

Michael watches me for a moment. 'Okay, deal,' he agrees, shaking my hand. 'But you won't win.' His palm feels rough but warm.

I laugh. 'I will win. I've never lost.'

'Maybe you've never played with anyone decent before.'

'Oh, he's got you playing chess, has he?' Diane comes strolling over, heels sinking into leaves and mud. 'Don't fall for it, Liberty. Never play games with Michael. He makes you think you're going to win and then he takes you to the cleaners.'

'I just told her she's going to lose,' says Michael. 'That's hardly misleading her, is it?'

'You won't win this game,' I say, eyes moving over the chessboard.

Diane pats my shoulder. 'Well, at least you're confident.'

'Sorry.' I blush. 'I know that makes me sound like an idiot. But it's true. And I have an especially good incentive to win.'

'Let battle commence,' says Michael.

Diane sits on another tree stump and watches us play. She's a good audience member, gasping at the appropriate moments.

Eventually, Michael gets me in a position where I can't win. I tip my king and grudgingly shake his hand.

'I don't believe it,' I say, searching the board. 'I totally didn't see that coming.' I shake my head. 'Wow. I really, really wanted to win that game.'

Michael nods. 'I know you did, Liberty. But it's for the best you didn't, if you get my meaning. Honest to God it is. Just … be patient, okay? Give us all a chance to get to know each other.'

'You played a very good game, Liberty,' says Diane.

'A great game,' Michael agrees. 'Big well done. Bravo. Quite the head on your shoulders. A worthy opponent. But I've got forty-odd years on you, when all is said and done. I've learned all the tricks.'

Diane claps her hands. 'Don't take it to heart, Liberty. I've never seen Michael lose at anything. He's pig-headed when it comes to competition.'

'But she was pretty brilliant, my daughter,' says Michael, swiping at tears. 'Oh goodness. Here come the waterworks again.'

'Listen, it's getting late,' says Diane, looking up at the greying sky. 'Michael, your audience are missing their front man. What are we going to do with you, Liberty? Have someone drive you home … or … what do you want to do? Have something more to eat? Does your doggy want something to eat? A bean burger or something?'

'Oh, I can't give Skywalker veggie burgers,' I say. 'They make him farty.'

Diane laughs. 'He's like most men then.'

'It's okay. I've brought him dog biscuits.'

'Listen, Liberty – you're welcome to stay overnight if you want. Whatever's happened in the past, you're still Michael's daughter. You'll always have a place to stay here.'

Michael nods, his face tired and craggy. 'But the choice is yours. We're not going to tell you when you can come and go. You're sixteen. You can make up your own mind. Have you enjoyed yourself today, young Liberty? A lot of new faces. A few connections in your back pocket, right?' He winks. 'I've been selling your band to the heavens.'

'You haven't even heard us all play together. What if we suck?'

'You're my daughter,' says Michael. 'You have an energy about you. Doesn't she, Diane? Too cool for school, the perfect rock and roll star.'

'Absolutely,' says Diane.

'So what's the plan, Liberty bell?' Michael clears away chess pieces. 'These party guests are going to start hunting me down soon. Shall I have Danny drive you back?'

'I want to stay,' I say. 'I'm hoping to persuade you to tell me stuff.'

'I'll mingle with the guests for you,' says Diane. 'I sense you two need a little alone time.'

Michael picks up a guitar that's propped against a nearby tree, idly plucking a string and tuning it as Diane walks away. 'A deal's a deal, isn't it? You lost the chess game. We'll talk another time.'

'Please, Michael.'

Michael sighs. 'Liberty, I never want to hide anything from you. And I know it's driving you mad, me holding things back.

But hurting you is the last thing I want to do today. And I just can't bring myself to do it.'

'I don't care. I can deal with it. Whatever it is.' I recross my legs, feeling rough bark on my bare knees and calves. 'Whatever you have to say, I'm ready for it. I've spent a lifetime waiting.'

Michael sighs. 'You're persistent. Like your old man. But I don't know where I'd even begin, to tell you the truth.'

'At the beginning.'

'The beginning. Okay. Maybe I can tell you a little of it. The beginning would start with … Lorna having cancer when she was your age. Did she tell you about that?'

'Sort of. I mean, we don't speak much about it. But she's always telling me this causes cancer, that causes cancer.'

'What kind of cancer did Lorna have, Liberty?'

'Um … I don't know. Terminal cancer? That's what the hospital told her. But she pulled through. She got better.'

'So Lorna didn't tell you what *kind* of cancer she had?'

'No.'

'A bit unusual, don't you think?'

'I just assumed … you know, that Mum doesn't like talking about it. Bad energy, or something.'

'Let me ask you another question,' says Michael. 'Your mother has a lockbox in the house. Right? A safe. Something like that.'

I hesitate. 'Yes. How did you know that?'

'Call it a hunch. And here's another hunch. Your mother doesn't have precious jewellery. Nothing that would ordinarily be locked away?'

'No.' I shake my head. 'She's not that sort of person.'

'So what do you think she'd need a safe for? Since she's not into diamonds and rubies or anything like that. You know your mother. Come on now, you're a smart girl.'

'She keeps our documents in the safe. Like … passports and stuff. Her medical records, I think. She wants to keep our life locked up in her safe little bubble. It's just her mentality. You know? Lock it all up safe and—'

'HEY, what's going on over here?' Cat Cannon stumbles over rough ground in high heels, coughing into her elbow. 'This is supposed to be a party. Where's my stage buddy?'

'Just taking a break, Cat,' says Michael.

'You're sixteen, right? You know my daughter went missing when she was about your age.' Cat watches me for a second, then her face breaks into a thousand heartbroken pieces.

'Hey.' Michael hops to his feet and pulls her into a hug. 'It's okay. I know. She'll turn up one day. All right? One day. She will.'

Cat starts to wail and cry. Then she abruptly snaps away from Michael, swiping at her eyes. 'No. I won't do this today. Not at your big party. No way. I gotta go, Micky. I gotta go home. If I don't, I'm gonna drink and you know how that ends up.'

'Danny will take you,' says Michael. 'He's at the gate. Limo ready and waiting. Okay?'

'Sure.'

Cat stumbles away, and Michael comes back to sit with me and picks up the guitar.

'We've had a good day, right?' he says. 'Shall we leave things on a high and talk another time?'

'*Please*, Michael.'

'Did you see how upset Cat was? Do you get how heavy all this stuff is? I just can't, Liberty. Another day, any other day. But not *this* day. Our perfect reunion day. I will remember this day for as long as I live. And I won't have it ending with you upset.'

'Can I stay here tonight, then?'

Michael looks up from the guitar. 'Lorna will go crazy if you do that. I mean, like certifiably crazy.'

I look at my tanned feet in flip-flops, toenails painted black. 'She already is crazy. Just … nobody admits it.'

We fall silent as Diane walks towards us carrying an earthenware plate of fresh focaccia bread sprinkled with rosemary and pink sea salt.

'Liberty wants to stay the night,' Michael tells her.

Diane tilts her head. 'Do you think that's a good idea?'

'Please don't send me home,' I say. 'I can't go back to my mother tonight. She'll lock me up and throw away the key and then I'll never see you again. Please. I've been without a father my whole life. I've only just got you back. I need more time. And I want to find out more about my mother. I don't want to leave without knowing everything.'

Music plays from the stage – an acoustic version of 'Should I Stay or Should I Go?' by The Clash.

'Irony,' says Michael. 'If you go there will be trouble. If you stay there will be double.'

Diane shivers in the night air. 'Well, I'd love you to stay over, Liberty. We have the turret room made up for guests. I'll can take you up there now if you like. It doesn't seem proper for a man to do it, does it?'

184

'Um … I mean, my best friend is a boy. He holds the toilet door with the broken lock for me sometimes. And he's gone to the school office to get me tampons before. But okay.'

'Well, you know what I mean,' says Diane. 'And I fancy heading in, too. I'm not much of a party animal. I'll show you the room.'

Michael stands to give me a hug. 'Night-night, sweetheart. It's good to have you home.'

'Will you stay up much longer, Michael?' Diane asks.

'You know how it goes, Diane. This lot won't let me get to bed before midnight. But I won't be later than that.' He kisses her cheek.

Diane smiles. 'Promises, promises.'

In the main house, Diane shows me to the turret room: a round room with a Johnny Rotten decal painted over a fake fireplace and bright white walls. I spend a moment looking at Johnny Rotten, following his lines and curves.

'Cool picture,' I say. 'I love the Sex Pistols.'

'One of Michael's set painters did it,' says Diane. 'He has a talent for decals.'

The bed looks comfortable, made up with red sheets, and there's a private bathroom and shower with towels and a basket of organic cookies. There's also a bookshelf with a few Zen Buddhism books on it, one tattered Dicken's novel and a book of Hans Christian Andersen fairy tales.

Diane follows my eyeline and goes to the bookshelf. 'Ah. Someone asked about this one.' She picks up the book of fairy tales. 'I'll bring it down.'

'This is an eclectic mix,' I say, looking at the books. 'Asian spirituality, fairy tales and Dickens.'

'Oh, Michael picks up all sorts of different books on his travels,' Diane tells me. 'I bet he hasn't even read half of them. But at least if you can't sleep, you can broaden your mind instead. We'll have a chat over breakfast tomorrow, okay? And work out how to handle things going forward.'

'You mean handle my mother?' I say.

'Yes.' Diane hesitates in the doorway, then comes to sit beside me on the bed. 'Look, I'm angry with Lorna. You may as well know. I'll never forget what she did. But I'm Catholic. We believe in forgiveness. The aim is to move forward.'

'Can I ask you something?'

'Anything, love.' Diane rests the book in her lap and strokes hair from my face.

'What do you think happened to Cat's daughter? Annalise?'

'How do you know about her?'

'Old newspaper articles. When I was looking up stuff about Michael.' I watch Diane closely. 'And … my middle name is Annalise.'

'God.' Diane's eyes widen. 'Why on earth would Lorna … Oh, who knows with that woman. Never mind.' She sighs. 'I have no idea what happened to Cat's daughter. She was a very sweet girl but a bit of a mess. I always thought perhaps a suicide, but they never found … you know, a body or anything. Cat's whole rock and roll lifestyle certainly took its toll on the poor girl. It couldn't have been easy being Cat Cannon's daughter. Maybe she just wanted anonymity and is safe and well somewhere. It's the happiest ending any of us could hope for.'

'My mother says something really bad happened to Annalise,' I say.

Diane shakes her head. 'I don't know about that. But I'll tell you something. Lorna knows something she's not letting on about that girl. You know what they say about mud slingers. They're the dirty ones. And it's odd that your mother gave you that middle name, to say the least. Like she has a guilty conscience.'

'My mother says Annalise stayed here,' I say. 'With you and Michael.'

'That was just Lorna pot-stirring, love,' says Diane. 'Divide and conquer. Cause trouble between Michael and Cat. Hell hath no fury.' She meets my eye. 'For what it's worth, I never believed what Lorna said about Michael. Not for one second. Do you think I'd still be with someone who was capable of something like that? I've had Cat here in floods of tears. If Michael knew anything, he'd have told her. Lorna makes me out to be some shy little fawn, hanging on to my husband's coat-tails. But I make my own money. I have my own clothing line business. I might not be Coco Chanel, but my jumpsuits are big sellers on the home shopping channels. If Michael was as awful as Lorna said, I'd have left long ago.'

'So why does my mother believe Michael had something to do with Annalise's disappearance?'

'Honestly, I think Lorna lost her mind a little bit and has never put all the pieces back together.' Diane lets out a long sigh. 'Lorna … she was like some fatal attraction thing. The poor girl had this fantasy in her head. She made up a fictitious relationship. And then when it all went wrong, she convinced herself Michael was this evil abuser. Which I'm telling you now, he isn't. Your mother hadn't long recovered from cancer. She thought Michael was her fairy-tale ending. When it didn't work out like that, well … as I said, hell hath no fury.'

'Do you hate my mother?'

Diane twists her wedding ring. 'Sometimes.'

I put my head in my hands. It feels weird that my hair isn't long anymore. Usually it would tumble through my fingers.

'Mum and I used to be best friends,' I say. 'I believed everything she said. But lately … I mean, it's just a joke how overprotective she is. And now Nick has moved in, it's chronic. Just so bad. Mum says something crazy and Nick is this nodding puppet going along with her. My head is all over the place. I don't believe most of what Mum says anymore. And I sometimes hate Nick for being too stupid.'

'It must be hard,' Diane ventures. 'When your mother … I mean, she's not the most stable of characters. Sorry.' She catches herself. 'Well, at least you've got a port in a storm here now. If things get too terrible you can come and stay with us.'

'Diane,' I say, head flicking up. 'How come you and Michael never had children?'

'I always wanted to,' says Diane, going to the door. 'But after Lorna took you, Michael just didn't want to go there. Too much pain. So we never did. You could say Lorna stole that from us too. Our chance of having a family. But it's okay.' She manages a smile. 'Maybe you can be our little girl. I know you're nearly grown-up, but teenagers still need a bit of guidance. Right?'

'I think I'm all guided out.'

Diane laughs. 'We'll be friends then. I can be your shoulder to cry on. Night-night, sweetheart.' Diane's hand lingers on the door. 'You know, I'm happy you're here. I'm sorry for saying that about your mother. It doesn't reflect on you at all. Okay? Have a good sleep. If you get cold, you just turn the radiator up here.'

'Okay.'

Michael and Diane are not what I expected. None of this is what I expected. I had hoped to have more answers by now. But one thing's for certain – I'm not leaving here until I do.

Lorna

It's 7 a.m.

Liberty's been away all night.

I'm waiting at the Heathrow arrivals gate, pacing like a mad woman. Sleep is still a stranger.

All night. Liberty's been there all night. In his house full of lies and hunting weapons.

Maybe she's dead already.

I throw up into my takeaway Starbucks cup and look up at the Heathrow arrivals board.

The board flashes and my eyes flash with it, twitching.

Then I see my her – my sister.

Dee strides through the arrival gates like the commanding soldier in an army. She wears a bright red coat around her soft shoulders. Shiny calf-length black boots. Her hair is cut short, flecked with blonde streaks and she wears dangly Perspex earrings and glasses with green frames.

For a plus-sized woman, my sister has bold dress sense. Most larger women try to blend in, but not Dee. She's not a blend-in person.

I throw my coffee cup into the trash (rubbish bin, Lorna) and walk towards her.

Dee's face tenses when she sees me. 'Oh, Lorna.' She hugs me, pulling me into lavender-scented softness. 'I'm sorry. I'm so sorry.'

I let myself fall apart, sobbing as my sister holds the pieces together. Then Dee lets go and finds my eyes with hers.

'Liberty will come back. She just has to find her own way out of the woods. Okay? A leap of faith, huh? We have to trust our kids. She's not stupid.'

'Don't you get it?' I say. 'He'll be getting into her mind, twisting her thoughts. You know what he does, Dee.'

'You knew this day would come. We both did. I could see it coming a mile off. You held on too tight to her and she ran.'

'I tried to keep her safe,' I say. 'That's all I ever did. I need a plan, Dee. He's too clever. I've been coming at this like an angry bull, and it's not the way. He sees me coming.'

'We need breakfast,' says Dee. 'This is too upsetting on an empty stomach.'

'Isn't it like 2 a.m. your time?'

'So call it a late dinner then. But who cares about me. *You* need breakfast. I bet you haven't eaten. I had to practically force food down you as a kid.'

'You know I can't eat when I'm upset.'

'Listen, I know how distressing this is for you,' says Dee. 'I know you never wanted to revisit the past. You nearly lost your mind back then. Honestly, Michael was worse than cancer for you. I thought you weren't going to make it. But things are different now. You have this Nick guy. Your own business.

A nice home. Liberty will get this out of her system and you'll all be better for it – you'll see.'

'How can you be so calm? He'll be telling her all sorts of things about me. How unhinged I am. A desperate groupie. And … the rest. All the rest. And then she'll hate me and never want to come home. And he has guns at that place—'

'Come on.' Dee puts an arm around my shoulder. 'You need to eat. And even if you don't, *I* need to eat.'

'We can't—'

'You said we need a plan, right? So let's go make a plan.'

In the first-class lounge, we're served poached eggs, mushrooms, roasted basil tomatoes, fruit and Buck's Fizz – or mimosa, to use the American.

If Nick were here, he'd be measuring grams of protein.

When the mimosas are placed on the table, I feel Dee's eyes on me.

'I don't want alcohol,' I tell the waiter. 'Thank you.'

'Are you sure?' Dee asks. 'It might calm you down.'

'No. I need to stay sharp.'

I choose to eat instead of drink. The food tastes of nothing, but I force it down. Dee is right – I'll be no good to Liberty if I'm fainting from hunger.

'Well done,' says Dee. 'This is just like when we were little, do you remember? Me making sure you finished your plate. You were so cute, always licking your plate clean.'

'You were the best big sister/mother in the world.' I look up. 'When I was with Michael, he said you resented me. That anyone in your position would.'

'Resent you? For what?'

'You having to bring me up when you were still a kid yourself. Mom being the way she was. Turning our childhood into one big hippy love-in.'

'A love-in?' Dee laughs. 'Where was the love? No, I never resented you at all. You were just a kid. I liked looking after you. You know how I am. A nurturer. And I don't resent Mom either. She had us too young and didn't want to miss the party. That's the thing with having kids, isn't it? It's not a mistake you can take back.'

'I would never change my time with Liberty,' I say. 'I'm so scared, Dee. That he'll take her away from me.' I start to cry. 'Dee – how am I going to get her back?'

'Okay.' Dee cuts up little pieces of food in her neat, tidy way. She always takes so long to eat. It's like a religious experience for her. 'Well, you can't go back to his house. That's a definite no. You can't get arrested.'

'I need the police to believe me,' I say. 'If only they'd search his property. We just need proof—'

Dee gives me sad eyes. 'There was no evidence. Nothing to make them search his grounds. In fact, it made them think you had something to hide. Remember?' She raises an eyebrow.

'I've got it.' I click my fingers. 'I'll talk to Cat. She knows the truth about Michael and she's clean now. Maybe I can ask her to go to the police again and they'll believe her—'

'Cat Cannon?' Dee pauses, mid-forkful. 'Annalise's mother?'

'Yes.'

'When you say she knows the truth …'

'She was the only one who believed me back then.'

'If the police didn't listen to Cat before, why will they believe her now?' asks Dee.

'Because she's stone-cold sober these days,' I say. 'I saw an interview with her in the *Guardian*. Clean as clean. She's even been ordained.'

'She's been what?'

'Ordained. You know. Like a Buddhist monk type thing. She was in this article. Celebrities who found God. Except Cat didn't find God. She found chanting.'

'Cat Cannon? A Buddhist monk? Wow. You can just never guess how life is going to turn out, can you?'

'You can say that again. I mean, look at me. I make monsters for a living.'

'Well, I hope Cat's finding peace. Isn't it better just to leave her be? I mean, her daughter is gone. Life must be hard enough.'

'She believed me about Michael,' I say. 'She knows her daughter stayed at the house.'

'Does she *know* though? For certain? Can it be proved?'

'She … not exactly. But she was on my side. She went to the papers with me. And the police.'

'So if it can't be proved …'

'She knows Michael lies,' I say, and I must say it loud because people turn to look at me. 'He tells people we never had a relationship. That I was just some one-night-stand groupie. That I never went to his house. But Cat met me on tour. She saw I was more than just a one-night thing. Diane was talking to me like I was a total whore.'

I begin to hyperventilate.

'Calm down,' says Dee. People are still staring. 'Who cares what Diane thinks, right? But … what exactly do you expect Cat to do?'

'Go to the police. Again. Tell them what I told her to say last time. Give it another try now she's sober. Maybe they'll believe her now she's not on drugs.'

'Maybe Michael did lie,' says Dee gently. 'To save his marriage. And maybe he lied about Annalise too. Maybe she was at his house and he didn't want anyone to know he had a teenage girl hanging around. Because she was so young and there would be implications. He wanted to sign her, right?'

'So he said.'

'Michael might even regret lying now. He might wish he'd told the truth. But now he can't back down without the police suspecting him of something sinister. And if he was honest about you, he'd ruin his marriage.'

'He regrets nothing because he feels nothing.'

'I don't think you should contact Cat,' says Dee. 'She's been through enough. For all you know, she might have forgiven Michael and made her peace with him. She's probably trying to let things go.'

'Like I should do, you mean?'

'I didn't say that.'

'You implied it. Look, Cat is the only person who ever called Michael out on anything. Everyone else is blinded by his magnificence. Too scared.'

Dee watches me with sad eyes. 'Lorna,' she says gently. 'I'm not sure this is the best way forward. We've been here before, haven't we? You trying to ruin his reputation.'

'That's not what I was trying to do. I was trying to make everyone see the truth.'

'You weren't trying to get your own back? Not even a little bit?'

I take a gulp of Americano, ignoring the burning.

'It didn't work,' Dee points out. 'Did it? It just made you look crazy.'

'But I'm not crazy. I'm *not*.'

Dee puts a hand over mine. 'I know, sweetie. I know. You're past all that now.'

Liberty

It's morning.

I've made it through a night at my father's house unscathed.

I have to say, this place is incredible in its own way. It's not my thing, all the fake turrets and marble and mismatched finery. I prefer simple. But the woods go on forever – miles of them.

As I climb out of bed, Skywalker whines and gives a few short barks, meaning nature is calling. I dress, pinning my smiley face badge to my denim jacket and making sure it's the right way up.

'This is the most important fashion statement I've ever made,' I tell Skywalker, patting the badge.

Skywalker looks at me like, 'What are you talking about, Willis?'

I smile. 'I know you don't get fashion. I'll take you out, okay?'

But when I try the door handle, it feels … stuck.

'It can't be,' I tell Skywalker. 'That's stupid. I'm being paranoid.'

I try it again. But it really is stuck.

'Hey,' I shout, pulling. 'HEY!' I twist the rattling metal handle back and forth.

Skywalker barks beside me, jumping about between my legs. He thinks this is a game, but the door won't budge.

'Skywalker, sit,' I say. 'Stay there.'

I'm preparing for a shoulder run when I hear a scrabbling sound at the door. Like witch fingernails dragging over wood.

I pause.

'Um ... hello?'

No one answers.

I watch a lot of Asian horror movies and right now I feel like I'm in one. The Johnny Rotten decal watches me from over the fake fireplace and the shadowy green trees whisper 'all alone' through the arched window.

I glance at the window, wondering if I can climb out. I'm a good climber.

The scrabbling gets louder, and I pick up a chair, wielding it like a weapon.

'Skywalker, heel.'

Doggie comes to my leg, one clawed paw standing shakily on my DM boot. He's trying his best to be a tough guy.

Scratch, scratch, scratch.

It's just the weirdest noise.

Okay. Okay, ready to charge the door ...

But suddenly the door flies open, light pouring in, dust clouds swirling up from the wooden floor.

'Oh my goodness.' Diane holds a palm to her chest and sounds out of breath. 'You're not going to whack me with that chair, are you?'

Diane wears navy blue cotton pyjamas with stars on them and her brown hair twists and flicks messily around her chin.

Without make-up she looks old and tired, with large grey bags under her eyes.

I lower the chair. 'There were weird noises outside. Like … scratching. I watch a lot of horror movies. I thought you were … I don't know, a Japanese girl with stringy hair over her face, crawling up the stairs to get me.'

Diane laughs. 'This door.' She rattles the handle. 'It gets stuck sometimes from the inside. I just woke up in a cold sweat, thinking Jesus – what if the door sticks, and Liberty thinks we've locked her in. She'll start believing Lorna and all her big bad wolf stories. You're up early.'

'I like early mornings.'

Skywalker sniffs at Diane's pyjamas and she strokes his head. 'Was he okay sleeping up here?'

'Yeah. Well, sort of.' I push hair out of my face, grab my denim jacket and pull Skywalker to the door. 'He needs to get outside, though. For his early-morning run-around. And toilet.'

'Of course,' says Diane. 'Listen, I've put some breakfast out for you downstairs. Do you like eggs?'

'Um … I'm vegan. Remember?'

'Right. Sorry. Okay. Wowsers. Can you give me some vegan breakfast ideas? What's left without eggs and toast with butter?'

'Mushrooms. And cereal with almond milk or oat milk.'

'I'll see what I can rustle up.'

'Thanks. Is Michael awake yet?'

'Not yet. He had a bit of a late one last night. He's feeling it today. Come on. Let's go downstairs and you can let your dog out for a run-around.'

Skywalker and I take a long time walking around Michael's

woodlands. The way I'm doing things, we explore methodically, kind of breaking the land up into chunks.

Skywalker, of course, wants to hare around in all directions.

'Come on, dogface.' I tug at his collar. 'We don't have forever. The longer we stay here, the closer Mum is to having a nervous breakdown.'

After an hour, Skywalker is done exploring the woods, so we head back for breakfast. On the path back to the house, Skywalker finds some old shotgun shells and picks up the gunpowder scent. I follow him to a hunting shed full of shotguns.

'Well, Mum was right about one thing,' I tell Skywalker, as he bounds inside the shed and sits perkily by the rack of hunting rifles. 'He does keep guns here. That's the countryside way.'

Skywalker is so proud of himself for finding the stash.

'Good boy.'

I throw him another biscuit for his sniffing talents. Then I pop chewing gum into my mouth and examine the rifles, looking down the barrels, testing them out.

'Wow.' I stand back, looking over the gleaming metal. 'Some of these are pretty mega. I mean, deer guns. You could kill someone with one of those.'

'Yeah, you could.' Michael's growly early-morning voice makes me jump. He stands in the cabin doorway, wearing green wellies, black jeans, a grey hoodie and a tweedy flat cap.

'Um … hi.' I try for a smile. 'Just checking out your rifle collection.'

'Careful with those now, little one,' says Michael. 'They're dangerous things. You know better than to play around with them, don't you?'

'I know,' I say, eyes gliding over the rack.

'Let's come away from these things, now. They're not toys. It's good to see you up and awake.' Michael gives me a clap on the shoulder. 'Did your doggy like the woods? Diane told me you were walking him.'

'Oh, yeah. He loved it.'

'I thought you'd got lost out here. I came to find you.'

'The walk took longer than I thought it would,' I say. 'These woodlands are huge.'

'Listen, you really shouldn't be in a gun shed like this on your own. No one should be messing around with guns unless they've had proper, safe instruction.'

'You think because I'm vegan I haven't handled a gun before? My mother has rifles.'

Michael laughs. 'Silly me. Lorna's armed to the teeth, no doubt. For the great war that's never coming.'

'Something like that. They're hunting rifles, but ... yeah. She doesn't hunt anything.' My hand wanders absentmindedly to the smiley face badge on my jacket, feeling to make sure it's the right way up. Fashion is all about getting the right look at all times, after all.

'What's that?' Michael notices my badge. 'The old acid house smiley face. That's a pretty big badge, isn't it? I've never seen a button that big. Is that the fashion among you kids today? I hope you're not into that whole scene. Drugs and all that.'

'It's just an emoji. A smiley face. Looking out on everything. A view on the world. You know?'

Michael nods, but I can tell he doesn't really get it. He's not supposed to – he's old.

'Listen,' Michael says. 'I was wondering if you wanted to see my little music studio today. Before you leave.'

'What I really want to do is talk,' I say. 'Really talk. About my mother and all the things she hasn't told me.'

'Yes, Liberty. A talk is long overdue. But promise me one thing. If you don't get to see the studio today, you'll bring your band up here sometime.'

I nod and nod. 'I'd love to. They'd love to. We'd all love to. Thanks.' I hesitate. '*Dad*.'

Michael gives me a gentle smile. 'Come on, daughter of mine, let's go have breakfast. And I'll start making my peace with you going back to Lorna today, if that's what you want. God, it's going to be tough. Like losing you all over again.'

'I'll come back,' I say. 'And if Mum won't let me … well, I'm sixteen years old. I'm allowed to leave home. It's sad. All these years we've missed. We've got a lot of catching up to do.'

'That we do, Liberty. That we do.'

Lorna

Cat Cannon opens her front door in a black Chanel dress, cigarette held between red fingernails. She stares at me like I'm a ghost.

The door opening only happened after a lengthy intercom interrogation, during which Cat accused me of being an investigative journalist and made me answer questions that she herself couldn't remember the answers to.

'It's 8 a.m. and you're all dressed in Chanel with your hair and nails done,' I say. 'Am I in a parallel universe?'

'Whoa.' Cat takes a long inhale of her cigarette and blows smoke up into wedding cake-style cornicing. 'You look different too. You know, I was thinking of you yesterday. A lot of stuff has come up this week. Come on inside. Jesus, I hardly recognize you. You were all skin and bone back in the day. Now you're like this strong, sturdy thing. And you grew your hair.'

I hold a clump of my thick, black hair. 'Michael liked it short, right? So I grew it long. What else was I going to do?'

'And what's with all the tattoos?'

'I thought I'd better take my identity back.'

'Yeah, I know that one.'

'I've changed a lot since Michael. I've gotten stronger.' I mean to sound strong too, but the words crack in my throat.

'Hey.' Cat gestures at me with a milk-white arm. 'Whatever pain you're in, I've been there and worse.' She offers me a cigarette. 'You know, I think some kind of cosmic force is pulling the past back right now. Come on inside.'

'Can I smoke inside? I gave up but ... right now ...'

'Sure you can smoke inside.'

'I read somewhere you couldn't smoke in these townhouses.'

'Yeah, you've gotta break a few rules, right?' Cat holds out a gold-stick Yves Saint Laurent cigarette lighter. 'All I do these days is smoke. It could be so much worse.'

'So you're all straight and clean now,' I say. 'Look at you. With your perfect fingernails and designer cigarette lighter.'

'I'm trying to buy respectability. It doesn't work.' Cat blows smoke as she tip-taps down the hallway on high, red shoes with blue soles. There's a picture on the flowery wall of Cat, dressed in saffron robes, hugging a stone buddha. On the glass she's scrawled:

Peace, fun and freedom. Everything changes.

'I read that you found religion,' I say.

'Who'd have thought, right?' says Cat, nodding at the walls. 'Life is crazy. Except Buddhism isn't a religion. It's a practice. And I couldn't do the short hair thing.' She runs her hand through neatly styled, platinum blonde hair. 'Shaving it every day ... you know. Just a pain.'

'What's the story with this place?' I ask.

'Oh, you mean because it's tasteful and traditional and

everything I'm not?' Cat laughs. 'I can't change anything here. It's in my ten-grand-a-month lease. Don't change the decor. And don't smoke.'

'I drove past your old house this morning.'

'Oh, yeah?' Cat nods and smokes. 'How's the old girl doing?'

'Not good. Graffiti. Parts burned down.'

'Everything changes. Right?'

'Yeah. It does.'

Cat shakes her head. 'Not a good time when I lost that place. Being broke is bad, but being a broke celebrity is the lowest you can ever get.'

'No, the lowest you can get is Michael Reyji Ray.'

Cat blows out a long stream of smoke, not meeting my eye. Then she says: 'He's not so bad. You know, I saw him yesterday.'

'What?' The word is chilly.

'Yeah.' Cat nods. 'He invites me to his anniversary party every year. I think Diane still hates me. But she hates me less with every year that passes.'

My fingers burn, and I realize I've smoked the cigarette down to the butt. 'How could you go to his party? That's *crazy*.'

'You still hate him, huh?'

'Of course I do. Don't you?'

'No.' Cat's eyes find mine. 'Not anymore. We've forgiven each other. Even Diane and I are sort of getting along. You know, she actually *talked* to me yesterday. We had a half-hour conversation about packing a flight bag. The eyedrops, rescue remedy, moisturizer. She's dull as ditch water, but at least she was trying. *And do you know, Cat, I've been taking probiotics all week for my flight tomorrow. And I keep a tub of them in my suitcase, packed in ice.'*

'I can't believe you're talking like this. Like you're *friends* with them.'

'I *am* friends with them. Nothing was ever proved, Lorna. And half the stuff you said about Michael ... I'm not sure even you believed it. You barely knew your own mind when you were with him. I don't believe Michael hurt my daughter. Truly I don't.'

My jaw hardens. 'Brainwashing. You always said you were too strong for him. But you're not. You let him in. You're drinking the Michael juice just like everyone else.'

'Michael hasn't got to me. He was there for me. He understood like no one else did. And he forgave me for getting everything twisted. Do you want a cup of tea?' Cat gestures to a country cottage-style kitchen.

'Nothing got twisted. He hurt your daughter, Cat.'

'NO.' The word booms around Cat's wooden kitchen. 'My daughter is okay. I don't know where she is, but she's okay.' Cat takes a deep inhale and exhale, eyes closed. Suddenly, her long eyelashes ping open again. 'Listen, honey. I accept you see things a certain way. But it's not the way I see things now. Michael and I are friends.'

Tears come. 'You and me were the only ones, remember? The sane-os. The only ones not buying into Michael's bullshit.'

'We *were* the bullshit, Lorna,' says Cat. 'Your crazy stalker brain told you stories and we both believed them. Because I needed answers, and you needed a reason to hate Michael.

But I'm in a better place now. Back then, I needed to believe Annalise had died. Because I couldn't face the truth.'

'Which is?'

'She ran away from me and all my chaos. From the embarrassment of being Cat Cannon's daughter. My job is to get healthy for her. So that one day she might come back to me. I feel like, maybe she's in India. Some place like that. A different country. Why are you here, Lorna? Just to stir up more shit?'

'You were at Michael's house yesterday,' I say, voice low. 'Right?'

Cat hesitates. 'Yeah. For his party.'

'My daughter is there. Michael has my sixteen-year-old teenage daughter. Did you see her?'

Cat blinks eyelash implants at me. '*Your* daughter? Are you feeling okay?'

'No, I'm not feeling good at all. My daughter is the same age Annalise was when she went missing. Doesn't that disturb you? She would have been at the party yesterday. Or … or somewhere in the house.' Nausea turns my stomach over.

Cat stubs out her half-smoked cigarette and lights another. 'You know, Michael's been a good friend to me. Who he has at his parties are his business.'

'He's a psychopath.'

Cat looks at red lipstick on her cigarette butt. 'I believed that too, once upon a time. But I don't believe it now, Lorna. I just don't.'

'They never searched his grounds. If they had …'

'There wasn't any evidence, Lorna. Doesn't that tell you something?'

'Yes. It tells me Michael has the police in his pocket. They wouldn't believe anything you said. Remember?'

'Yeah, well, I had no proof.' Cat lifts her big blue eyes. 'The police tore me apart. Opiates are no good for a clear and concise testimony. Which wasn't my testimony anyway – *you* told me to say it.'

I look her right in the eye. 'Cat. I was telling you the truth then and I'm telling it now. About Annalise. About everything.'

Cat pulls hard on her cigarette and shakes her head. 'Uh uh. No way. No way. Listen, Lorna. I believed all that "Michael is a psycho" stuff because I needed a reason that wasn't my fault. Denial. Closure. Whatever you want to call it. But Annalise is out there somewhere. I know she is.'

'Cat.' My voice is soft, tears coming. 'I was with Annalise when it happened.'

'Hey.' Cat holds up a hand. 'Let's not go there, right? You've vomited this story at me too many times. You were so crazy back then, Lorna…'

'Who wouldn't be? I was a teenager living with a psycho.'

'Listen, I know Michael wasn't totally straight with the press,' says Cat. 'But Jesus, after the things you said about him. I mean, you were all out to ruin him. Destroy his career, marriage, his whole life practically. And have him rot in jail. Michael's not such a bad guy. You're wrong about him. He's not perfect but he has a good heart.'

'He's brainwashed you,' I accuse.

'Do I look like the sort of person who can be brainwashed?'

'Totally,' I say. 'You're in pain. You want something. Those are the only two ingredients he needs.'

'So explain Diane. She's been with him over twenty years. Is she brainwashed?'

'Of course she is. She's a good Catholic girl who hates divorce. She has to believe her husband is perfect.'

'Why have you come here, Lorna? Just to spread more shit about Michael? I'm the closest to peace I've ever been.'

'I want you to help me,' I say. 'You're clean now. Tell the police that Michael lied about Annalise. And about me living with him. They'll believe you. It won't be like before.'

'What is there to remember?' says Cat. 'I never knew anything. I just repeated what you told me.'

'You know Annalise stayed with us.'

'That's what I thought, but … you know, I was on heroin. I don't trust any of my memories from back then. And nor should you. You weren't in such a great place.'

'Cat. Michael has my daughter. She's at his house right now. She's the same age Annalise was when she went missing. Does that mean nothing to you?'

Cat puts long, bony fingers on my shoulder. 'He hurt you. I get it. He's a married man who used you for sex. That's the bad part. But he also raises millions for charity. He called me every single day after Annalise went missing. He even asked me to go and stay with him.'

'Of course – he wanted to keep you close. Of course he did. My daughter—'

'This is starting to sound crazy, Lorna. I mean … you spying

209

on Michael again. After all this time. It's weird. It sounds like you're having a total psychotic break.'

'Talk to the police. Tell them—'

'Tell them what? Michael's my friend.' Cat clicks open a Chanel handbag and passes me a card. 'Here. Take it. It's a card for my psychiatrist. She really helped me a lot.'

Liberty

The kitchen breakfast table is laid with hunks of wholemeal bread, a bottle of olive oil and roasted mushrooms. Skywalker eats a bowl of chopped-up steak on the slate floor, chewing slowly because his stomach is already full of dog biscuits.

'So I'm hoping Michael and I can talk after breakfast,' I say, watching Diane pour coffee.

'About your mother?'

'Yes.' I pour olive oil on fresh bread.

'Well, I'm sure—' Diane smiles at the door. 'Here he is. The great man himself.'

Michael strolls into the kitchen wearing a black V-neck T-shirt, suit jacket and tight jeans. His hair is shower-wet and he's now clean-shaven.

'And here *she* is.' Michael jogs around the table and hugs me. 'My little girl. Right here at my breakfast table. Unbelievable. A dream come true.'

'I'd better get on,' says Diane, putting gentle hands on my shoulders. 'I've got more packing to do.'

'Sit down at the breakfast table for once in your life,' says Michael, scanning the breakfast offerings.

'Michael, I have a day ahead of me you wouldn't believe,' says Diane. 'My flight leaves after lunch. What's the point of me watching other people eat when I have a million things to do?'

'Well, you could eat something yourself,' Michael laughs. 'For a change.'

Diane puts hands to her skinny waist. 'There aren't enough calories in the day for breakfast.'

'Come on. Our charming guest here wants you to stay. Are there any eggs, Diane?'

'Michael. Liberty is vegan. I'm not going to put out food she can't eat.'

'Right.' Michael scratches the back of his neck. 'Uh … well, mushrooms look great.'

'Hang on.' Diane ties her apron string tighter. 'I'll put some chocolate croissants in for you, Michael. Okay? I know how you are with a hangover.'

Michael laughs. 'A fussy bastard. Is that what you mean?'

'You said it. Liberty, does this look all right for you? Is there anything else I can get? What do you usually have for breakfast?'

'This looks great,' I say. 'Sometimes I have a fruit plate. But it's okay.' I think of Mum.

Michael seems to read my mind. 'Do you need someone to drive you home today, Liberty?'

'It's okay,' I say. 'I can catch the bus. I don't want to put anyone out, and Skywalker is a pain in the back of a car. Paws everywhere.'

'It's a long way to go on your own, love.' Diane tidies napkins. 'Are you *sure* we can't drive you?'

'Don't suffocate the girl, Diane,' says Michael. 'She'll have had enough of that from her mother. If she wants to catch the bus, let her catch the bus. Liberty has a good head on her shoulders. And she's sixteen years old. Practically an adult. She made it here by herself. She can make it back.' He gives me a clumsy pat on the shoulder. 'Let's go for a walk after breakfast, shall we? See the studio? Have a catch-up?'

'Yes. That would be great.'

'You'll love the music studio. It's this beautiful little cottage out in the woods. You can see all my equipment – it's a musician's dream. And we can have a bit of a jam session and chat at the same time.'

'Sure. Okay. Sounds like a great idea. And we'll *definitely* talk today?'

Michael laughs. 'Yes. Who's your favourite musician?'

'Joan Jett.'

'Joan Jett, Joan Jett … she plays a Gibson Melody Maker, right?'

'Yes.'

'I have one of those out at the studio. You can play it. See how it feels.'

'Wow.'

'I have a whole load of stuff out there, Liberty. Some real heirlooms. I'm a bit of a collector. I buy so many instruments. Last month, I bought Gene Simmons's Axe Punisher bass guitar.'

My eyes widen. 'From Kiss?'

'Yep.'

'Wow.'

'When you and your band record your single out there,

you can play whatever instruments you want. Can I still say single? Or is it track now? Singles are from the good old days of record players.'

'I have a record player,' I say.

'No.' Michael leans back, eyes widening. 'Really?'

'And a cassette player. I'm interested in all sorts of sounds. Every medium has a different feel to it.'

'Just you wait until you see my stuff,' says Michael. 'It'll be like all your Christmases coming at once.'

'Do you have a drum machine?'

'Come now, young Liberty. Of course I have a drum machine. I have five different drum machines – one of which is a cool little number from the Eighties that Scruff took on tour with him.'

'That's ... wow. *Wow*.'

'What's mine is yours,' says Michael. 'I mean that. You can use the studio whenever you like. When I was your age, the band and I put our pennies together to buy an hour in a crappy room with egg boxes and tin foil on the walls. A lot of arguments, trying to get the material right in the time. But it was the first step, you know? Getting the sound down. After that, we conquered the world.' Michael's eyes go all teary. 'Like father, like daughter. Right? Have you ever been in a music studio before?'

'Never,' I say. 'Mum would never let me. It's like ... my dream.'

'Well, that's me,' says Michael. 'The man who makes dreams come true.'

Once upon a time …

My pale, unhappy face bounced up and down in the gym mirror, cheeks hollow, lips blue-white.

Stay slim. Stay in shape. Stay young and beautiful if you want to be loved.

It was a regular habit now, running on a machine in Michael's gym room, exercising amid boxes of tiles and stacked-up plasterboard. My skinny arms and legs flailed around. I was not, and never had been, a natural runner. I hated the running machine and I hated exercising inside like a lab rat, but I was determined to keep my figure for my man.

I used to be a feminist. What happened?

Suddenly, my legs flew out from under me and I caught myself on the digital running display, hitting the emergency stop. This was happening more and more lately – head rush and near fainting during exercise.

I knew I was overdoing it, but the consequences of getting fat didn't bear thinking about. Michael had told me over and over again how much he hated fat on a woman. His type was frail to the point of anorexic. Fat on women repulsed him, even though he himself was plump around the middle now the tour had finished.

As I struggled to get my breath back, I saw Michael, dark and looming in the wall-to-wall mirrors. He wore a black T-shirt, jeans and Ray-Ban sunglasses. His arms were crossed and his lips tight.

My whole body tensed. I recognized the signs. Something was up and I was to blame.

'What?' I asked, stepping down from the running machine.

Michael took off his sunglasses. He had that dark look again. Shoulders hunched over, eyes hard and cold.

'I've been here the whole time,' I said, voice going high and scared. 'The whole time. I got up and came straight down to exercise. I didn't even have breakfast—'

'Your sister's at the gate.'

'Dee's here?'

Michael nodded, jaw hard.

I shook my head. 'She can't be. She's in New York.'

'She must have got on a plane,' said Michael. 'I hear it's quite the thing these days. Air travel.'

'I didn't tell her the address,' I said, words rushed. 'How could I? I wouldn't even know how to get here myself. I swear to you, Michael. You won't even let me call her.'

'Well. She's here.'

'This is nothing to do with me. It's not my fault, Michael. Please—'

'The girl says she won't leave until she sees you. If you want to associate with that press rat, be my guest. But pack your bags.'

'Michael, she's not a press rat. She wouldn't have said a word about us. It was someone on your staff. It had to be—'

'Don't you DARE accuse my staff. Don't you dare.' Michael

clicks his fingers at the door. 'Go tell her she needs to leave. I want her off my property, Lorna. This is *my* home.'

'Fine. Okay, I'll tell her.'

Michael's eyes softened then. 'Listen – I've been through what you've been through. Remember? Family can be the worst of them. The very worst. You can't choose your family. But you can cut them out now and move on with your life.'

There was a colourful splodge at the gates. As I got nearer, the splodge separated into a purple coat, bright red woolly hat and blue knee-high boots.

My sister.

Dee's mouth dropped open when I got close. 'Lorna. Jesus. Are you okay? You're so thin.'

'I'm fine. I've been exercising. Staying fit. Michael has his own gym here.'

'Have you seen a doctor lately?'

'I don't need a doctor. I feel great. It's just … I mean, it's brilliant here. All my dreams coming true.'

'Your accent sounds weird. You sound like Michael.'

'No, I don't.'

'Yes, you do. You sound just like him. A little clone. What's happened to my sister?'

'You have to go, Dee. Michael doesn't want you here.'

Dee started to cry. 'I've flown all this way to see you. You look so … *thin*. Your cheeks … God. Worse than when you had the cancer. What is he doing to you?'

'Nothing,' I said. 'I just told you. Things are amazing. I'm living with a rock star. I have everything I've ever wanted.'

'Oh, come on, Lorna,' Dee said. 'Who are you kidding? This place is a building site, not a house. And he's *married*.'

'I know he's still married. He and his wife are separated, but they can't divorce because of the press.'

'They're not separated,' Dee said. 'He was at an awards ceremony with Diane just last month. I saw it in the papers.'

'Michael has to do that stuff,' I said. 'You know, keeping up the married-man image. He doesn't want to. He and Diane don't have sex anymore. He doesn't love her. He loves me.'

'He's brainwashed you,' Dee snapped. 'He's keeping you out here like a little bird in a cage, while he goes back and forth to his wife. Why can't you see it?'

'Life with a rock star is complicated. It's not like a normal relationship. If I want to be with Michael, I have to accept that.'

Michael's words, not mine. But I didn't have many of my own words left by then.

Dee reached through the bars to take my hand. 'Your hands are so cold. And your eyes – you're not yourself.'

'I am.' I snatched my hand back. 'Look, I told you. I'm happy. I have everything I could ever want. You're just being a jealous bitch.'

'You don't mean that,' said Dee. 'This is the first time I've seen you in months. You never call. I had no idea where you were. I had to stalk you to find this place and now you won't even let me in the house. It's like you died or something. He's controlling you.'

'No, not at all,' I said. 'But this is Michael's house, Dee. I don't get to choose who comes and goes.'

'And you think that's normal?'

'I understand where Michael's coming from. After that press story, he doesn't want you here. He's very protective of his privacy.'

'Wait – what press story?'

'Michael thinks you sold a story on us.'

'No, I didn't! I didn't sell any story. I'd never do that.'

'Well, something came out about us in the press. About how we got together after the New York gig.'

'If you're in a real relationship with him, it shouldn't matter that the press know, should it?'

'It's more complicated than that. We have to be discreet until the divorce comes through.'

'No,' says Dee. 'You need to be discreet because you're seeing a married man, and that married man doesn't want his wife to know about you.'

'No. That's not why.'

'Lorna, do you think it's normal that we haven't seen each other in over a year?'

'I wrote.'

'Wrote? When? I didn't get any letters.'

I chewed at my thumb. I had written. But I'd given those letters to Michael ...

'And now you won't let me into where you're living?' Dee continued. 'This is craziness. I think you need some psychiatric help. He's done something to you. Taken away your brain.'

'No, he hasn't. I'm exactly the same as always.'

'You're not. You're different. This isn't healthy.' Dee glances at the house. 'He's not healthy. Lorna, a girl went missing after being seen with him. A German girl. Look at this.' She pulled a folded newspaper clipping from a patchwork bag and began to read. 'Karla Muller was last seen with Ray in the VIP area at Glastonbury. Muller appeared to be intoxicated as she danced with the singer.'

Dee turned the clipping to show me the photograph: a pretty, brown-haired teenager with a nose piercing and sharp cheekbones, hanging on to Michael with her eyes half closed. She wore a Michael Reyji Ray T-shirt over a skinny frame. The thing I hated most about the picture was Michael's eyes. They watched the girl like a wolf watches a sheep.

'Girls throw themselves at Michael all the time. He has to be nice.'

'And listen to this,' Dee continued. 'A member of Michael Reyji Ray's staff told police that Muller left the festival with Ray.'

I leaned closer to read the article, jabbing at the text. 'This is all bullshit. Press bullshit. Michael is tired of it. People always trying to take him down in the newspapers. It's not Michael's fault that these girls are fantasists. Imagining they're madly in love with him.'

'Were you at this festival?' Dee asks.

My shoulders stiffen. 'I don't go everywhere with Michael. I'm not his ball and chain. He had enough of that from his wife. He prefers me to stay here. Out of the limelight. We're not into publicity, showing off. What we have is real. All *this* stuff.' I slap the newspaper page. 'It's fake. Made up. Listen, I'm sure that girl will turn up. You don't need to worry about my safety. Michael looks after me. He is so gentle and loving and kind, Dee. Honestly. He can be the sweetest guy.'

'Can be?' says Dee. 'Or is?'

'He takes care of me,' I insist. 'I mean, sure, he has his moments. No guy is perfect. Everyone is a little bit afraid of their partner sometimes. But when we're in a good place, I swear to God it's like a spiritual connection.'

'Okay.' Dee crossed her arms. 'If this is all normal and you're in a beautiful relationship, open up the gates and let me in.'

'You know I can't do that, Dee.'

'Why?'

'Because Michael doesn't want you here.'

Dee gives an outraged laugh. 'And what about you?'

'Please don't put me in this situation, Dee. Where I have to choose between you.'

'*He's* putting you in that situation, Lorna. Not me. This is crazy.'

'I'm happy with Michael. I love him. We're going to get married and start a family and live happily ever after.'

Dee's face changed then. Her expression became soft and her voice low. 'Okay, Lorna,' she said. 'There's not going to be a baby. There will never be a baby. Michael is married and all you are is the other woman. Okay?'

'You're wrong. You don't get it. You're measuring our relationship by an everyday yardstick, but Michael isn't an everyday guy. It's different. We're soul mates.'

'There will be no miracle happy ending here, Lorna,' said Dee, choking up. 'But if you won't come home with me now, I'll be waiting.'

'I should go.' I glanced back at the house.

'He's controlling you, Lorna,' said Dee. 'I see it, but you don't. I'll be waiting every day. Okay? Every single day.'

She reached through the bars and took my hand.

'Dee, it's okay.' I tried to smile, but tears came. 'Really it is. I'm so happy. Crazy in love.' I glanced back the house and saw Michael at the door, arms crossed. My voice rose three octaves. 'Dee. Dee, I have to go. Please don't worry. I love you.'

Liberty

Michael's music studio really is lost in the woods. It takes us maybe ten minutes to reach it via a winding woodland path, and with every step, the summer sun grows dimmer above thick trees.

'This is your studio?' I ask, looking over the cottage, shadowed by giant fir trees. The little building has blacked-out windows, like a limousine. It looks weird, the soulless modern panes in olde worlde sugar-cube crumbling walls. And it's so far away from everything. I can barely see the main house anymore.

'You were expecting something different?' Michael asks.

'Yeah, kind of. I thought your studio would be like square and glass walls and metal beams and stuff. Totally modern.'

'Music lives better in old buildings,' says Michael. 'Places with soul and character. I have a real soft spot for this little cottage. It was the farmhouse that came with the land. The big place was built afterwards. But I always loved it out here. It's totally secluded; you wouldn't find it unless you knew where to look. I wouldn't even need soundproofing if these owls didn't hoot away at night.' He hesitates. 'You know, this cottage burned down once upon a time. I wonder if your mother ever told you about that?'

'No.'

'No. I imagine she wants to put all that behind her. Anyway. Forget I mentioned that, Liberty. It's all in the past and something beautiful came of it. Make the best of every tragedy, right? You just wait until you see inside. It's magic in here, I tell you. The best studio in the whole country.'

'Humble as always, Michael Reyji Ray.' Diane totters through the woods, dressed in a black fitted suit and neon-pink high heels. The outfit is a little dated, and I can picture Diane wearing it better as a younger woman.

'Trust me, Diane,' says Michael. 'Liberty is gonna flip her lid over this equipment.'

'Is she indeed?' says Diane. 'Well, listen. I've come to say goodbye before I head off.'

'You're going?' I ask.

'I have a plane to catch,' says Diane, kissing Michael on the cheek and giving me a long hug. 'So I have to skedaddle. Liberty, it was amazing to meet you. Don't be a stranger. Okay? Why don't we have a girls' shopping trip when I get back? Get this man to spend some money on us?'

'Where are you going?' I ask.

'Milan. I'm meeting some designers.'

'Diane has a new handbag range,' says Michael.

'I think you'd approve, Liberty,' says Diane. 'It's vegan. Fake leather all the way.'

'This woman won't sit still, I'm telling you,' says Michael. 'Good cause after good cause. She puts me to shame.'

'Oh, I don't know about that,' says Diane. 'You give millions to your charities. I'm just the little wife who sells ethical clothing.'

'A little wife who's always jetting off and leaving her husband.'

'What'd I do if I stayed home all the time?' says Diane. 'You like me being gone once in a while. Admit it.'

'Only because it's so fun when you come back.'

Diane takes out her phone. 'Come on, let's have a photo of you two before I leave. You two are peas in a pod. You're the spit of each other.' She hesitates. 'I don't see Lorna in you at all, Liberty. You're all Michael.'

'So how about it, Liberty bell?' says Michael. 'A selfie with the old man?'

Diane laughs. 'It's not a selfie, Michael. A selfie is when you take a photo of yourself.' She shakes her head at me. 'He thinks he's so down with the kids. Okay – stand together, you two.'

Michael puts his arm around my shoulder and grins from ear to ear, every bit the proud father.

When Diane shows us the photo, Michael's eyes well up. 'Wowsers. Look at the pair of us. Together again. We do look the same, don't we? You have to say it.'

I look at the picture. He's right. Same tanned skin, straight white teeth, long nose, thick, dark eyelashes and eyebrows. And now black-brown hair, bleached blonde. Like Diane says, two peas in a pod.

'Father and daughter, reunited,' says Diane.

Michael nods, but he's too choked up to answer.

'Kids, I'm so sorry.' Diane checks her Rolex. 'I really have to run. Don't look at me like that, Michael. You know who you married.'

'I know, I know,' says Michael. 'A woman who can't sit still.'

Diane gives him a hug, then me. 'What a pleasure it was to meet you, Liberty.'

I let out a long breath as she heads off. 'Okay, Dad. Tell me everything.'

'Okay. Let's go inside. I'll show you the instruments. And we'll talk.' Michael pulls open the heavy cottage door. 'It gets stiff, this old thing. But it has to be metal. Wood goes rotten out here.'

I stand on the threshold, eyes wide.

'I like to do things differently, Liberty. Come on inside now, there's a girl.'

Lorna

I roar down our street in Nick's green MG, tears streaming down my face.

He's got to Cat too. He's poisoned her mind. She's drunk the Michael magic potion ...

I slow as I reach our house, heart racing.

Who the hell is that?

An orange-jacket delivery guy lurks outside the house, looking around the tall gate then peering through the crack. He won't be able to see inside. The crack is sealed. I glued the rubber strip on myself with modelling glue.

I screech to a halt, bumping two car tyres onto the sidewalk (pavement, Lorna) and leap out.

We never order goods by mail because I don't like strangers hanging around the gate. Or strangers, full stop. Nick calls me paranoid, but he's given in to my cynical world view and now buys his protein bars and neoprene sleeves in town.

The delivery guy's jacket boasts: 'Same Day Guarantee'. He has a cosy-looking blond beard all around his face and neck like a furry scarf, and he holds a small, grey parcel.

'Hey.' I jog up to him. 'This is my house. We never have parcels delivered. You must have the wrong place.'

'Iron Bridge Farm, right?' The courier has an oddly high voice, considering his large beard. I see two broken front teeth.

'Yes, but I told you. We never have deliveries.'

'It's definitely for you.' He hands me a small package, then unsnaps the plastic device from his belt. 'Miller, right? Sign here.'

I squiggle my finger on the signed for device, staring at the parcel. Then I let the courier shove it in my hand.

The parcel feels light, like a piece of cedar wood, the edges squared but soft. I rip open the thick, grey plastic, making a big, jagged black mouth.

What the hell is this?

A book.

I slide the novel out of the plastic, my fingers slippery, unreliable, not my own.

The Tales of Hans Christian Andersen.

This is my book. One of the study resources I took on tour with Michael, before I abandoned school entirely to live with him.

An angry tear falls onto the cover. Where the hell did this come from? Who sent it?

Someone has folded a small, plain paper between two pages as a makeshift bookmark.

My hands shake as I flick the book open. The bookmark has been placed at the end of *The Little Mermaid* story. It's the part where I stopped reading the book years ago on a flight with Michael, but the bookmark can't be mine. The paper is too new.

The story is about love and sacrifice, I remember telling Michael.

Would you sacrifice yourself for me?

Of course I would …

There are bright yellow highlights on the bookmarked page. Did I make these highlights? No. I don't think so. But then again, my memory of that time is terrible.

I read the neon yellow sections:

The knife trembled in the hand of the little mermaid; then she flung it far away from her into the waves. She cast one more lingering, half-fainting glance at the prince, and then threw herself from the ship into the sea, and thought her body was dissolving into foam.

'After three hundred years, thus shall we float into the kingdom of heaven,' whispered one of her companions. 'Unseen we can enter the houses of men, where there are children, and for every day on which we find a good child, who is the joy of his parents and deserves their love, our time of probation is shortened. The child does not know, when we fly through the room, that we smile with joy at his good conduct, for we can count one year less of our three hundred years.'

More tears come, falling onto sandy-coloured, porous paper.

A story of love and sacrifice.

This is all Michael. He made this bookmark and he high-lighted this section.

It's a message.

He wants me to give myself up. Diane must be gone – Cat said something about her taking a flight. Michael is calling me back with the strongest bait he could get.

If I give myself up now, he might let Liberty go.

Liberty

Wow.

Michael's music studio is … wow.

I suck in a breath.

'You like it?' Michael asks.

I nod and nod. 'Who wouldn't? It's amazing.'

'Diane isn't too interested,' Michael chuckles. 'Not her sort of thing. But you're a musician. You get it.'

I walk around, hands running over instruments and recording equipment. 'Totally amazing.'

The space is open plan, like Peter Gabriel's recording studio. No separation between the sound engineer equipment and the recording area. The mixing desks are within the rehearsal room. Not that I've ever been to Peter Gabriel's studio, but I've seen YouTube videos.

I feel like I'm in a playground.

Skywalker sniff, sniff, sniffs at the floor, suspicious of its texture.

'It's a great space, isn't it?' says Michael, closing the door behind us. 'I'm guessing you've never been in a real music studio before?'

'Never. My mother isn't keen on me exploring that particular avenue. This is like … amazing.'

'Better than you were expecting?'

'A hundred times better.' My boots squeak on the floor. 'You have everything. You've got a TR808 …'

'Oh, yeah. Of course. I'm a musician who also happens to be a millionaire. What else would I spend my money on?'

I look around the studio. 'Can I record something?'

'Don't you want to wait until the rest of your band are here?'

'Nope. I want to play around with all this stuff right now.'

Michael laughs. 'If it means I get to spend more time with you, you can do anything you like. You can even have a rock and roll moment and smash a guitar.'

'As if I would. I'd never hurt an instrument. It would be sacrilegious.'

'Let's get everything set up then,' says Michael, going to a mixing deck and flicking switches.

I grab a guitar.

Something happens when I play music. It's like being carried away. Time just … goes. Before I know it, a lot of time has passed. We've recorded three of my songs, and I'm still free-styling, messing around with the sounds.

'I'll tell you one thing, Liberty,' says Michael, leaning back in a white swivel chair. 'You're the best thing I've heard in a long time. A very long time. And that guitar suits you down to the ground.'

'It's the coolest guitar ever.' I'm holding Joan Jett's guitar of choice.

'You want that guitar?' says Michael. 'It's yours.'

'No way. You mean it? No way.'

'Of course I mean it. You're my little girl. You've missed enough birthday and Christmas presents. Anyway, you need a good guitar. It's a necessity for you. To play like that at your age … I have to tell you, I'm pretty blown away.'

I look down at the guitar, plucking strings. 'Thank you. That means a lot, coming from you. Do you know what? How long have we been out here? It must have been hours.' I shake my head, fretboard-toughened fingers finding chords. 'I feel guilty.'

'Because of your mother?' Michael plinky-plonks a few notes on the piano.

'Yes.' I hang up the guitar and shake out my fingers.

'So on that note, pun intended, I think now is the right time to have our talk.'

I nod. 'Okay. Just let me give Skywalker some fresh air.' I go to the studio door and heave it open so Skywalker can scamper outside. Michael comes to stand beside me, and we both watch dogface sniff a tree then pee against its trunk.

'Once we do this, there's no turning back,' says Michael, returning to the piano. 'Your life is going to change forever. You'll never see the world the same way.'

My nodding gets slower. 'Yes.' I let out a long breath. 'Yes, I know. And I'm ready. I came here because I wanted things to change. Things can't stay as they are. And that means knowing the whole truth. About everything. Whatever my mother is hiding, I need to know.'

'Okay.' Michael stares at piano keys. 'But you should be

prepared for something. You're not going to like your mother very much once I tell you. You might not like me much either.'

'I'm prepared for that.'

'Well then.' Michael slides his hands from the piano keys. 'Here goes. We talked about Lorna's cancer before, didn't we?'

'Yes.'

'And that she never told you what kind of cancer she had.'

'Yes.'

Michael laces chubby fingers together. 'She told me all about her cancer. The operation, the radio-chemotherapy, how it all made her feel. Where the cancer started. It's a bit weird, don't you think, that she hasn't told you, her own daughter, what kind of cancer she had?'

'Maybe she wants to put it behind her,' I say, rubbing Skywalker's ears as he comes to stand beside me. 'Positive outlook. Don't mention the C word.'

'What about her new partner? Has she told him, do you think?'

'I don't know. I don't think so. I don't get why it matters.'

'Oh, it matters so much, Liberty bell. So much. It changes everything.'

'Why?'

Michael watches me for a moment. 'Lorna had uterine cancer.'

'Is that ... the womb?'

'Exactly. Uterine. Uterus. She had cancer of the womb. They removed her womb, Liberty. The whole thing. Before you were born.'

There's a long silence, broken by a wood pigeon squawking outside.

'So … how did she have a baby?' I say eventually.

'She didn't.'

There's another long silence.

'She's not your real mother, Liberty. She's just a girl who liked me a heck of a lot and couldn't let go. When I had a baby with someone else, it drove her mad with jealousy. So when she saw a chance to hurt me she took it. By stealing you.'

I stare at him. 'No. My mother … I mean, she has her faults. But she would never do that. Take another woman's child? No way.'

'Lorna was a young kid who thought she might die, Liberty. And then she was told she could never have children. She wasn't in her right mind. And she was obsessed with me and my music. Hearing my voice during the chemo and all of that. And then she finally met me and thought I could wave a magic wand and make it all okay. Marriage and children. The whole fairy tale. I treated her badly. I admit it. I should have known better. The whole thing sent her a bit mad. Being sick can make people do crazy things. Lorna was sick in the body and sick in the head. I don't know if it was all the treatments, but her head wasn't right. Liberty, look right into my eyes, baby girl. Your mother isn't your mother. She stole you from this house on the day you were born.'

'No,' I blurt out. 'That can't be true.'

Michael puts his hands on my shoulders. 'Now tell me, do I look like I'm lying?'

I look into his eyes. They are totally sincere. 'No.' I turn away. 'But none of this makes sense. Is … is Diane my mother?'

'Oh, Liberty bell. I wish she were. But Diane knows nothing about any of this. She thinks Lorna is your real mother. To tell Diane the whole truth would just hurt her even more. And trust me, she's been hurt enough.'

'So who is my real mother?'

'Listen – let's go back to the house. Okay? We'll talk more there.'

Once upon a time ...

How much do you trust your own mind?

Living with Michael was never as solid as other memories. Not hard and vivid, like growing up in the US or Dee's apartment or meeting Nick. When I was sixteen, reality was something Michael built for me, brick by brick. So memories, reality, perception – it became a jumble, a blur, a big cloud of renovation dust. Everything hazy. But here's a memory that's clearer than the rest:

One day, through that twirling cloud of plaster, Cat Cannon's daughter banged on Michael's front door.

I was sleeping upstairs, even though it was nearing midday. Depression and a touch of anorexia equals big-time lethargy, in case you've never experienced the two together.

Bang, bang, bang.

It was the sound of a fist pounding, I was sure, but Michael would handle it. I rolled over in bed. There was nothing for me to do in a situation like this. My role was to stay quiet and out of the way.

Bang, bang, bang.

Michael still hadn't got a doorbell or intercom fitted. After all, technically no one was living in this pile of scaffold and gnawed brick.

Bang, bang, bang.

Probably it was a tradesperson. Worse-case scenario, a journalist.

I heard Michael's footsteps beat the flagstones and the door creak open.

'Michael?'

The voice was young, breathy, female – and horribly familiar. What the hell was *she* doing here?

'You made it here all by yourself?' I heard Michael reply. 'I was going to send a driver.'

I threw off the covers and ran to look over the stairs.

Annalise stood in the entranceway below, kohl-lined eyes filled with giddy excitement. She wore an oversized Michael Reyji Ray T-shirt with a belt and Indian sandals. Slumpy canvas bags lay at her feet.

I couldn't see Michael's face, but I sensed excitement from him.

I cantered down the stairs, catching myself on the stair rail.

'Hey,' I said.

Michael didn't turn around. 'Good morning, Lorna.'

'Annalise,' I said. 'What's with the bags?'

'Annalise has come to stay with us,' said Michael.

'She's … what?'

'She's going to live here for a while. You're okay with that, right, Lorna? Another girl around the place. Like sisters.'

I swallowed. *I already have a sister. I just never see her.*

'She's staying here?' I asked.

'She can't live with her mother right now,' Michael explained. 'Cat's falling to pieces. And poor Annalise has nowhere else to go so she's gonna stay here. She's a friend. We take care of our friends.'

'A *best* friend,' said Annalise, laughing and giving Michael a kiss on the cheek.

I looked at Annalise then – taking in her youth and prettiness and twig legs.

'The best-friend role is taken,' I told Annalise. 'By me.'

Michael laughed good-naturedly. 'Hey, girls. It's not a competition.'

But instinctively I knew it was. And Michael was loving every minute of it.

'How long is she going to stay for?' I asked, voice tight.

'Michael, doesn't Lorna want me here?' Annalise asked in her pretty London boarding-school accent.

I glanced at Michael too. 'It's not that. I just … I wish someone had told me.'

'Annalise will stay as long as she needs to,' said Michael. 'Lorna, you need to accept it.'

Annalise risked an excited glance at Michael. Then she looked around the vestibule at the plasterboard, ladders and paint cans. Even with all the mess, it was probably less chaotic than Cat's place.

'Is my room upstairs?' Annalise asked.

'Yeah, upstairs,' said Michael. 'Lorna – grab Annalise's stuff, will you? Come on now. Lend a hand. Make the girl feel welcome.'

I wanted to swallow but couldn't. My throat was tight as a drum.

Michael linked Annalise's arm and escorted her up the stairs, leaving me with the bags. I dragged the luggage over the floor and bumped it viciously up each step, bump, bump, bump.

'Does her mother know she's here, Michael?' I asked.

Michael turned to give me hard eyes. 'No. Annalise needs a little peace and quiet from Cat.'

'But she's only fifteen. She shouldn't be staying somewhere without her mother's permission.'

Annalise grabbed Michael's hand. 'Age doesn't matter. It's just a label. Right, Michael?'

Blood rushed to my face. Those were Michael's words, not hers. *Age is just a label.* When had he said them to her? He'd said things like that to me in bed, soon after I joined him on tour. *Age is just a label. Marriage is just a label.* Had he and Annalise been to bed together?

'Cat's not going to be happy when she finds out,' I said. 'Don't you think it's sort of weird? Moving in a fifteen-year-old without her mother's permission?'

Michael's eyes blackened. 'If you say a word, ONE WORD about this—'

'I didn't say I'd tell anyone,' I said. 'But Cat's going to find out eventually. You two are friends.'

'NO ONE is going to tell Cat that Annalise is here,' Michael boomed. 'It's our secret, and if you're loyal to me, Lorna, then you keep my secrets too. Mention this to Cat and you're out of here.'

I watched Annalise climb the stairs, holding Michael's hand, and spots and flashes danced in my vision. 'I loathe you,' I told her. 'Making big lovestruck eyes at him. You won't take my place, do you hear me? Michael is mine. You won't take him away from me.'

'You're, like, so into ownership,' said Annalise. 'Everyone is free. No one belongs to anyone. Michael isn't your property.'

'Well, if he's not mine, he's not yours either.'

'Lorna, you're being jealous and ridiculous,' said Michael. 'Annalise is a good friend of the family. Stop acting up.'

'You want me to share you now?' I said, starting to cry.

'You're being paranoid,' said Michael.

I turned to Annalise. 'How long *do* you need to stay here?'

'I don't know. Michael. How long am I staying here?'

'As long as you like, love. Like I said. You're practically family.'

'But there's hardly any space here,' I insisted. 'Only a few of the rooms have been finished.'

'Annalise will stay in the room that's just been decorated,' said Michael.

'The room next to yours? No way. Why does she get to be next to you and I don't?'

Michael laughed. 'This is silly. A room is just a room.'

For a moment, no one spoke.

Then I had a horrible realization. 'That room has only just been decorated. You did it for her. The bedroom right next to yours. This is not just looking after her for a while. You've planned this. You're moving her in.'

I stormed down the landing, throwing open the bedroom next to Michael's. It was decorated with sickly pastel-pink bed linen and rose wallpaper. There was a huge Victorian wardrobe with mirrored doors. I had a vision of what might be inside that wardrobe: flowery dresses and crepe shoes, all bought by Michael for Annalise. His English rose.

I screamed at Annalise, 'I won't share him. If you go anywhere near him, I'll kill you.'

'Take a chill pill,' said Annalise, shaking her head at Michael. 'Is she always this crazy?'

Michael put an arm around her shoulder. 'She's had a few problems in the past. But she'll get used to the change. And you'll be best friends in no time.'

'But *you're* my best friend,' Annalise laughed.

'Well, I'm honoured. And now I've got an English rose to add to my collection.'

Michael and Annalise smiled at each other then, a special look, and I wanted to claw at Annalise's face and rip the smile away.

'What do you think this is, Michael, a girl band?' I demanded. 'The punk princess. The English rose?'

'What are you talking about, Lorna?'

'You've taken things too far this time.' I felt tears sting. 'I hardly ever see you. You're gone half the time, and when you're back we hardly ever talk. It's all sex. But at least I've been the *only* girl. I've always had that. If Cat's daughter stays here too, what's left?'

'You're not making any sense,' said Michael. 'You sound crazy. Annalise needs a place to stay. Don't make it out to be something sinister.'

'Michael. I can't handle this. I just can't. It's too much.'

'I treat you like a princess. Everything you could possibly wish for.'

'But bringing another girl to live with us?' I chewed at my nails. 'Michael, I'm at my limit. I swear to you.'

'Jesus,' said Michael. 'Calm down, Lorna. You know how I feel about hysterical women. I'd have stayed with Diane if I wanted hysterics.'

'You're still married. You still do photoshoots with your wife. This house.' I gestured to the plasterboard piled up against a wall. 'It's still a dust cloud because you're different, you don't do things like other people. And I just have to put up with it. Because I'm not important enough to renovate your house for. I put up with all of it, Michael. Everything. Because I love you. But this is too much.' I started pacing back and forth.

'A million girls—'

'Would be grateful to live with you. I know. But only if they're the *only* girl living with you. Isn't that what you always tell me when you've been gone for weeks? That I'm your special girl, your only girl, the only one who lives in your big fancy house? Just me?'

'Lorna, you're being selfish.'

'Michael, she can't have that room,' I said. 'She can't have the nearest room to you. It's not right. I'm your *girlfriend*.'

Michael's eyes darkened. 'Lorna. Don't throw those labels around. You don't own me and I don't own you. This is my house. I make the decisions. I'm not going to put her up in a room with bare boards and plaster dust.'

'But Michael—'

'Wait for me in the lounge.'

'Michael—'

'Now.'

When Michael came down to the lounge twenty minutes later, his eyes were dark and his shoulders hunched.

Without a word, he punched me in the eye and I fell to the floor.

'You don't question me,' he said. 'Ever. Not in *my* house.'

The punching was so normal by then that I just lay there without complaint. He'd knocked me down plenty of times by then. One punch was nothing.

'Christ, Lorna,' said Michael, stalking back and forth. 'Why can't you just be normal?'

Eventually I got to my feet, rubbing my cheek. 'Have you slept with her?'

'What are you talking about, Lorna? No, I haven't slept with her. She's fifteen, for God's sake. How could you even think that?'

'Just promise me you won't sleep with her, Michael. Promise me.'

'You're being jealous and paranoid, Lorna. Where's my fun girl gone, huh? You're turning into a nag. A few more months and you'll be just like Diane.'

I started to cry, turning away from him. 'Well, what do you expect me to think when you move another girl in here?'

'Come here.' Michael pulled me into a hug. 'You're my one and all. Okay? Annalise won't stay here long.' He tapped me on the head. 'That pretty little brain of yours. Thinking too much as always. Don't make this out to be more than it is, okay? It's just a few days.' He looked right at me then, eyes sincere. 'You know who I am, Lorna. I'm not perfect. Maybe I'm not even that good some of the time. But you know who I am. A man who loves you very much. Listen – I get angry because I care. I'm scared, you know? Just a scared little boy at heart. Scared you'll stop loving me. I don't mean to show it with my fists. It's just how I was brought up. Tell me you love me. Tell me you love me and you'll never leave me.'

I started crying. 'Of course I love you.'

'Hey.' Michael squeezed me tight. 'I'm one of the good guys. I have a big heart. Too big a heart, letting Cat's daughter come to stay. But what could I do? We can't let her be out on the street, can we?'

'No. I guess not. It'll just be a few days, right?'

'Just a few days.'

Lorna

I'm standing on a swivel chair in Liberty's bedroom, pulling climbing ropes from the top shelf of her wardrobe.

Darcy is toddling around the room, sticking more Post-it notes on things.

Guitar. Poster. Desk.

Being in my daughter's room, with the Suzi Quatro and Jean Seberg posters on the wall, arthouse French movie DVDs lined up in alphabetical order on the wardrobe shelf, it's tearing my heart out.

'Lorna.' Nick is in the doorway, his body covered in Darcy's Post-it notes. 'I'm still not getting this. You think Michael sent you this book.' He holds *The Tales of Hans Christian Andersen,* frowning as he flips pages. 'And it's some kind of message?'

Abdomen. Forehead. Left buttock.

Dee is beside Nick, also covered in Post-it notes.

Neck. Shoulder. Stomach – big.

'Of course it's a message,' I say. 'There was a slip of paper in the book.'

'Maybe it was your slip of paper,' says Dee. 'From years ago. You used to do that. Make bookmarks out of whatever was close to hand. Maybe Michael's just returning your property to you. Sort of like saying, good riddance.'

'No. The paper is too new. And there are highlights.'

'You used to make highlights.'

'The parts about sacrifice? Why would I highlight that?'

'You were very dramatic as a teenager,' said Dee. 'You used to gravitate towards misery.'

'Why can't you two see it?' The chair turns under me, nearly throwing me off. 'Michael made those highlights. He wants me to go back. Diane is gone now. She's taking a flight somewhere. Cat told me. Now she's out the way, Michael wants me to take Liberty's place. He thinks I'm still the same meek, mild idiot he knew all those years ago. That I'll just walk in and do whatever he wants. The gates will be open now. He'll be waiting for me.'

'So why the climbing rope?' says Dee, helping Darcy stick a Post-it note on her chest.

Left breast.

'You never know with Michael,' I say. 'I want to be prepared. Everything's always slippery. But one way or another, I'm going to end this today and bring Liberty home.'

'Jesus, Lorna,' says Nick. 'This is all sounding a bit vigilante.'

I climb down from the chair with Liberty's climbing rope and shoes. 'Don't you get it? Michael has made a trap. He's a control freak. If I don't do what he wants, he'll hurt my daughter.' I put a hand to my mouth, emotion suddenly overwhelming me. 'And the police will do *nothing*. Liberty has run away from home.'

'Has she?' says Dee. 'It seems to me she's facing things. Maybe it's you who's running away, with all these high fences and gates. I mean, look at this place. It's Fort Knox. This is running, Lorna. Liberty's tackling everything head on. And she'll be just fine.'

'No. She won't be.'

'Liberty is clever,' says Dee. 'She can work out fact from fiction.'

'She's no match for him.'

'Are you sure?' says Dee. 'Because the last time I checked, Liberty was a girl genius. All those sudoku and chess challenges she does on Facebook … she's like lightning.'

'I don't know what she does on Facebook,' I admit. 'She blocked me.'

'How come?'

'I sent a few messages, you know. Telling some of her classmates that Liberty wasn't allowed out in the evenings. Just in case they got the wrong idea.'

Dee raises an eyebrow. 'All those human rights marches you used to go on. Now you're a Nazi dictator.'

'Can you blame me?'

'Yes, I can blame you,' says Dee. 'I blame you for this whole thing. If you hadn't kept Liberty locked up, she'd never have run away.'

'But I'm her parent,' I say. 'It's my job to keep her safe.'

'Where'd you hear that?' says Dee. 'Some 1950s parenting manual? Liberty's not a child. She's a sixteen-year-old whose mother is stalking her Facebook profile and harassing her friends. She's been locked behind these high gates most of her life and it still happened. The thing you were most afraid of. Maybe it's not about keeping Liberty safe from her father. Maybe it's about empowering her to look after herself.'

'Liberty's been away *all night* and now most of the day. The police will do *nothing*.'

'What can they do?' says Dee. 'No crime has been committed.'

'Are you seriously saying that to me?' I demand. 'You were there. You know what he did.'

'I wasn't there, Lorna,' says Dee. 'I know Michael was controlling and you were too vulnerable to stand up to him. That's the only thing I know for sure.'

'You don't believe me about Annalise?' I say. 'Is that what you're telling me?'

'I believe … something really bad happened that night. And seeing Michael, yes, I know he has a temper. For sure.'

'Okay.' Nick takes a step back. 'This is all sounding way too paranoid. Does anyone want a cup of tea? Or an omelette?'

'No, Nick, no one wants an omelette. Michael sent me this book. You think he did that for no reason? He's telling me to come back. To sacrifice myself for Liberty.'

'You get that from a couple of highlights?' says Dee. 'Highlights you might have made yourself? What if you're wrong? You'll be committing a criminal offence, going back there.'

'Dee's right,' says Nick. 'If you go back to his house and start trying to climb over the gate or something, the police will arrest you. And then what? You'll be stuck in a cell, maybe overnight. What use will you be to Liberty then? Sit tight. You have to wait. Maybe I should go there, Lorna. I'm sure if Michael understands how upset you are—'

'That's very sweet of you, Nick, but forget it,' I say. 'Michael will play you like a fiddle. You won't stand a chance. You'd just come back telling me what a great guy he is.'

'I'd never do that. I like my balls where they are.'

Dee snorts with amusement and I glare at both of them.

'I'm going back there,' I say. 'Neither of you are getting it. The police won't be there this time. Michael's as good as told me to come back. I lived with him for a long time. I know how he works. If I don't do what he wants ...' I close my eyes and take deep breaths. 'Oh God, I hope Liberty is okay. Please let her be okay.'

'She'll be okay,' says Dee. 'She loves you and you love her. Just be patient. I know this is torture, but she has to come home sometime.'

I shake my head. 'Michael's not going to let her just leave. He has his prize. A way to hurt me. Do you think he's going to let that prize walk out of the door?'

'What are you saying?'

'The only way Liberty is leaving is if I make out like I'll trade places.' I loop climbing rope over my shoulder, pushing past Nick and running down stairs two steps at a time.

'This is idiotic,' calls Dee over the banisters. 'You'll just get arrested. What exactly do you plan to do at Michael's house anyway? Beat him up?'

'Do exactly what Michael wants.'

Or at least pretend to.

Neither Nick nor Dee know about the samurai steel kitchen knife inside my jacket.

Liberty

I watch my DM boots squash leaves and flatten twigs as Michael and I head through his private woodland. It's afternoon now, and the air is warm around the feathery fir trees. Bright blue sky frames the main house up ahead.

I sense Michael's eyes on me.

'Michael,' I say. 'I think I know who my real mother is.'

Michael slows, his shoulders stiffening. 'Let's have some lunch before we start down that road. I haven't given you so much as a snack in hours. I've been a terrible father. I can't have my little girl not eating.'

'I'm not sure I can eat right now, truthfully.'

'Well, that little pooch of yours will want something, won't he? Come on. Back to the house with you.' He quickens his pace.

Skywalker trots behind us, a good pack member following his leader. I can tell he wants to explore everything, and sometimes he sneaks a little sniff of a tree or the ground.

The trees thin out and bright sunshine struggles onto the woodland floor. We turn a corner and the turreted main house appears ahead of us, magnificently fake and multicoloured.

I stride to catch up with Michael. 'So about my real mother…'

Michael slows again then, rubbing at his craggy face. 'Yeah?'

'I think … she's Annalise, isn't she? The girl who went missing.'

Skywalker trots behind us, his paws making a gentle puff-puff sound on loose soil and fallen fir frongs. We come out of the woodlands into full sunshine.

'What makes you think that?' Michael asks, turning to me then, eyes sharpening.

'I was born around the time Annalise went missing,' I say. 'I've checked all the dates. I have her middle name, which is weird and no one has ever explained it to me. And I was watching Cat Cannon at the party. I look a little like her. These two crazy canines.' I point to my teeth. 'And it also explains why you're putting off telling me. Because Annalise would have been really young. Like, far too young when she had me. And I might think badly of you for it.'

Michael stares at me then, eyes dark and curious. 'You, Liberty bell, are a very clever girl. Maybe too clever for your own good.'

'I'm not that clever. I just pay attention.' We carry on walking. 'I'm right though, aren't I? And Annalise was underage when you were together. Fifteen.'

Michael sighs. 'Annalise was a beautiful thing. Such a beautiful thing. You know, love … it can be ageless. We have a soul age too. Not just an earth age. Annalise was an old soul. I loved that girl so much. People get caught up in labels when it comes to relationships, Liberty. Age. Gender. Race. But you love who you love. I've never believed in putting limits on that.'

'Does Diane know?'

'No. And it would kill her if she found out.'

'You should tell Diane the truth. You owe her that.'

'Diane can NEVER find out about Annalise. Do you hear me? Never.' Michael's sudden fury knocks me sideways.

'Okay, okay.' I hold my hands up. 'Chill out.'

Michael's face loosens. Then he starts nodding and manages a laugh. 'You're right. Sorry. It's just I want to protect Diane, you know? She's been through enough pain thanks to me.'

'How could you sleep with someone so young? You must have been … what? Nearly forty? And to get her pregnant too. I mean … that's pretty bad. Not to mention illegal.'

Michael snaps his head towards me. 'You've made your point, okay? Things happen. Love happens. Have you ever been in love, Liberty?'

'Lots of times. But always with people I've never met. Like David Bowie.'

We're nearing the main house now, and Michael is still walking fast.

'You'll learn in time,' he says. 'Love is complicated. You don't choose it. You fall for who you fall for. Look, I'm not proud of being with such a young girl. But Annalise and I were like Romeo and Juliet. Star-crossed lovers. Soul mates.'

'Even though you were married and she was underage?'

'Diane and I were separated for a few years. The years Lorna and Annalise happened.'

We cross the moat, me looking at Michael's turreted mansion.

'Diane told me that you two never separated. She said my mother made that part up.'

'Women sometimes kid themselves,' says Michael. 'Listen. The world of adult problems is … complicated. Don't you get caught up in all the rules and have to's. Love is beautiful. In whatever form it takes.'

'I don't get how you can make out that a relationship between an adult man and a fifteen-year-old girl is okay,' I say. 'It's not beautiful at all. It's a power imbalance.'

Michael pulls open the front door with force. 'So what are you, Liberty? Just a little Lorna parrot? Is she telling you what to think now? Has she sent you here and put words in your mouth?' His eyes go wild suddenly, swimming in their sockets. 'Just get inside the house, for goodness sake.'

I take a step back. 'I say my own words. And I know my own mind.'

Michael studies me for a moment. Then he shakes his head. 'Sorry. You're right. Look, I didn't mean to lose it. But it was such a hard time, you know? For everyone. And I don't know how to explain Annalise to you. I didn't expect you to work out she was your birth mother.'

'So what were you going to do? Just keep me hanging on, desperate to know who my real mother was?'

'To tell you the truth, Liberty, I didn't have much of a plan at all. Come on, let's get things back on track. You're a great artist. You and I should be talking about music, not arguing.'

'Do you have any idea what happened to Annalise?'

'Nobody knows, love.' Michael considers the front door, with its iron studwork. 'Cat and I have spent millions of dollars searching for her.'

'I saw Cat at the party. Does she know—'

'Cat doesn't know about you. And I for one am not going to tell her. She's just given up drinking. I don't want to send her straight back to the bottle.'

'Oh, so you have a *virtuous* reason. Nothing to do with not wanting her to know that you slept with her fifteen-year-old daughter?'

Michael gives me big, earnest eyes. 'Look, maybe I sound like I'm excusing my behaviour. You're right. Me and Annalise – it wasn't right. She was too young and it wasn't okay. When you're a rock star … people make you into this sort of godlike figure. Normal rules don't apply. It warped my thinking. But losing you … it was God's punishment, you know? For the life I was living. It put me straight. And I've been straight ever since. Can you forgive your old man for being the devil who made all those mistakes?'

'I don't know. I'm still trying to get my head around everything.'

'You don't know?' More anger flashes across Michael's face. It's so quick this time that I'm not sure if it was ever really there. But now Michael is smiling and putting an arm around my shoulder. 'Of course you don't know yet. This must be so hard. You've lost a mother, found a mother, then lost her again – all in one day. It's a lot to deal with. Can you see now why I didn't want to tell you who your real mother was? There's so much pain there. For all of us.'

'What do *you* think happened to my real mother?'

'God forgive her, I think that beautiful girl took her own life. She was a child having a child. And then to have her baby taken from her, stolen by a jealous rival … it broke her.'

I shake my head. 'I can't believe Lorna did that to her. Stole me away.'

'I think evil is the word for it.'

'So … what was my birth mother like? I mean, by the sounds of things you knew her better than anyone.'

Michael drops his sunglasses down onto his face. 'And I'm ashamed of it, Liberty. God help me, I am. But Annalise was quite something. She had the most beautiful singing voice. It was from another world. She felt music in a way I've never seen before. For a soul like that to just disappear … utterly tragic. In my opinion, Lorna destroyed that girl just the same as if she'd held a gun to her head and pulled the trigger.'

'Maybe Annalise isn't dead. If no one has ever found her … I mean, it's possible she's still alive, isn't it?'

Michael shakes his head. 'She would have been found by now. I think she hurled herself off a cliff somewhere and was swept out to rot at sea. Let's get ourselves into the house and we'll talk some more.'

I turn and click my fingers at Skywalker. 'Come on, boy. Come on. Stop being a dead weight.'

'What's he doing, that dog of yours?' says Michael, frowning. 'Get him inside, would you?'

Skywalker is lying on the brick moat bridge, nose to the ground.

I shake my head. 'I've trained him, but he's still a rescue dog. He's always doing crazy stuff. This is probably a protest. He wants to go back and run around the woods, sniffing everything.'

'He looks like he's having a rest,' says Michael. 'Get the old boy moving.' He whistles. 'Come on, doggy. Let's be having you.'

I walk back to Skywalker, standing over him. 'Come on, friend. On your feet. Let's go inside and feed you.'

Skywalker doesn't move.

'Is he in a huff with you or something?' Michael asks. 'Maybe we'll just leave him out here. He can catch his own lunch. But you and I should go inside. Let's go now, Liberty. Come on.'

I kneel to Skywalker, hand on his back. Skywalker is almost totally still, the only movement being the gentle rise and fall of his chest.

'Skywalker?'

He doesn't respond.

'Something's wrong,' I say, crouching. 'He feels too cold.'

I give Skywalker a shake, but his body is unmoving like a corpse. 'Michael, something's wrong. He's ... sick or something. We need to take him to a vet. Can we use your car?'

Michael's eyes turn shadowy. 'Poor little doggy. Let's get him into the house and have a vet come to us. That's the best way to do things. Here – I'll carry him.' He scoops Skywalker into his arms and half walks, half staggers into the house.

'Wait.' I jog after him. 'If we take him to a vet surgery, they'll have all the equipment—'

'There isn't anywhere like that for miles, love.' Michael walks sideways through the front door with Skywalker in his arms. 'We're way out in the country. But I know a vet who lives in the next village. He can come here. That's going to be a lot quicker.'

'How quick are we talking?' I stay close, stroking Skywalker's head as I follow Michael into the entranceway.

'Let's put your doggy in the guest bed upstairs,' says Michael, climbing the staircase. 'Put a blanket on him. Warm the poor fellow up. And I'll call a vet. No more talk of leaving now. We have everything we need right here.'

Michael takes us right up to the turret room – the same one I slept in last night – and lays Skywalker on the bed.

'Stay with him, Liberty,' says Michael. 'Stay right there.'

'Please, I really don't think ... if he needs his stomach pumped, he'll need a veterinary surgery. We're wasting time.'

'Sit on the bed with him, love. Or he'll get upset. Don't move from there, okay? You're not going anywhere.' Michael leaves, closing the door behind him. There's a clicking sound.

'Wait.' I go to the door. 'I don't think this is the best way—'

But the door is stuck. I shake and rattle the handle.

There is another clicking sound, and the door opens. Michael fills the doorway. His eyes aren't nice guy eyes anymore. There are no crinkles. They are empty, churning black holes.

'I told you to sit down on the bed, love. And not move. There's a girl. Sit right on that bed or there'll be trouble. Lorna will be here any minute.'

'What?'

'I've sent Lorna a message. She'll be on her way here right now. So you just wait up here in the princess tower until she arrives.'

'I don't understand.' I start to cry. 'What did I do? Why are you being so mean all of a sudden?'

Michael leans his face right close to mine, so I can see his fury up close. Then he intimates my voice: 'I don't *know*. I'm still trying to get my *head* around it. An older man and such a young girl. She was only fifteen. It's a *power* imbalance.' He pulls back then, eyes still churning. 'Of *course* it's a bloody power imbalance. What do you think this world is? One big hippy festival? Do you think my father played fair when he beat the living daylights out of me and my brothers? That's the way the world really is, Liberty. You get strong or you die. That, baby girl, is the only lesson in life worth learning.'

'I'm leaving.'

'No, you're not. You're staying right here until Lorna comes. You're my flesh and blood and you'll do as you're told.'

'Why do you even want me here? You sound like you hate me. What good am I to you?'

'My goodness, Liberty. You might be good at chess, but you didn't inherit my brain. You're here so Lorna will come here.'

'What?'

'You're the bait in a trap I've waited years to set. Lorna belongs to me. I trained her to be the perfect, compliant mate but she ran away and now she thinks she's in charge. She needs to remember who owns who.'

'So that's your problem? That she got away from you? That's what all this is about?'

'Lorna didn't get away,' Michael snaps. 'Did she? She's on her way here right now. I got her in the end.'

I stand.

'Let me get past.'

'Without your dog?'

I turn back to Skywalker. His chest moves up and down, but only slightly. The rest of him is totally still.

'He doesn't look well, does he?' says Michael, snapping his reasonable face back on. 'Best you stay with him. Wait until your mother gets here. I can't let you go running around on your own. What kind of parent would I be?'

'Did you do something to my dog?'

'He's probably eaten something he shouldn't.'

'Will you call a vet at least?'

'Not until Lorna gets here,' says Michael. 'Let's hope your mother has a spring in her step.'

My eyes dart around the doorway. 'Please. Let me phone a vet or—'

'Sit down.'

'Please, I—'

'SIT DOWN.'

I plop down on the bed, my hand going to Skywalker's fluttering chest.

Once upon a time ...

I'*ll bet you feel so lonely, you could die.*

I hummed the David Bowie song to myself as I carried a food tray to my bedroom.

I'll bet you feel so lonely, you could die.

Michael was entertaining journalists in the lounge, so I'd been told to stay out of sight.

'*It's not the right time to show you off. I still haven't finalized the divorce. We've got to keep you a secret just a little bit longer ...*'

I'd been in the gym room all morning and was about to undo all my good work by eating potato chips and chocolate fudge cake, washed down with Coca Cola. Michael hated me eating junk food, but he still kept cupboards of it in the kitchen for himself. Comfort food. In the absence of love, food would have to do.

Michael hadn't visited my bedroom since Annalise came to stay.

Yes, Annalise was still here. Days had turned into weeks and now months. I could hear her at night, sometimes singing in a nightingale voice, sometimes moaning. She was moaning because she was sick, Michael said.

As I reached the landing, I noticed something – Annalise's bedroom door was open. It was never open.

I set my tray down, stuffing a handful of potato chips into my mouth. Instinctively, I glanced at the stairs in case Michael was watching.

'Annalise?' I knocked softly on the open door.

Annalise was on the bed, her back to me, looking out of the window. She was staring at the large concrete hole that was destined to become a swimming pool, and the acres of fir tree woodlands beyond. Her room was a mess – piles of chiffon dresses on the floor, books, underwear …

Annalise was a mess too. Her long, brown-blonde hair was unwashed and unbrushed. She'd put on weight – which pleased me. Her middle was round and large, something I knew Michael would loathe.

'Are you okay?' I asked. 'I heard you making noises again last night. Michael says you're sick.'

Annalise didn't answer. Just sort of gawped at me, staring with her big, dumb fish eyes.

'Okay,' I said. 'I get it. I'm not Lord Michael. Only Lord Michael is good enough to waste your words on. But listen, you can't stay here forever. Don't you think it's time to pack your bags and go home to your mother? Michael's getting tired of you being here. He … he told me.'

A lie.

As I turned to go, Annalise said, 'I'm not going home. I'm going to stay here with Michael. We love each other. We're having a baby. And when the baby comes, Michael says we'll all be one big happy family.'

I put my hands on my hips. 'What are you talking about? What baby?'

'Michael and I are having a baby.'

I laughed. 'Don't be stupid. You're living in fantasy land. I'm his girlfriend, get it? His real, actual girlfriend. You're just some silly girl with a crush who's come to stay.'

'*I'm* the mother of his child.'

I laughed again. It was so ridiculous. But then Annalise put hands to her stomach. It was round and solid-looking under a flowery summer dress.

I stared at her. My hand went to my own stomach, and to the scar running across my abdomen.

'Who's the father?' I asked, swallowing thickly.

'I told you. Michael.'

'Come on, Annalise. Who's the *real* father? Is that why you left your mother's house? Because you were pregnant and didn't want her to find out?'

'Michael is the father,' said Annalise again. 'We're in love. He's going to divorce Diane and marry me.'

I laughed. 'You're just a dumb kid making up stories. You probably got pregnant by some roadie on tour and now you want Michael to be your happily ever after. Been there, got the T-shirt. But I got there first. So it's not going to happen for you. Michael loves *me*.'

I stormed right downstairs to the lounge, where I found Michael entertaining two journalists – both women. They were laughing, while Michael topped up champagne glasses and offered cucumber sandwiches.

I hesitated, feeling sickly terror. Interrupting Michael when he had guests … there would be consequences. I felt them in every sinew of my lean body. But I couldn't stop myself.

'Michael.' My voice was shaking.

Michael's eyes lit with anger when he saw me in the door-way. 'Excuse me, ladies. My assistant has come to bother me when I'm meeting important people.' His words and lips were tight. 'Lorna here is my Girl Friday. She's here to do the very dusty and thankless job of stocktaking merch out there in the cottage. I should lock the door to keep her out there. She's always sneaking into the house for tea breaks.'

The two female journalists laughed.

'I need to talk to you,' I said.

Michael's black eyes burned. 'Not now, okay?'

'No. Now.' I smiled at the journalists. 'Sorry. Urgent stock-taking business.'

'Back in a minute,' Michael told the women. 'Top up your champagne glasses, ladies. I don't want to see them run dry.'

We went to the kitchen and Michael said, 'This better be an emergency or you're out of here. I mean it.'

'Annalise says she's pregnant and you're the father.'

'What?' Michael blinked at me. 'She said *what*?'

'She says you're the father of her child. It's not true, is it?'

'Of course it's not true.' Michael glanced back at the kitchen door.

'She looks pregnant.'

'What are you girls doing talking to each other anyway?'

'Is she pregnant, Michael?'

Michael hesitated. 'Listen, she might be.' He put a hand on my shoulder. 'But I'm not the father. That's total nonsense. No way. This is worse than the tabloids. She's just trying to upset you, love. Make you jealous. She's young. You're the grown-up here, okay? I'll talk to her.' He gave me a quick disconnected kiss. 'All right? Go back to your room.'

'She has to leave, Michael,' I said. 'I mean it.'

Fury settled into Michael's forehead and cheeks. 'Of course she bloody well has to leave. That girl is in a whole world of trouble, Lorna. She's going to be begging for her mad mammy by the time I'm finished with her.'

I felt uneasy then, noticing Michael's balled fists and hunched shoulders. Michael had lost his temper with me many times, but I didn't like the idea of him hurting someone else, especially someone so young. I imagined Annalise falling to the floor, protecting her pregnant stomach.

She's a liar, a voice said. *She's not even pregnant. She's a liar and she tried to hurt you. She deserves everything she gets.*

I looked away from Michael. 'Just a telling-off, right? You won't hurt her.'

'I'll handle it how it needs to be handled. She'll be out of this house today. And stop eating those crisps. You'll end up with a fat arse.'

He patted my bottom and sent me upstairs, where I ate more junk food to ease my guilt.

Later that day, Annalise's bedroom was empty. There was no mess of hippy and babydoll dresses over the bedroom floor. A decorator guy was stripping rose wallpaper from the walls and the linen had been torn from the bed, revealing a bare, unloving mattress.

'She's gone back to her mother,' Michael told me when

I found him downstairs eating breakfast. 'I gave her a talking-to and we both decided she needed to leave the house.' He threw his knife and fork noisily at his half-eaten fried breakfast plate and stood up.

'Where are you going?' I asked.

'To the cottage. The renovations are really coming along out there, but I have to oversee every detail. Honestly, you turn your back for a moment on those guys and they do everything back to front.'

Michael stayed in the cottage all day. When he came back that night, he didn't come to my bedroom. He didn't come the next night either.

I knew I was in a lukewarm bath that was getting colder by the day. But it was freezing outside and I didn't have the courage to get out.

Liberty

Skywalker is lying deathly still on the bed, his chest making the tiniest movements.

'Good boy, Sky,' I say, wiping at tears. 'You're such a good boy. Just ... stay cool, okay? Stay cool.'

I can't stop crying. I'm pretty sure this is trauma. Seeing Michael transform like that, from like this good guy to a dead-eyed monster ... it's totally freaked me out.

Crazy how can someone can seem so charming, but have all that rage going on just below the surface. Malevolent intentions can be so well hidden.

I've explored every corner of the turret room, checking every angle.

At first, I pulled and hammered on the door, shouting my head off. But it was stupid. I knew it was stupid. Who would come? Michael?

After the futile door hammering, I threw a chair at the door, but all I succeeded in doing was smashing a probable antique into pieces and hurting myself in the process.

I put a cheek to Skywalker's soft fur. 'Now I know why Mum is so scared, huh? Why she runs from him. Crazy is scary.'

I go to the window, pressing my nose right against the glass.

It's a good view – I can see right over the woodlands, all the way to the gate. The sun is setting and although I can't feel the temperature drop in here, I shiver.

Michael strides out of the trees on his short little legs, carrying two rifles in his arms with a box of ammunition balanced on top. He's dressed all in black: jeans, shoes, T-shirt and sunglasses.

My heart is beating so hard. So he's been to his gun shed. I expected that. Arming himself before my mother arrives. I'm shaking so hard that my vision is blurry.

This is what you wanted, Liberty. A change. Liberation. Right? Be careful what you wish for.

Michael has crossed the moat now and is heading into the house.

I scuttle back to Skywalker, crouching back beside him as I hear Michael climbing the stairs.

'Hello, Liberty, love.' Michael's chubby body appears in the arched doorway. I expect him to still be holding the rifles and ammo, but instead he carries a tray.

'Where did the guns go?' I ask.

'What guns?' Michael's outline reminds me of a frog stretched out – large belly over skinny legs. A frog carrying a tray of sandwiches and bottled water. He surveys the room, eyes darkening when he sees the smashed-up chair. 'You've made a real mess up here, haven't you? A real mess.'

Michael puts the tray down on the bed and the bottled water leans precariously. 'Lorna hasn't come yet. I thought she'd be here by now. How are you, anyway? You must be getting hungry. I brought you a little supper.'

'My dog needs a vet.'

'Oh, your poor little pup.' Michael shakes his head. 'He's still not himself, is he?' He crouches beside Skywalker, putting a hand to his chest. 'He's in a bad way, if he's still not moving.'

I shrink back. 'You did it,' I say. 'You poisoned him. At breakfast, or … when we were in the music studio.'

'You really are sounding crazy, love, saying things like that,' says Michael.

'You *were* carrying guns. I saw you.'

'Now you're sounding *really* crazy.'

'Just let me out.'

'Listen, Lorna will be here soon. You'll stay here until then, won't you?'

'I need to get my dog to a vet.'

'God, Liberty, I mean, all the vets' offices will be closed by now, won't they? And is he really all that bad?'

'Of course he's that bad. He's barely moving. There are out-of-hours services. For emergencies.'

'Well, listen, I can't take you anywhere now, not with Lorna on her way. I hope she hurries along. When she gets here, we might be able to do something for your doggy. Okay, love?'

'We need to go *now*.'

'We can't, love. Sorry.'

'Is this what you did to Annalise and that other girl? Lock them in?'

'What other girl?'

'The German girl. The one who went missing after your show.'

Michael's head flicks towards me. 'You've been reading too

many newspapers. They're full of lies. Don't believe a word of them. A girl went missing. What's that got to do with me?'

'Two girls going missing? Don't you think that's a big coincidence, considering you're clearly a psychopath? What – did they both starve to death up here?' I start to cry.

Michael pushes his sunglasses into his shaggy white-blond hair. I see cold, hard, dark eyes within a puffy, tanned face.

'Liberty. I've just brought you a meal. You're hardly likely to starve to death. This is all sounding very dramatic. And no one's locking you in. The door handle gets stiff, that's all.'

'Skywalker could die.' I start crying. 'He's just an innocent animal. What did you give him?'

'How do you know he's been poisoned, love?'

'It's happened before. He ate chocolate. He had to have his stomach pumped. He nearly didn't make it.'

'Maybe he ate something out in the woods,' says Michael. 'Animals can be dumb, can't they?'

I stand, and Michael places himself between me and the door.

'Remember your doggy now,' he says. 'You can't leave without him, can you?' Michael scratches at his black and white stubble. 'And even if you did, I don't think you'd get too far. I'd have to come after you. I've got a few all-terrain bikes out there; I'd catch you in no time.'

'Why are you trying to hurt me like this?'

'I'm not trying to hurt you, Liberty. I think you're being a little full of yourself. It's Lorna who's going to get hurt.'

'Why?'

Michael's shoulders hunch forward and his voice drops two

octaves. 'I told you. Lorna was my little pet, just like that doggy is yours. And for her to leave … it was the worst betrayal. She can't get away with it. Not while I'm still breathing.'

'Please,' I say. 'My dog is sick. He could die.'

'Just stay where you are. Stay right there and wait for Lorna. When she comes, do everything you're told. And you might just come out of this okay. You don't want to end up disappearing like your real mother. Right?'

More tears come. 'What did you do to her?'

'They never found your mother's body,' says Michael. 'Did they? You know that part. So for all the world knows, she could still be alive. Nothing to suggest otherwise. But you know, I've got acres of woodlands out there. Acres. If I ever wanted to hide a body, that's what I'd do. I'd hide it out there. Chop her up first and scatter the limbs around. I don't think I'd ever get caught if I did that. Sit yourself down, Liberty, there's a girl.'

I sit.

'Let's wait for Lorna to arrive,' says Michael, closing and locking the turret room door. 'This is the best view in the house.'

Once upon a time ...

I woke to Cat Cannon's loud voice, raised to screeching pitch.

'WHERE IS SHE, MICHAEL? WHERE IS ANNALISE?'

Whoa. I felt early-morning sun on my eyelids, bright and warm, and a downy duvet over my bony body.

I sat on the edge of my single bed, trying to get a handle on what was going on.

'She *did* stay here.' Cat's voice shattered into heartbreaking howls. 'What are you doing with these girls, Michael? What are you *doing* with them?'

I tiptoed down the stairs, my Michael Reyji Ray T-shirt hanging over bony legs.

Cat was in the hallway, hands on hips, lips bleeding red lipstick, eyes bloodshot. She looked unusually svelte in a Vivienne Westwood spikey shoulder suit, pale skin glimmering under Michael's chandelier.

Michael's face was inches from Cat's, furious. He wore striped pyjama bottoms and a shabby grey T-shirt, white-blond hair sticking up around his head.

Cat was equally furious, glaring back at him.

Seeing me on the stairs, Michael said: 'Go back to bed, Lorna.'

Cat turned to me then, eyes huge and desperate. 'Lorna. Is Annalise here?'

'She was,' I said. 'But she left. Michael asked her to leave.'

Cat spun back to Michael. 'You fucking liar. You LIAR. I knew it.'

'You're going to believe Lorna?' said Michael, giving an outraged laugh. 'Come on, Cat. She barely knows what day of the week it is. You have to listen to me – Annalise was never here.' His voice had turned smooth then. If there was one thing he could never do, it was to out-temper-tantrum Cat. They were equally matched when it came to aggression.

'But … she stayed in the room next to you,' I said, feeling even more insane than I usually did.

Michael turned to me and barked: 'Go back to bed, Lorna! Sleep it off.'

'I *knew* she was here,' Cat raged. 'I knew it. You're a fucking liar, Michael.'

'I. Don't. Lie,' said Michael, voice low, shaking his head in disgust. 'Listen – okay, Annalise came to my door a while back, bags on her shoulders. But it was months ago. She's not here now, end of.'

'Why didn't you tell me she came by?' Cat demanded.

'You two are always arguing,' said Michael. 'Some drama going on. How was I supposed to know she didn't go back to you? What was there to tell? She came here. She said she was going home. She left.'

I tensed then, knowing Michael was twisting the truth.

Annalise had come here. But she hadn't left straight away. I thought about Annalise's rounded stomach under that cottony dress.

'If you slept with her—' Cat began.

'Don't you start throwing accusations around,' said Michael, pointing an angry finger. 'What kind of parent are you anyway? Three days out of rehab and you think you're Mother Superior? Like you haven't neglected that girl her whole life?'

'I haven't been the best mother. I know I haven't. You think I don't feel guilty? It doesn't make me love my daughter any less.' Cat's red fingernails clenched into fists. 'WHERE IS SHE, MICHAEL?'

'You should know the answer to that,' said Michael. 'You're her mother. Don't put your bullshit on us. You're the one who's taking care of her.'

'Lorna, when was she here?' Cat demanded.

'Um …' I was a dumb, frozen rabbit in headlights. I hate myself for that now. Absolutely hate myself.

Michael's voice turns quieter. 'Earlier in the year some time.' He turned to me. 'A long time ago. Wasn't it, Lorna?'

My stomach churned. When Michael's voice went quiet like that, I knew I was in trouble. And he wasn't lying – Annalise had left earlier in the year.

I felt myself nod.

'Listen.' Michael put an arm around Cat's shoulder. 'She'll turn up. You know she will. She'll be staying with a friend somewhere. Do you want to call the police?'

Cat's eyes faltered. 'Do you think it's come to that? She

always turns up in the end. You know what the police will do. Call Social Services.'

'She'll surface soon,' says Michael. 'She always does, doesn't she? Like you always say, she's fifteen going on forty. A real little grown-up.'

'But it's been so long now. Months and months.' Cat looked Michael right in the eye then. 'Tell me the truth, Michael. Do you know anything, *anything* you're not telling me?'

Michael's jaw set hard. 'Now pull yourself together. And stop throwing accusations around.'

Cat started crying, tears pouring down her face, red mouth opening and closing.

I couldn't bear it, and for once my decency overcame Michael's control.

'Cat, why don't you try the hospitals?' I said.

'Hospital?' Red nails shot to Cat's mouth. 'You think something happened to my baby?'

'She said she was pregnant.' I glanced at Michael. 'So maybe she visited a hospital. For a check-up or something.'

'She was pregnant?' Cat glares at Michael.

Michael gave me an angry smile, and I knew I was in trouble. 'Annalise wasn't pregnant, love,' he said. 'She just made all that up. A big story to get attention. They were jumpers stuffed around her middle. Didn't you notice?' Michael scratched his nose. 'Cat, she came here and left. That's the whole story. At the end of the day, Cat, I'm not her parent. You've let your daughter live away from home for all these months.'

'She said she was staying with a guy from the tour. I was in rehab. I thought she was okay …'

'Cat, you're wasting your time here,' said Michael. 'I've got work to do. Show yourself out.'

Michael headed past me, up the stairs.

Cat loitered in the hallway for a few desperate minutes. Then she said in her gravelly opiate voice, 'Is he telling the truth, Lorna?'

I shuffled on the stairs. 'Annalise did leave, Cat. A long time ago. She … she told me she was pregnant. But I guess she wasn't.'

Cat shook her head in disgust. 'One thing I can't stand. A woman who lets a man think for her.'

'I don't do that,' I said.

'Yeah, you do.' Cat left then. I watched her American 1968 Ford Mustang drive over gravel onto the winding woodland path and away.

Later I was in the gym room, red-faced, trying to run away from the morning.

Michael came striding in and I tensed, mid-run.

I expected him to punch me, then drag me up to the turret room and leave me without food for the next few days.

If I was lucky.

I braced myself. Self-defence was useless. It only made him angrier.

'Turn that thing off for a minute,' said Michael, pressing the treadmill emergency stop. 'I've got something for you.' He gave me a stubbly kiss on the cheek and held out a sheaf of magazines.

I flinched at the kiss, still wary. 'What are these?' I asked, head rushing, seeing glossy models in white dresses.

'Wedding magazines. Time to plan our future, right? I've decided to divorce Diane. It's been long enough. Keeping the poor girl hanging on isn't doing either of us any good.'

'You're kidding me.'

'I'd hoped for a smile at least,' said Michael, squeezing my hand. 'It's what you wanted, isn't it? You and me, happily ever after.'

He was right, I should have been smiling. If this were a normal relationship, I would have been.

I said the truest thing I could, without aggravating Michael's temper: 'It's weird timing. I thought you'd be mad at me. About Cat.'

'Forget about Cat,' said Michael. 'She's a drug addict who should take better care of her daughter.'

'And Annalise?'

'Like mother, like daughter. She'll be living with junkies somewhere and she'll find her mother again in time.'

He gave me a hug, but it felt hollow.

'So now you'll have something to focus your mind on,' said Michael, giving me the magazines. 'Right? Not Cat coming here and shouting about her daughter.'

My eyes couldn't quite meet his.

I wanted to ask him more about Annalise. When she left, had she said where she was going? Was there anything we could tell Cat?

But I knew what Michael would say. You're spoiling this moment, Lorna. You're being ungrateful. Why would you bring up something like that now when we're talking about getting married?

And I couldn't pull myself out of the pit.

I hate myself for that now.

I hate myself for so many things I can never change.

Liberty

My mother is at the front gate. At least, I think it's her. I can see the tiny speck of a person dressed in black, its size and movements female.

I watch the speck and feel sick.

Michael watches too, face pressed to the glass. There's an air of a victory about him. A knight swaggering around after winning a joust.

'What will you do now she's here?' I ask, my voice flat.

'I'm going to say hello,' says Michael. 'Good news, Liberty. Your mother is behaving herself. She's come alone. This is long-awaited, let me tell you. She's been laughing at me. Thinking she was in charge. But not anymore.'

'She was never laughing at you,' I say. 'She didn't want anything to do with you.'

'She's obsessed with me,' says Michael. 'Living so close by.'

'That's not why she chose to live close by,' I say.

'Oh?' Michael's eyebrows shoot up. 'You have some insight there, do you? So tell me, Liberty. Why did Lorna camp on my doorstep all these years like a lovesick fan?'

'She was playing you at your own game.'

Michael snorts. 'Lorna could never play any kind of game. Look at her, walking right in here, a rat in a trap. Not a thought in her stupid little head about how to get out of this one. No, she's getting what's in store for her and she knows it.'

'You're wrong,' I say. 'She *was* playing a game. She thought close by would be the last place you'd look. And she was right. She out-thought you on that one. You didn't find us.'

Michael's eyes darken. 'No, she didn't out-think me. You're here, aren't you? Lorna left herself wide open as usual. Not a clue how the game was played. Do you know something, Liberty? I set Lorna up before she even *thought* of going to the press. When she still thought I was her hero. Just in case she ever turned on me, I had photos of her I could use.'

I turn back to the window, watching my mother.

'She doesn't look afraid.'

'She's afraid,' says Michael, going to the door. 'She's about to lose everything.'

Once upon a time ...

'Wake up.' Michael loomed over the bed; short, dark and sinister.

I tensed under the bedclothes, eyes open enough to take in the grey early-morning sky and hear the high winds whipping around my turret bedroom.

Wedding brochures were stacked on my bedside table – something to keep me occupied after Cat's visit.

It hadn't worked. I hadn't slept well since Cat turned up. Annalise leaving so suddenly was bugging me. I hadn't questioned it much at the time because I was too busy counting my blessings. And her stomach – the fullness hadn't looked like a bundle of jumpers. Not at all. She'd been wearing a very thin dress and I'm pretty sure I saw her sticky-out belly button through the cotton.

Then there was the fact that Michael had suddenly got preoccupied with the cottage. He'd often stay out there all night, claiming to have some amazing musical inspiration.

'Lorna,' said Michael, his voice urgent now. 'Lorna, wake up. I have something for you.'

Michael's voice sounded weird. Not drunk. Not angry. Just weird.

I pretended to stir even though I was already wide awake.

Michael was holding something in his arms: a bright-blue Adidas hoodie.

'It's for you,' said Michael, leaning forward with the bundle.

At first I was confused. Then I saw what was wrapped inside the royal-blue cotton and sat bolt upright.

'Jesus. It's a baby.'

'She's for you,' said Michael, pushing the bundle into my arms. 'A little girl.'

I saw a dark-haired, tiny child, little white milk marks on her cheeks, soft sunken diamond shape in her skull. She looked so much like Michael. And she was covered in blood.

I sat bolt upright. 'Shit, Michael, what's going on?'

Michael paced the room, white-faced.

'Michael, this is your baby. Where did she come from?'

'She is a blessing from God,' said Michael.

'She's … Michael, where is this baby's mother? Why is the baby all bloody?'

Michael started talking about life and death, pacing back and forth, rambling about the universe, God and continuation. There was a streak of blood on his forehead.

The baby blinked at me, a little bit cross-eyed. I breathed her in. I checked around her blankets, but couldn't see any cuts or injury.

'Has she … has the baby just been born?'

'Yes.' Michael stopped pacing. 'This little baby is going to do great things. She is Reign Janis Michael and she'll heal the sins of the world.'

I held baby Reign as Michael paced and jabbered. Maybe

he's taken a shitload of drugs, I thought. Either that or he's losing his mind.

'Michael. You really need to tell me what's going on. Where is this baby's mother?'

'Her mother doesn't matter,' said Michael. 'Reign is yours now. You'll take care of her. You always wanted a baby. It's another Michael miracle.'

Michael paced and rambled a little more, then stooped to kiss Reign's head in a disconnected, jerky way.

Reign started crying then, but Michael's eyes stayed blank like a shark.

My handsome rock god crumbled into dust, lies and propaganda. In his place stood a short, mad toad.

'Where *is* her mother?' I demanded.

'You're her mother, Lorna. I've decided that you will have the honour of taking care of her. A baby. Just like you always wanted.'

'You can't just take a baby from one person and give her to someone else. You need to tell me who her mother is. And *where* her mother is. Is she here?'

Michael turned to me then, his dark eyes flashing and angry. 'Don't you realize what an honour this is?'

There was blood in his white-blond hair too, I realized.

I shuffled against the wall, holding on to that little bundle for dear life. 'I'm … uh, am honoured.' I glanced at the door, working out if I could get past him.

'This is it now, Lorna,' said Michael. 'The world will change forever. This baby is the second coming of Christ.'

Okay.

So he really had lost it.

As Michael paced and rambled, I shuffled to the edge of the bed and scanned the tall gates out of the window.

'I need to call my sister,' I said.

Michael stopped pacing then. 'You're not going anywhere.'

'I don't want to leave,' I lied. 'I just want to *call* my sister.'

'You don't need to call that press whore.' He went to take Reign from me, and for a moment I thought we'd have to fight. There was no way I'd let him hold this fragile little bundle. He'd was clearly on something. But I was saved by a thin, guttural female scream from outside.

I tensed, holding Reign close to my chest.

Michael went to the window, and I saw him in profile, nose long and hawk-like, eyes blacker than ever.

'Stay here,' he said.

Michael left, and I started shaking uncontrollably.

'I'll get you back to your mother,' I told Reign, sniffing back tears. 'Okay? I know he's lost it. I'm not going to let him take you.'

I headed to the rain-splattered window, holding Reign close to my chest, looking to see Michael. Under a bright full moon, at the edge of the woods, below spooky dark tree branches and pouring rain, I saw a lone figure, ghostly white.

A first I thought Michael had magicked himself out of the house at lightning speed, but then details floated into place. The figure was curvy and female and watching the house, an anguished look on her face.

My teeth started to chatter.

Annalise.

She stood half naked in the rain, soaking wet in a black Michael Reyji Ray T-shirt, thighs white, feet bare. When she saw me at the window, she let out a scream that could shatter glass. Then she started shouting something, but I couldn't hear her. I opened the rickety little turret window.

'Pleeeeease,' Annalise screamed. 'Give me back my baby. PLEASE! I won't try to run again. I promise. I'm sorreeee.'

Michael appeared then, striding over the moat bridge. He had a shotgun under his arm.

'What are you doing out of the cottage?' he shouted. 'I told you what would happen if you left that cottage.'

'Give me my baby.'

'I *warned* you. I've been warning you for months. I told you about the other girl, didn't I? The one who got out. She's chopped into pieces.' He held up the gun and took aim.

Annalise ran then, disappearing into the trees. Michael followed.

I was frozen to the spot. Utterly frozen. *Run*, a voice said. *Don't wait here, a sitting target.* But I just couldn't move.

Then there was a cracking sound, like fireworks.

That's when I ran. I bounded down two sets of stairs, baby Reign held tight to my chest. I ran straight down the path and into the woods, hardly seeing or hearing as rain lashed down.

On the winding woodland path to the gate, baby Reign squirmed and whimpered under the rain, flinching and grimacing as cold drops fell on her brand-new skin.

Please. Please don't cry.

As we neared the gate, Reign let out a long, loud howl.

Then I heard Michael. 'Lorna.' His voice was fifty layers deep with anger. 'Don't you move an *inch* with my baby. Stay right there.'

Lorna

I see pine forest. Twisty castle turrets behind green branches. I lived here once. It feels like a lifetime ago.

The gates are wide open, just as I expected. Of course they are. Michael knows I'm coming. This is his cat-and-mouse game, after all.

'Michael?' I call out. 'I know you're there.'

Michael appears through the trees, all charming eyes and rock-star swagger. He carries a rifle under his arm. Casually, like a country gent out on a fox hunt.

My stomach drops.

He has no hold over me. He has no hold over me.

I take in the deep lines on his face, the chubby little hands, the rounded body shape. He's changed so much. It's crazy to think I slept with this man. That once upon a time, I was so attracted to him that I waited at the window, desperate for him to come home. But he's still powerful, even if he's lost his good looks.

'Lorna,' says Michael, like a host at a dinner party. 'Good to see you. You got my message, then? How does it feel to be back after all these years?'

'You can turn off the charm,' I tell him, my voice shaking.

'You're not the handsome prince from my adolescent fairy tales anymore. All I see is a short, fat little con man.'

The smile slides from Michael's puffy face. 'You know, I was worried you'd got held up. You really took your time.'

'Sixteen years.' My legs shake as I move closer. 'Where's Liberty?'

Michael doesn't move an inch. 'You look different, I gotta tell you. Are you a tough girl now, or do those tattoos come off in the wash? It's a little warm for that army jacket, isn't it?'

I hesitate. 'What?'

'I mean, the sun is shining.' Michael gestures to the blue sky. 'What do you need that big coat for?'

'I'm … cold.'

Michael laughs. 'You always were a terrible liar. Come on, Lorna. What do you have stashed in that jacket? A knife or a gun or something?'

'I don't have a—'

'Yeah, you do. Take it off.' He lifts the rifle.

I swallow and feel my eyes close. Then I pull my jacket off and throw it to the ground. It falls open, showing the long kitchen knife loose in the inside pocket. There is it, lying on the ground. My feeble attempt to end Michael's horrible, destructive life. I failed to out-think him once again.

Michael holds the gun up and pretends to take aim. 'If you're dangerous, maybe I should shoot you now. Trespassing with a weapon.'

'Where's my daughter?'

Michael steps forward and jabs the rifle barrel to my fore-head, eyes black and furious.

'She's in your old bedroom.' He pushes it hard enough for me to remember all those times he turned into a hunch-shouldered demon and knocked me to the ground. 'But I don't like your tone. Who's in charge here, Lorna? You or me?'

'You,' I say, and the word is meek, just like the old days.

I could try and fight him, but I can't risk it. Fury makes Michael strong and he has a gun.

'Poor Liberty,' says Michael. 'She's told me all about you. How you kept her as your prize for all these years. Locked up at home.'

'I was keeping her safe.'

'It didn't work.'

'I know it didn't. But I'm here to take her place. A sacrifice, right? Will you let her go?'

'You need to do something first.'

'What?'

'Tell Liberty the truth.'

Uneasiness stirs inside me. 'So that's what you want. To destroy every bit of me. Every single bit.'

'You tried to do the same to me, didn't you? With those press stories. The difference is, I'll succeed where you failed. You'll be nothing to Liberty after today.'

'People will see through you in the end. Even Diane.'

'Diane will never know about this.' He moves the rifle barrel against my sternum now, jabbing hard. 'Let's go see Liberty now. You've got some explaining to do. Time to tell that little girl the truth. You know me. I can't stand lies.'

'And if I don't tell her?'

'You already know the answer. It's buried in my woods.'

Lorna

I remember the stairs to the turret room so well. The shallow steps curling around the stone pillar, finishing with one deeper step at the top – careful with that one, it can trip you.

The bedroom door is the same too. Mock medieval castle to satisfy Michael's regal delusions. And on the other side of the door …

My little girl.

Liberty sits on the turret room bed, curled over Skywalker. She looks up when the door opens and cries when she sees me.

'Liberty.' I feel myself smile. 'You're okay. Everything's going to be all right.'

'It's not all right,' says Liberty, eyes on fire. 'It'll never be all right again.' She grips Skywalker's fur.

Michael pushes hard metal against my spine. 'Don't you have something you want to tell her, Lorna?'

The words come out in a gabble. 'I'm not your real mother, Liberty.' My face crumples into tears. 'And your real mother – something real bad happened to her. And I left her. I ran.'

So much for marching in here and taking my daughter back. Michael is in charge, just like always.

'You left Liberty's real mother to die, didn't you, Lorna?' says Michael. 'She burned to death.'

I close my eyes and when I open them again, the world spins a little. I nod. 'Yes.'

Just like the old days.

Liberty starts to sob, hugging the furry mass on the floor. 'You lied to me my whole life. And *he* hurt my dog. You're both monsters.'

I turn to Michael, spinning away from the gun. 'You hurt her dog? How could you do that?'

'Careful now, Lorna. You'd better manage that temper of yours. You don't want this rifle going off. It would be a terrible thing for Liberty to see, wouldn't it? A real trauma.'

'What did you do to Skywalker?'

'Nothing. He must have eaten something out in the woods. I had nothing to do with it. I love animals.'

'Like hell you do.'

'How about *you* should have come quicker,' said Michael. 'If you had, her doggy could have got help in time. Poor little Liberty. Quite the day she's had. Finding out the real wicked witch around here is you. And now her pup dying.'

'Let Liberty go now. Let her *go*. You've done enough damage. I'm here. I did what you wanted.'

'Liberty can leave whenever she likes,' says Michael, pushing the door wider. 'I'm not a kidnapper, despite what the press might say on the subject.' He gives me a meaningful look. 'It's not like I'm locking her in.'

'You did,' says Liberty, lifting her head, chin out. 'The door—'

'I told you, this door gets stiff sometimes,' says Michael. 'You've got yourself confused. Don't let Lorna make *me* out to be the bad guy, now. If it weren't for Lorna, your real mother would still be alive. Lorna lied to you your whole life.'

Liberty scrabbles to her feet, chest heaving. 'The door was locked. It was *locked.*'

'There's no need to look so angry, love,' says Michael. 'I thought you were happy up here, looking after your doggy. I brought you food. Don't make out like I'm some big bad jailer.'

'So ... I can leave now, then?' Liberty asks, voice suspicious.

'You could always have left. Like I said, the door does get stiff sometimes. You know, Lorna had this same room. She'll tell you. Off you go then, if that's what you want. Lorna and I will stay here and catch up.'

'Go, Liberty,' I tell her. 'Go.'

I want to say something profound. Some big motherhood wisdom. But I'm not wise. I messed everything up. She's better off without me.

Liberty scoops Skywalker's bulky body into her arms. I wonder if she knows she's never going to see me again.

'Liberty.' My eyes soften. 'Sweetheart. Leave Skywalker here. If he really is in such a bad way, he deserves a peaceful end. If you're carrying him—'

'Leave him here with you two maniacs?' says Liberty. 'I'll be with him until the end. No matter what.' She staggers to the door, legs impossibly skinny under Skywalker's weight. 'I hope you two are very happy together.'

I watch Liberty walk sideways down the stairs. A moment

later, she's on the moat bridge. I see her through the turret window, long body heading into the trees, half walking, half stumbling with Skywalker in her arms.

'Happy?' I ask Michael. 'Now you've destroyed me completely?'

'I'm never happy,' says Michael. 'But today I'm something like content. Having you home again after all this time.'

'So what happens when Diane comes back? I hear she took a plane today.'

'Yeah, another trip abroad. More handbags.' Michael scratches his chin. 'I'm not worried about Diane. I've got pretty good at clearing up messes. She won't even know you were here.'

'How can she not have seen through you by now?'

'Don't make me out to be the bad guy,' says Michael. 'It was you who started this war. You took my daughter.'

'She's your daughter in name only,' I say. 'What kind of life would Liberty have had with you? You lost your mind when she was born. Having something real blew your image apart. It sent you mad. How could you have taken care of her?'

'Will you shut up, Lorna? For the love of God. Jabbering away. What happened to you? You were so much quieter before.'

'I want to see Liberty walk out that gate.' I go to the window.

'You know, once upon a time I thought you were perfect,' says Michael. 'You did everything I told you. But then you ruined everything. You were one big lie.'

'I wasn't a lie. I was obedient. But I grew up pretty quick the night you threw a baby into my arms. Why did you do it, Michael? Why did you let Annalise give birth, then take her baby away?'

'I wasn't going to leave the baby with her birth mother, was I?' says Michael. 'No – you had to be the one to take care of her. You were an extra-marital affair but at least you were over sixteen. If people thought the baby was yours, PR could do damage limitation. A crazy one-night-stand groupie pregnancy.'

'You're disgusting,' I say. 'You kept a pregnant fifteen-year-old a secret in that horrible, half-built cottage for months. You let her give birth out there alone. All to protect your image. And when she tried to run away—'

'Look, it was her own fault,' says Michael. 'She wouldn't get an abortion. And then she blabbed to you about the pregnancy. What did you expect me to do with her? She was a ticking bomb.'

'If you wanted her out of the way, why not just kill her before she gave birth?'

'I couldn't do it,' says Michael. 'I thought about it and I couldn't. You know what, Lorna? Maybe I'm not a complete monster. Liberty is the only thing that's ever made me human.'

'Very touching.'

'Annalise should have done as she was told,' says Michael. 'If she hadn't run out of the cottage it never would have happened. I warned her what I did to the other girls.'

I feel sick. 'Other girls?'

Michael lowers the gun. 'Girls I met at the shows and took to the cottage.' He watches the window. 'Why isn't she at the gates yet?'

'The gates are closed,' I say, following his eyeline. 'Why are they closed? You need to open them. How will Liberty get out?'

Michael doesn't say anything.

Realization dawns on me. 'You're not going to let her out.'

'Of course not. Come on now. What if she talks?'

'You separated us.' I feel furious with myself. 'In case we fought you. You couldn't have two against one.'

'Very good, Lorna. You're getting how it works.'

'The police know Liberty's here—'

'According to the testimony of a crazy woman.'

'Let her go, Michael. Open the gate.'

'Are you telling me what to do now? Where do you think that will get you?' He lifts the gun.

'Nowhere,' I say, my voice breaking. 'But … you had a party yesterday. People will have seen her here—'

'So what? Liberty came to my house. Then she left. There's nothing to suggest any harm came to her here. Everyone at the party saw us getting on like a house on fire. And you know how the police feel about searching my woods. They wouldn't want to offend me by doing that, would they?'

I lunge for Michael, my hands finding his throat. He struggles to move the rifle under my chin but I press my body against his so he can't get a good angle.

'You can't do it, Lorna,' says Michael. 'You might be stronger now, but you can't kill another human being. It's wired through you like writing in a stick of rock.'

'You're wrong. I could do it for Liberty.'

'Do it then.'

'You really think I won't?' My hands tighten.

'You can't kill me,' says Michael, his voice becoming raspy. 'You know why? Because I'm not real. There's nothing here to kill, Lorna. And you know it. This is just a body. Michael Reyji Ray lives beyond this body. The idea of him is loved by millions. You kill me and I'll become a martyr. Liberty's mother will have caused the death of a legend. The world will tear your daughter apart. The fans will hunt you both down like dogs.'

I feel my hands fall and hear a scream of frustration – mine. He's right. Always so many moves ahead. The brilliant chess player. Defended on all corners.

'Let Liberty out the gates,' I say. 'Make her look crazy. Tell the press she's a liar. You know you can do that. Just let her go. And I won't fight you anymore.'

'That's a given.' Michael looks out the window. 'The problem right now is Liberty's not at the gate.'

'What?'

Michael whips around to face me. 'Where is she?'

'I don't know.'

His shoulders turn into a furious hunch and he lifts the rifle, taking aim. 'What are you two playing at?'

'Nothing. I don't know any more than you.'

Michael shoves me hard onto the bed and points the rifle. For a minute, I think he's going to do it. I think he'll shoot me. But instead he turns and marches out of the room, slamming the door behind him.

I leap off the bed and run to the door, but it's locked or stuck. Immovable.

Goddamn it!

I pull on the metal-studded oak door, fists pounding, trying to smash through solid oak. But it doesn't work.

It's just like the old days.

I'm trapped and Michael holds all the cards.

Once upon a time …

Rain poured from a jet-black sky, catching in the tree branches and falling in cold, mean drops on the baby's forehead and cheeks. I tried to shield her, hold her against me, but the rain just kept coming.

Michael was behind us, his brown moccasins slapping on wet mud.

'Where do you think you're going with my child?' said Michael, his voice low and hard.

My whole body went rigid, stiff hands clutching Reign for dear life. If I was just me, I would have fought or run. But I couldn't risk anything with a baby. Some kind of natural instinct.

'I was looking for you,' I lied. 'Reign was crying. She wanted her father.'

'Come with me,' said Michael, his voice softening. 'Reign shouldn't be out here in this rain.'

'Yes,' I said. 'I know. You're right, Michael.'

I tried for a smile, as though Michael's spell hadn't been broken. But it had. I now saw not the love of my life, my hero, my obsession, but a bitter middle-aged man with a lined face and hard, empty eyes.

'Watch your step now, Lorna,' said Michael, as though he were a gentleman. 'That's a precious thing you're carrying. More precious than both of us.'

'Did Annalise give birth out in the cottage?' I ask, cold bare feet flinching on stones and twigs.

'What does it matter?' said Michael. 'You're this baby's mother now. Think of it as a holy birth. This baby is of the world, not of us. But you have the honour of taking care of her.'

I looked up and realized we were going deeper into the woods.

'Michael.' I started to panic. 'Why aren't we going to the house? This baby needs to be warm. It's raining.'

'Hush now,' said Michael, his voice hard. 'Stop your noise. We're going to the little cottage.'

'What? Why would we go there?'

'Because I'm king and this is my castle and I'm telling you, that's where we're going.'

The cottage loomed up ahead then, like something from a horror movie: foggy, dark and cold.

I started yelling then. Begging. Pleading with a man who couldn't care less.

'Michael. This is your daughter. Please, she's crying. You can't put us out here in the cottage. It's cold. It's a half-built shell.'

'Shut up now, Lorna. Get yourself in there.' He flung open the metal sheet door.

The cottage was as bare and ghostly as the night I'd slept in it. No renovations had happened. There were no walls, no first floor, no staircase: just one big space criss-crossed with beams, flaking with old plaster. The windows had been shuttered closed on the outside. The floor was concrete.

'You said you were making music out here,' I said. 'When you left me alone all those nights. Where are the instruments?'

'Just shut up and get inside, Lorna,' said Michael.

I could see Michael's dark eyes, glinting under moonlight. They were cold and dead and they told me I had no choice. I walked right into the cottage, into the dark and shadows, clutching the baby.

'Stay there.' Michael slammed the metal door shut, and I heard the click and crunch of the padlock falling into place outside.

'Wait … MICHAEL!' I stumbled around in the dark. 'MICHAEL! MICHAEL!'

No answer.

Reign cried louder.

As I clung to her, trying to figure out what to do, I heard a low moan from the back of the cottage.

I backed towards the door, tipping around like a spider with a broken leg.

I held baby Reign tight. 'It's okay, baby. It's okay.'

But it wasn't.

The noise had come from a big, black shadow hunched over in the corner, and every muscle in my body locked tight. I honestly thought it was a ghost. Truly.

'*Lorna.*' The voice was cracked and deep.

I blinked and stared at the hunched shadow, and it became a girl: bare-legged, head bowed, body bent over itself. A dark pool grew under her on the cement floor.

'Annalise?'

Annalise lifted her head. A wet, black T-shirt with Michael's face on it hung over her shivering body.

She croaked, 'He shot me.'

I began to see better. More things around the cottage. A double mattress in one corner with darkly stained sheets and a pile of damp-looking blankets. Next to the mattress was a bucket – probably the same bucket I'd peed in when Michael made me sleep out here. And there were magazines and candy bar wrappers strewn around.

Annalise's face turned soft. 'Can I hold the baby?'

'Of course. Was she … did you give birth out here?'

Annalise nodded. 'My baby was born in this hellhole.' Then she started to cry. 'And she'll die here too. Michael didn't want anyone to know I was having his child. So when I boasted to you about the baby … Michael said I couldn't stay in the house anymore. I had to be punished.'

'You must have been so frightened.'

'He kept me prisoner out here. I had to do whatever he wanted. It was a nightmare.' She cries harder. 'But I don't expect pity from you. I know you hate me.'

'No, I don't hate you. Michael's not what I thought. I'll get us out.'

'You won't get us out,' Annalise croaked. 'This is a prison. Do you think if there was a way out, I wouldn't have found it? Michael's been keeping me out here for months.' She cried harder.

'You've been out here for *months*? Oh God.' I stared at her. 'He's … You've been living out here?'

Annalise nods.

'Why—'

'I told you. Michael couldn't have anyone knowing about the baby. So he couldn't have me staying at the house anymore. He hid me out here. He said when the baby came, I could come back, but … it was a lie. All the nice stuff – it's just a mask. He's a monster. You haven't seen the half of it. He's not human at all. He does what he wants with me. Whatever he wants.'

'You're bleeding.'

'Forget about that. It's too late.' Her eyes looked longingly at Reign. 'Please can I hold her?'

I carried baby Reign over and placed her in Annalise's arms. 'Let me try and stop the bleeding.'

'Forget about me. It's all over.'

'No. I'll get us out.' I bang at the solid metal door and window panels. 'And then I'll get you to a hospital. They'll know what to do.'

'You'll never get past Michael. Don't even try to go against him. You have no idea what he's capable of.' She cried jerky, gaspy sobs.

'You got out before,' I said. 'You were in the woods. I saw you from the window.'

'Michael left the cottage door open when he took my baby away. I think the birth messed with his head.'

'Wait.' I sat upright. 'I smell smoke.'

An orangey brightness flickered in Annalise's pupils and under a metal-plate window. Smoke twirled into the cottage, thin strands at first, then thicker and thicker.

Suddenly, a *BOOM!* rattled the metal window and fire

exploded up one wall, tearing around the window frame towards the ceiling.

Annalise sat up straight, clutching the baby tight.

'It must be lightning,' I said. 'From the storm.'

'No,' said Annalise, looking around, trying and failing to get up. 'This is Michael. He's locked us in here and he's burning the place down. Don't you get it? Anything that hurts his image … it has to go. We have to go. All of us.'

'He wouldn't—'

'I wasn't the first girl Michael kept out here,' said Annalise. 'He told me about them, Lorna. When they tried to escape, he cut them up and buried them in the woods. He said he'd do it to me if I tried to get out.'

I got to my feet and hammered on the windows. 'Let us out. LET US OUT!'

'There's no way out,' said Annalise flatly. 'Not unless he lets us out. Here. I can't hold her. The baby. Take her.'

I took the baby and Annalise slumped forward, arms limp and loose. Her breathing sounded raspy. Shallow.

'I've been told that before,' I said. 'That there's no way out. But there's always a way.'

Annalise didn't reply, but I heard her little sparrow breaths in the darkness.

'There's always a way out, Annalise,' I say again.

More raspy sparrow breaths.

'If you really, really want to live.'

Was I already going a little bit insane?

Yes. Pretty sure I was.

Liberty

I didn't walk to the gate, like my dad wanted. Of course I didn't. That would have made me a pawn in Michael's chess game, when in fact it's me who's been playing him this whole time.

Michael is a good tactician but I'm better. I've been pulling Michael's strings, putting him where I want him.

Now I'm one move away from checkmate.

They say chess is about thinking many moves ahead. But to me, the most important part is analysing your opponent, working out what kind of player they are.

Michael is the 'win at all costs' kind of player. He doesn't care if he breaks the rules, as long as no one sees him do it. As soon as I worked that out, things were simple. Make Michael feel like he's winning and he'll move into the right places.

I watch Michael from my crouched position, one of his shotguns on my lap, hidden behind the cottage. Skywalker sits beside me, ears pricked and alert.

Guess what, Dad? I am not a dumb, scared little teen desperate for a record contract. My dog isn't really sick. And you're not the only one who can act.

'Well done, boy,' I whisper, stroking Skywalker's silky head. 'If there were acting awards for playing dead, you'd win an Oscar.'

Skywalker watches Michael, ears fierce, body primed.

'Not yet. Just a little longer, okay?' I grab Skywalker's collar, hand tense and controlled. Poor boy, he's desperate to run around after playing dead for so long. But not yet.

Skywalker and I have been practising the 'dead weight' command for over a year. When I say 'dead weight', Skywalker plays dead until I tell him to stop. It's taken months of training.

I watch Michael go to the gate. I can't see his face, but I can picture it: lips tight, blank eyes twitching. He'll be furious.

Where is Liberty? She should be at the gate ... Where'd she go?

Oh Michael, Michael.

I did warn you I never lose. That chess game we played? I beat you twenty different ways in my head. But I let you win on the board because this is about the big game. The game my mother lost. The 'tell the world who Michael Reyji Ray really is' game.

Michael is looking around the railings now, probably wondering if I've climbed them with a dead dog on my shoulder.

'I have to give him credit,' I tell Skywalker. 'The birthday cake in the freezer was clever. He's a quick thinker. But every slice looked the same. If it was from different years, some pieces would look older than others.'

Skywalker makes a noise and I clamp his mouth closed. 'Not yet,' I whisper. 'Just wait. Nearly time.'

Skywalker has been key to winning this game. Yesterday he

sniffed out human remains in Michael's woodlands and found the gun shed – both important moves. I've trained Skywalker to be a cadaver dog. That means he can smell human remains, even from sixteen years ago. Some of the remains in Michael's woodlands will belong to Cat Cannon's missing daughter. The other sites – there were three in total – I have no idea. I geotagged the locations, anyway. The police can dig them up and examine the DNA.

'Okay,' I say, standing. 'Stay, Skywalker. Stay right there.'

Skywalker drops to the floor, watching me.

Perfect.

I stumble onto the woodland path, breathless, frantic, the grade-A drama student.

'Dad!'

Michael sees me through the trees and freezes. Surprise crosses his puffy little face. He jogs towards me, but slows to a huffing walk when he sees the shotgun under my arm.

'Liberty,' he says. 'Where'd you get that gun from?'

'Your gun shed. I smashed the lock off.'

'Let's not be silly. Why didn't you go to the gate, love? You need to get your doggy to a vet, don't you? Where's your doggy? Give it to me, let's not be silly now.'

'I couldn't leave,' I say. 'Not without knowing what happened to my real mother. Where her body is buried.' My words are stumbly and tearful. I'm a good actress, if I do say so myself. 'And ... and I'll shoot you if you don't tell me.'

'It doesn't matter now,' says Michael. 'Your real mother is dead. Okay? A real tragedy. Come on now. Go to the gate.'

Of course he wants me to go to the gate. There's a camera at

303

the gate. Michael needs CCTV footage of me appearing to leave. That way, if the police ever ask about me being here, he can show them evidence that I left willingly.

'I need to know the truth,' I say, making the words choked and frightened. 'Did Annalise die here? Is this where she's buried?'

'If I tell you, will you go to the gate?'

'Yes.'

'Okay. You're right. Annalise died in these grounds.'

'And you buried her in the woods?'

Michael hesitates.

'You must have done,' I say. 'Where else would her body be?'

'Okay, Liberty. Yes, I buried her in the woods. And I'll do the same to you if you don't do as you're told.'

'Skywalker,' I click my fingers. 'Here boy.'

Skywalker trots to my side.

Michael takes a big, surprised breath. 'Your dog. He's ... he's up and about, is he?'

'Oh, yeah,' I say. 'He's fine. So listen. I've got a deal for you.'

'A deal?' Michael's black eyes glimmer. 'What are you talking about, a deal? Go to the gate. And give me that bloody gun, for goodness sake. You'll hurt yourself.'

'This is the deal.' I take out my phone from my denim shorts pocket.

'Where did you get that phone from?' says Michael. 'Did your mother—'

'I've had my phone the whole time,' I tell Michael. 'I'm calling the police now. I'm going to tell them that you held me captive and that there are human remains in your woodlands.

Which my dog sniffed out. But before that, give me the key to the turret room so I can let my mother out.'

'Liberty.' Michael's face goes rigid. 'Give me that phone. Right now.'

I press the button to wake the screen.

Predictably, Michael lunges for me.

Skywalker leaps forward, snapping and barking. He's not so cowardly after all. I told a white lie about that. Actually, the police let him go because he was too aggressive and bit an old lady carrying a bag full of fireworks. Also, I've been attack-training him for months with a bite sleeve and a mannequin in black jeans and sunglasses.

To Michael's credit, he only looks frightened for a moment. Then he steps back and reconsiders his position.

'Give me the gun, Liberty.'

'Give me the key, Michael.'

'You're not going to shoot me, so just hand it over.'

'I will shoot you.'

'No, you won't.' Michael walks right up to me, planting his chest at the end of the barrel. 'You'd feel too guilty. It'd tear you up.'

'Pretty much the opposite of you then.'

'You were the closest thing I came to feeling anything. Did you know that? The day you were born … I understood, just for a moment. What it was like to feel like everyone else does. It was awful. Horrible. Like torture.' His mouth moves in that odd way of his. 'So you can understand. I'm in no hurry to connect with that part of myself again. But I don't wish you dead, Liberty. You're a part of me and I want you to live on.'

'I don't want to be a part of you,' I say.

'I know that, Liberty. I never had any more children, did I? You have to say that for me. Give me the gun now. We can still make this right. If you pull that trigger, you'll create a legend. A rock star scrubbed out by the daughter of a crazed groupie. And then do you know what will happen? The whole world will tear you *and* your mother to shreds.'

Michael grabs the barrel and pulls the whole gun from my hands.

'Get back,' he shouts, eyes dark and furious. 'Get back. Get *back* or I'll shoot the damn thing. Now I'm telling you, Liberty. Walk to the gate.'

'You won't shoot. You're on camera.'

Michael stiffens. 'No, love. The gate camera can't see us from here.'

'Smile.' I put a hand to the smiley face on my T-shirt. 'You're being live streamed. The whole world can see you, Michael Reyji Ray. As you really are. Mask off. This badge is a camera. That's the thing about image, isn't it? One bad picture and it's all over.'

Michael's face contorts with rage. He is a man on the edge. He has nothing to lose. He takes aim and pulls the trigger.

Once upon a time ...

Fire crept up the walls, eating at the roof timbers. Tiles fell and smashed.

'You just need a reason,' I told Annalise, my voice high and afraid. 'A reason to live. Or you won't make it. You have a baby. Make this baby your reason.'

But Annalise didn't move. Her breathing was barely there now, and she didn't flinch as tiles dropped.

It's something no one ever prepares you for, hearing another human being take their last breath. Shallow breathing became stop, start, and then nothing at all.

'Annalise?' I knelt beside her, my warm forehead to her cold one, trying to put life back into her.

Baby Reign had fallen asleep by then, into a blissful otherworld. A place nobody could hurt her.

'You have a reason to live,' I whispered, tears falling. 'You can't give up.'

But it was too late. She was dead.

Baby Reign started crying and I pulled myself together.

'You'll be my reason to live, then,' I told her, my own tears falling on hers. 'Okay?'

The space around the metal front door was burning, blackened and warped and white-hot with thick, black smoke billowing in around the frame.

More hot tiles smashed to the floor.

I put a screaming Reign down on the damp mattress and looked around the burning building. Hope dwindled, but hope had dwindled before and I'd pulled through. And I decided, just as I had on the hospital bed, that I was going to survive. Not to see some make-believe pop idol this time around, but to protect this baby from her father.

As I prayed, the rain started – soft at first, then hard and heavy, pummelling the roof, falling through holes and steaming on the cement floor.

There were still flames everywhere, but the wooden frame around the metal door had turned black and charcoal-like. I hurled my body into the heat. The pain did not scare me. Nor did the choking, chemical smoke. My body had been washed with chemicals before.

I didn't think the door would give way, but it did, exploding in sparks and wood splinters. Air rushed into the cottage, and with it fire, eating away at the walls. The doorway was an angry, burning ring, raging and tearing.

I took one last look at Annalise's stiff, dead body. Then I picked up the baby and walked right through that burning doorway into cool, dark woods.

For a stupid moment I just stood, staring at the burning cottage. The roof was ablaze and tiles were falling. Then the roof collapsed and I ran through the woods. Reign bobbed in my arms.

Finally, I made it to the gate and hit the release mechanism. The gates opened slowly, whirring like screams in the silent night, but eventually they were wide enough and I slid through the growing gap and onto the lane outside.

It was a long way to the main road. About a mile down a straight, tree-lined path. Street lights twinkled up ahead like stars. There were big, swaying fir trees either side.

I began to half walk, half run down the path, the baby bundle held close to my chest, eyes fixed on those twinkling lights.

Then I heard it. The roar of a quad bike.

I began to jog, taking hasty glances over my shoulder.

Warm, distant headlights flickered in the woods, then appeared on the path behind me, a long way behind but gaining ground all the time, lighting up the bumpy road.

I knew I couldn't outrun the bike. Any moment, Michael would screech up behind me, shoot me and take the baby. Or maybe shoot both of us.

I carried on running.

'Lorna!' called a voice. 'Lorna!'

It sounded like Dee's voice. My sister. But of course, it wasn't really Dee. I was hallucinating. Or I was sleeping. This was a nightmare, after all.

But the shape got bigger and bigger and I saw it really was Dee, coming down the lane towards me.

'DEE!' I screeched the word and baby Reign gave a start and began to cry.

'Lorna.' Dee reached me, drawing in great lungfuls of air. 'I saw the fire. I've been waiting ... wait. What are you holding?'

'A baby.'

'Jesus Christ.'

'It's Michael's.'

The quad bike headlights flowed behind us like waves.

'Let's get in the car, Lorna,' said Dee.

'What car?'

'My car. It's parked right over there.' Dee pulled me to a dark blue car parked by the side of the lane.

'How are you even here?' I asked, taking a horrified glance down the lane at Michael's approaching quad bike. 'And you have a car. How?'

'I told you I'd be waiting. Get in.'

We climbed into Dee's car and I pulled the passenger door closed.

'You have a baby,' said Dee matter-of-factly.

I clicked the car lock down just as Michael's quad bike roared up beside us. I saw him through the car window: his pale, dead-eyed face turned to us, more furious than I'd ever seen him.

I heard his scream through the glass: 'GIVE HER TO ME.'

'Drive, Dee,' I shouted.

'Lorna, if you have his child—'

'Please. Please trust me. I'll explain later.'

Michael's fists pounded on the window.

I clutched Reign. 'Drive, Dee, drive. Please. PLEASE!'

'Okay.' Dee nodded. 'Okay.' Dee put the car into gear and we screeched away towards the main road.

I didn't look back. When we pulled out of Michael's lane, Dee revved the accelerator and we raced into dark, early-morning countryside. Eventually, I started noticing the world around me and the quaint little village name signs. Huntingdon. Abbey Fields. Taunton Wood. And there were trees, too. A sunrise.

'So what's going on?' said Dee, glancing at the sleeping bundle in my arms. 'You have Michael's baby. You're a baby thief. Have you lost your mind?'

'This *was* Michael's baby,' I said, kissing Reign's head. 'But she's mine now.'

Dee sucked at her cheeks. 'Okay. Let's figure this out. We'll take the baby to a hospital or a doctor or … I don't know, some safe space. And then have someone tell Diane to come get her. And we have to do it now, Lorna. Diane must be going out of her mind—'

'Diane isn't the mother,' I said. 'The mother is dead. Michael shot her.'

Dee swallowed. 'Lorna – what the hell are you talking about?'

'Cat Cannon's fifteen-year-old daughter is this baby's mother. She gave birth out in the woods. And then she bled to death.'

'I saw a fire,' says Dee.

I started crying. 'Annalise was in that fire. I had to leave her. She died before I could get her out.'

'Oh my God.' Dee gripped the steering wheel. 'If this is true, you have to go to the police.'

'No. No way.'

'Why not?'

'You think anyone will believe that Saint Michael Reyji Ray shot someone? That he kept a teenager in some makeshift prison cottage in the woods, where she gave birth to his child? I know him, Dee. He'll talk his way out of it. And the police will make me give this baby back. No one will believe me. Who am I? Just some crazy American groupie.'

'Well, what are we going to do about the baby?'

I clutched at Reign, my arms like steel cable. 'I'm gonna take care of her.'

'You?'

'Me.'

'How's that going to work?'

'I'm going to hide. Somewhere clever. Somewhere he won't find us. I'll say she's mine. That I gave birth to her. No one in this country has seen my medical records. They don't know I can't have children.'

'Don't you think ... I mean, shouldn't you give the baby to the authorities and let them ...'

'Let them what? Give the baby back to Michael?'

We drove for a long time. I could have stayed in Dee's car forever, that day. It felt safe, but the world outside ... oh so scary.

'Why were you waiting in the lane tonight?' I asked.

'I've been waiting for months,' said Dee. 'I wasn't going to leave you.'

'You've been parked on Michael's lane for months?'

'Every night. I sleep out here. I'm practically an expat now.'

'You've been waiting this whole time?'

'Of course. You're my little sister. I'd do anything for you.'

I stared out of the windscreen, smiling.

'What's so funny?'

'I had the real thing this whole time. While I was chasing after illusions of love in thin air.'

'It's not your fault. Michael's a lot older than you. He took advantage.'

I gave a weird laugh. 'Michael will try and ruin me now. He'll make me out to be crazy.'

'He already has.'

'What?'

'The press. I guess you haven't seen the stories ... you've been stuck in a Michael bubble. Well, according to the papers you're a crazy stalker groupie. Michael's PR team must be doing damage limitation. Or Michael's trying to convince his wife that you're nothing to him. There are articles about you, the unhinged cancer survivor, stalking Michael and his wife.'

'He's such a liar.' I hold the baby tight. 'He won't mess with this baby's mind, like he does everyone else. No way.'

It was spring, I realized. A time of rebirth. The leaves never looked so green.

Lorna

I throw myself at the oak door over and over again – *bang, bang, bang.*

When my shoulder burns with pain, I try the other shoulder.

Bang, bang, bang.

'Mum?'

The word sails through oak door, high and light.

'Liberty?' I put my ear to the door. 'LIBERTY?'

There is a crunchy clack sound and the door opens. I catch myself on the door frame.

Liberty stands at the top of the stairs, bleached-blonde hair flopping across her forehead, long, skinny legs in cherry-red DM boots.

She has blood on her hand – the same hand that holds the door key. Skywalker sits by her side. He has blood on him too, around his muzzle and on one ear.

'It's okay, Mum,' says Liberty. 'We can go home now.'

'What happened?' I grab her bloody hand. 'Are you okay? Did he hurt you?'

'This is Michael's blood,' says Liberty.

'Where is he?' I push past her, scanning the stairs. 'Where is he, Liberty?'

'Injured,' says Liberty. 'We should go.'

'Injured? Injured how? What happened?'

'Michael tried to shoot me. But the gun exploded in his hand. And then Skywalker went for him. Some protective instinct. I taught him how to attack, but I've never seen him go crazy like that before.'

'Where *is* Michael?'

'Out there.'

'Show me.'

'Honestly, Mum, you don't want to see.'

'Yes, I do.'

Liberty leads me into the woods. My hand shakes in hers, but she is just fine – cool as a cucumber.

'I'm warning you,' says Liberty. 'It's pretty disgusting.'

On the path near the cottage, Michael is a bloodied heap looking blank-eyed at the sky. His black T-shirt and jeans are covered in blood. I mean, soaked. And his throat and hands are a mess. He twitches and I step back, pushing Liberty behind me.

'Jesus Christ.'

'I know,' says Liberty. 'Skywalker really went for him. A foot soldier. Protecting his pack leader.'

With my boot, I push at the bloody cloth thing that was once the love of my life. The thing is heavy and sand-like.

'It was self-defence,' says Liberty. 'Michael tried to shoot me. But I'd already stuffed chewing gum down the gun barrel. The gun exploded and took half his hand with it, then Skywalker attacked him.'

'You … what?' I put hands to my head. 'You put chewing gum down the barrel of his shotgun? How?'

'Actually, I put chewing gum down the barrels of all Michael's guns,' she says. 'I did it yesterday. Chess tactics. You have to disable the enemy defences.'

'And then—'

'Well, I pointed the gun at him. That way, he wouldn't know I'd disabled it. You know? He had to be his own undoing. I have it all on camera.'

'Jesus, Liberty, we need to get out of here.' I grab her arm and pull her to the gate. 'My van … it's on the drive. Let's get the hell away from this place and call the police. It's not safe. *You're* not safe.'

Liberty laughs. 'Have you not worked it out yet, Mum? I can look after myself.'

Lorna

Liberty and I drive through countryside in my workshop van, with all the silicon body parts and masks in the back.

The landscape looks the same as it did that day, when Dee drove me away from Michael's house with baby Liberty in my arms.

'So … are you going to tell me how all this happened?' I ask. 'I feel like I'm missing at least twenty different things.'

'I decided to fix things,' says Liberty. 'It felt safer doing that than carrying on as things were.'

'Liberty, I'm not sure you're thinking straight. Maybe seeing the dog attack someone has affected you… You're talking like you *planned* this.'

'I did plan it. I've been planning it for about two years.'

'What? How? You've only just found out who your father—'

'No. I found out when I was fourteen. I broke into your safe and found your old medical records and your old surname. I worked it all out. That you couldn't have been my real mother. Then I did newspaper research and found pictures of you and Michael.'

'But you told me you only just found—'

'A white lie. Once I got Skywalker trained up, I was ready to visit Michael's house. I was hoping you might give me your blessing. That was the original plan. Have Skywalker sniff out the remains, show footage to the police, then ask them to dig. But you said no.'

'Wait a minute. The woods. Skywalker—'

'I trained Skywalker to find human remains. My science teacher gave me a human placenta to use. And Skywalker found that same scent, you know dead human flesh, in three different sites in Michael's woods. They're all marked up, ready for the police. I geotagged everything. And then I got Michael on camera, admitting my real mother is buried in his woods.'

'How?'

'On a button camera. And my phone.'

'You have your *phone*? You've had your phone this whole time?'

'I told you. I know your safe code, Mum. It's my birthday. Not all that safe really.'

I shake my head in disbelief. 'I could have called you this whole time?'

'I wouldn't have answered.'

'So ... you believed me about your father? That he was dangerous?'

'Of course I believed you,' says Liberty. 'All the psychological indications suggested you were telling the truth. Michael, on the other hand, was a clear case of words not matching actions. I mean, a so-called environmentalist keeping a collection of polluting classic cars. Talk about a mismatch.'

'Weren't you scared?' I ask. 'Walking right into his house, thinking he could have killed … well, your mother?'

'Terrified,' says Liberty. 'I nearly didn't go through with it. But I had my phone with me. I had Skywalker.'

'What if Michael had found your phone and taken it?'

'That wouldn't have happened,' says Liberty.

'Why not?'

'I would have set Skywalker on him. I made sure we were never separated.'

'He owns a collection of *shotguns*, Liberty.'

'I know. But I told you. Skywalker sniffed them out and we put them out of action.' She taps her nose. 'Chess player, mother. Chess player. Many moves ahead.'

'Mother. You're still okay to call me that?'

'Of course I am. I told you. I've known for years we're not related. It's never mattered to me. And when I found all those articles – all that stuff you said about him – I pieced everything together. Who my real mother must be, what must have happened to her. I know you well enough to know you wouldn't lie about what happened to Annalise.'

I stare at her. 'And what … you just didn't care that I'm not your real mother? You didn't say a word to me about it?'

'I've known my whole life you were hiding something. It was a relief really. I mean, it could have been much worse. And what's biology anyway? Michael Reyji Ray is my biology. A man who wears sunglasses indoors. Biology doesn't make sense. It doesn't take care of you. It doesn't love you. It doesn't mean anything.'

'And you worked out who your real mother was?'

'Yes,' says Liberty. 'If Annalise was staying with Michael, like you said in those articles, I figured there must be some kind of sexual relationship going on. And if she got pregnant with me underage, it would have given Michael a reason to, you know ... get rid of her.'

'And how do you feel about that? That your real mother died? And *how* she died?'

'How do I feel? Awful. Terrible. It's really sad. But it's okay. I got you as a mother instead.'

Happily ever after ...

'If they do leave us in the forest, we'll find our way home,'
said Hansel to his sister.

C*rash!*

The final piece of fencing falls down and light floods into the kitchen.

Nick and I watch from the kitchen, listening to the radio play 'It's a Wonderful World'.

'There it goes,' I say. 'Our old, safe little space. Bulldozed.'

'The best decision you ever made, Lorna,' says Nick. 'It feels great. All this light.'

'I'll tell you a bad decision,' I say. 'This vegan cheese. I should have paid more for the cashew nut stuff. I mean look at this.' I give the yellow cube a prod. 'It feels like a pencil eraser and smells like feet.'

'Liberty won't mind,' said Nick. 'She'll be feeling too happy about her exam results to notice the finer details of her vegan feast. Assuming she got the results she wanted.'

'Of course she will,' I say. 'Neither of us need to worry about Liberty and exams.'

'Lucky her to be born with that brain,' says Nick. 'My parents gave me a clip around the ear on my exam-results day.'

'The house feels good with the fences down, doesn't it?' I look at the tree-lined street and blue sky. Then I see Liberty and her bandmates bounding towards the house, talking and laughing, dressed in tight jeans, oversized boots, leather and hand-printed T-shirts.

'There they are,' says Nick. 'The next Oasis. I've never seen so much ripped denim.'

'All change today, right?' I say. 'The start of something new.'

Nick starts singing the song from *High School Musical*, about this being the start of something new.

I cover my eyes. 'Don't let those guys hear you sing that.'

'Liberty knows who I am,' says Nick. 'Lame and proud. And we're getting on better for it.'

The radio music fades into the six o'clock news:

The death toll rises today as more human remains are found at Huntingdon Wood.

Nick kisses my head. 'I know it's horrible. But at least everything is out in the open now. The truth heals.'

'It is horrible,' I agree. 'But it's also like putting down a heavy backpack. The world knowing. And being able to talk with you about it. I thought you'd run away screaming. I have to pinch myself that you stuck around.'

'I'd never leave you. You know that.'

'I wish I'd told you the truth when we first met. You're right. The truth heals. And now everything's so much better. With Liberty. With everything. We have the family we want.'

'We're doing great. We're all doing great.'

I like living with a personal trainer. It's very motivating.

The remains, believed to be female, were discovered this afternoon in the private woodland belonging to singer Michael Reyji Ray. Two female bodies have already been identified at Ray's Sussex home as those of Annalise Cannon, daughter of singer-songwriter Cat Cannon, and Karla Muller, a German teenager who went missing at the height of Ray's fame.

It is thought Michael Reyji Ray killed the women, dismembered their bodies and buried them in his grounds. Annalise Cannon's body was partially burned.

Ray died at his home earlier this year, whilst holding his daughter and ex-partner captive. He sustained fatal injuries from an exploding shotgun and a dog attack. A video of Ray threatening his daughter with a shotgun has had over 10.6 billion views.

Michael Reyji Ray's wife, Diane Ray, has now moved out of the singer's former home. Mrs Ray, heard speaking here from her new home in New York, claims to have been fooled by the singer:

'This has shattered my whole world. I was married to Michael for twenty years. He was a caring and loving partner. The man who killed those girls is a man I never met. I'm still hoping to wake up from this nightmare.'

Nick flicks the radio off. 'Focus on the positive, yeah?'

I nod. 'Agreed. You know, I feel sorry for Diane. She was a victim too.'

'She chose to look the other way, didn't she? I mean, she must have had some idea of who Michael was.'

'She was the sort of woman who believed in supporting her husband, no matter what. He was a god to her. Michael played on that. He played everyone.'

'Well, I think she deserves to be locked up,' says Nick. 'If she hadn't helped protect his image, Michael might have been caught a long time ago.'

'Maybe. But I don't think she had a choice. Michael was a predator. He preyed on weaknesses. It's like telling someone in a prison cell they should get out. They don't know how.'

I watch Liberty lean her bike against piled-up fencing. Her eyes are wide with wonder and she silently mouths: 'Whoa'. Then she clatters into the house on long, teenage legs, followed by her bandmates.

'You got rid of the gates,' says Liberty, flicking her hair – pink and blue today.

Liberty's bandmates congregate awkwardly behind her.

'Hi, Abi,' I say. 'Hi, Freddy.'

'Hello, Mrs Armstrong. Hello, Mr Armstrong.'

'The garden looks good, right?' I coax.

'Very cool,' says Liberty. 'But what does Darcy think about it? It's a big change. You know how she feels about change.'

'You can ask her,' says Nick, turning to the staircase. 'She's home already. Darcy. DARCY! Tell Bibberty what you think of the fences.'

Darcy comes carefully down the stairs one at a time, concentrating on each step. Then she lifts her head, sees Liberty and her bandmates and says, 'You mustn't wear double denim.'

Everyone laughs, except Freddy, who's wearing double denim.

Liberty takes Darcy's hand. 'Have you seen the garden?'

Darcy squints at the sunshine, and takes a long time to scan the new, open front lawn and street.

'Yes.'

'Do you like the change?'

'I can see the postbox.'

'Yes. And you'll be able to see me coming home,' says Liberty. 'So you don't need to worry anymore.'

'So we all like the change, right?' I say.

'I love it.' Liberty gives me a hug tight enough for me to feel her bones. 'You're the best, Mama. Thank you.'

'What about your exam results then, Libs?' Nick asks. 'Good news?'

'I did okay,' says Liberty. More hair flicking.

Freddy shows beautiful white teeth. 'We all got As across the board, Mrs Armstrong.' His smile falters. 'Except for one C in my case. Home Economics. The teacher warned me soufflés are tricky under exam conditions. I should have listened.'

'Well done all of you. Wow. That's *amazing*.' I grin at Liberty. 'How did I get the honour of regular dinners with a girl genius and her genius friends, huh? Lucky me.'

'The food looks wonderful, Mrs Armstrong,' says Freddy. 'Thank you for all your hard work.'

'Yes, thank you, Mrs Armstrong and Mr Armstrong,' says Abi.

They're such good kids. I can't think why I was so afraid of Liberty hanging out with them.

'I hope you're hungry,' I say. 'And everything is vegan. Plant-based. Nick and I have been obsessively checking supermarket labels.'

'Plant-based?' Liberty's eyes widen. 'As in plants cruelly ripped out of the ground? I'm not up for torturing vegetables anymore, Mum. I've decided to only eat foods that have fallen naturally to the ground. Fruit, basically.'

I stare at her. 'But … I bought this vegan cheese and shredded two knuckles grating it over the salad. Do you know how hard it is to prepare rubber cheese?'

Liberty and her bandmates snigger. Nick is laughing too. Darcy watches everyone's faces closely, completely confused.

'Oh, right.' I put a hand to my cheek. 'It's a hilarious joke. Very funny.'

Liberty throws a long arm around my shoulder. 'I have to tease you sometimes, Mama. Or you'd take life too seriously. Thank you for the dinner. It looks amazing. And thank you for taking the fences down.'

'It's okay,' I say. 'It was hard. It's made me realize you'll leave me one day.' My lip starts to wobble and I feel hot tears welling up.

'But not today.' Liberty squeezes my shoulder. She shakes her head at her friends. 'Parents. They're so emotional, aren't they? Must be the hormones. Hey, Mum – what time is Cannon getting here?'

'Cat?' I check my watch. 'You really should call her Nanna or Grandma or something … I don't know … more respectable.'

'She won't let me. She says it makes her feel old.'

'She'll be here any minute.'

'Cat won't make us chant before we eat again, will she?' asks Liberty.

'Oh, please no,' says Nick. 'It took *hours* last time.'

'Come on, guys,' I say. 'You know Cat comes from a good place. And she's been amazing for Liberty's band. Not many teenagers get to record at Britannia Studios.'

'Yeah, I got lucky with one of my long-lost relatives,' says Liberty. 'The other one … not so much. But hey. You can't choose your family, right?'

I think, *usually you can't.*

But if I had to choose Liberty again, and everything that came with her, I'd choose her a million times over.

Thank you for reading

If you have a minute, please review.
I read all my reviews (yes, the bad ones do make
me cry) and good reviews mean everything.
Reviews don't have to be fancy. In fact, just one
word is great (as long as it isn't 'shit' ...). And they
do more good than you could ever imagine.

Suzy K Quinn xx

Acknowledgements

This book was completed just as Covid-19 hit the UK, so thanks go to more people than I can possibly include in a few paragraphs.

Thank you to hospital workers, supermarket workers, delivery drivers and everyone who is keeping our world running and risking their own health during the process.

Huge thanks to my amazing editor, Emily Kitchin, for doing a stand-out awesome job with this book and fielding questions about hairy covers. Thank you to all the team at HQ for being heroic and upbeat during a global crisis. Thank you to my partner, Demi, and my sis, Cath, for being the very best readers and critics. And thanks to all my readers.

Peace and love to you all – and hopefully by the time you read this, the pandemic will have passed, and we will be an even more connected and caring world.

Turn the page for an extract from the
gripping and addictive psychological thriller
from Suzy K Quinn, *Don't Tell Teacher...*

Prologue

We're running. Along wide, tree-lined pavements, over the zebra crossing and into the park.

'Quick, Tom.'

Tom struggles to keep up, tired little legs bobbing up and down on trimmed grass. He gasps for breath.

My ribs throb, lighting up in pain.

A Victorian bandstand and a rainbow of flowerbeds flash past. Dimly, I notice wicker picnic hampers, Prosecco, Pimm's in plastic glasses.

No one notices us. The frightened mother with straight, brown hair, wearing her husband's choice of clothes. The little boy in tears.

That's the thing about the city. Nobody notices.

There's a giant privet hedge by the railings, big enough to hide in.

Tom cries harder. I cuddle him in my arms. 'Don't make a sound,' I whisper, heart racing. 'Don't make a sound.'

Tom nods rapidly.

We both clutch each other, terrified. I shiver, even though it's a warm summer's day.

Tom gives a choked sob. 'Will he find us, Mum?'

'Shush,' I say, crouching in my flat leather sandals, summer dress flowing over my knees. 'Please, Tom. We have to be quiet.'

'I'm scared.' Tom clasps my bare arm.

'I know, sweetheart,' I whisper, holding his head against my shoulder. 'We're going away. Far away from him.'

'What if he gets me at school?'

'We'll find a new school. One he doesn't know about. Okay?'

Tom's chest is against mine, his breathing fast.

He understands that we can't be found.

Olly is capable of anything.

Lizzie

Monday. School starts. It won't be like the last place, Tom knows that. It will be hard, being the new kid.

'Come on, Tommo,' I call up the stairs. 'Let's go go go. We don't want to be late on our first day.'

I pack Tom's school bag, then give my hair a few quick brushes, checking my reflection in the hallway mirror.

A pale, worried face stares back at me. Pointy little features, a heart-shaped chin, brown hair, long and ruler-straight.

The invisible woman.

Olly's broken ex-wife.

I want to change that. I want to be someone different here. No one needs to know how things were before.

Tom clatters down the polished, wooden staircase in his new Steelfield school uniform. I throw my arms around him.

'A hug to make you grow big and strong,' I say. 'You get taller with every cuddle. Did you know that?'

'I know, Mum. You tell me every morning.'

I hand him his blue wool coat. I've always liked this colour against Tom's bright blond hair and pale skin. The coat is from last winter, but he still hasn't grown out of it. Tom is small for his age; at nearly nine he looks more like seven.

We head out and onto the muddy track, stopping at a blackberry bush to pick berries.

Tom counts as he eats and sings.

'*One, two, three, four, five – to stay alive.*'

'It's going to be exciting,' I coax as Tom and I pass the school playing field. 'Look at all that grass. You didn't have that in London. And they've got a little woodland bit.' I point to the trees edging the field. 'And full-sized goalposts.'

'What if Dad finds us?' Tom watches the stony ground.

'He won't. Don't worry. We're safe here.'

'I like our new house,' says Tom. 'It's a family house. Like in *Peter Pan*.'

We walk on in silence and birds skitter across the path.

Tom says, 'Hello, birds. Do you live here? Oh – did you hurt your leg, little birdy? I hope you feel better soon.'

They really are beautiful school grounds – huge and tree-lined, with bright green grass. Up ahead there is a silver, glimmering spider's web tangled through the fence wire: an old bike chain bent around to repair a hole.

I wonder, briefly, why there is a hole in the fence. I'm sure there's some logical explanation. This is an excellent school … But I've never seen a fence this tall around a school. It's like a zoo enclosure.

I feel uneasy, thinking of children caged like animals.

A cage is safe. Think of it that way.

The school building sits at the front of the field, a large Victorian structure with a tarmac playground. There are no lively murals, like at Tom's last school. Just spikey grey railings and towering, arched gates.

A shiny sign says:

STEELFIELD SCHOOL: AN OUTSTANDING
EDUCATIONAL ESTABLISHMENT
HEADMASTER: ALAN COCKRUN, BA HONS
SEMPER FORTIS – ALWAYS STRONG

The downstairs windows have bars on them, which feel a little sinister and an odd paradox to the holes in the fence. And one window – a small one by the main door – has blacked-out glass, a sleeping eye twinkling in the sun.

The playground is a spotless black lake. No scooter marks or trodden-in chewing gum. I've never seen a school so clean.

We approach the main road, joining a swarm of kids battling for pavement position.

Most of the kids are orderly and well-behaved. No chatting or playing. However, three boys stand out with their neon, scruffy shoes, angry faces and thick, shaggy black hair.

Brothers, I decide.

They are pushing and shoving each other, fighting over a football. The tallest of the boys notices Tom and me coming up the lane. 'Who are *you*?' He bounces his football hard on the concrete, glaring.

I put a hand on Tom's shoulder. 'Come on, Tommo. Nearly there.'

The shortest of the three boys shouts, 'Oo, oo. London *town-ies*'.

I call after them, 'Hey. Hey! *Excuse* me—'

But they're running now, laughing and careering through the school gates.

How do they know we're from London?

'It's okay, Mum,' says Tom.

My hand tenses on his shoulder. 'I should say something.'

'They don't know me yet,' Tom whispers. 'That's all. When they get to know me, it'll be okay.'

My wise little eight-year-old. Tom has always been that way. Very in tune with people. But I am worried about bullying. Vulnerable children are easy targets. Social services told me that.

It will be hard for him …

As the three black-haired brothers head into the school yard, a remarkable change takes place. They stop jostling and pushing each other and walk sensibly, arms by their sides, mouths closed in angry lines.

Tom and I walk alongside the railings, approaching the open gates.

It's funny – I'd expected this new academy school to be shiny and modern. Not to have grey brick walls, a bell tower, slate turrets and bars.

I sweep away thoughts of prisons and haunted houses and tell Tom, 'Well, this is exciting. Look – there's hopscotch.'

Tom doesn't reply, his eyes wide at the shadowy brickwork.

'This is my *school*?' he asks, bewildered. 'It looks like an old castle.'

'Well, castles are fun. Maybe you can play knights or something. I know it's different from the last place.'

'Castles have ghosts,' Tom whispers.

'Oh, no they don't. Anyway, big nearly-nine-year-old ghost-busters aren't afraid of ghosts.'

We move towards the school gates, which are huge with spikes along the top, and I put on an even brighter voice. 'You're going to do great today, Tom. I love you so much. Stay cool, okay? High five?'

Tom gives me a weak high five.

'Will *you* be okay, Mum?' he asks.

My eyes well up. 'Of course. I'll be fine. It's not your job to worry about me. It's mine to worry about you.'

Tom turns towards the soulless tarmac and asks, 'Aren't you coming in with me?'

'Parents aren't allowed into the playground here,' I say. 'Someone from the office phoned to tell me. Something to do with safety.'

Two of the black-haired boys are fighting in a secluded corner near a netball post, a pile of tussling limbs.

'Those Neilson boys,' I hear a voice mutter beside me – a mother dropping off her daughter. 'Can't go five minutes without killing each other.'

The headmaster appears in the entranceway then – an immaculately presented man wearing a pinstripe suit and royal-blue tie. His hair is brown, neatly cut and combed, and he is clean-shaven with a boyish face that has a slightly rubbery, clown-like quality.

Hands in pockets, he surveys the playground. He is smiling, lips oddly red and jester-shaped, but his blue eyes remain cold and hard.

The chattering parents spot him and fall silent.

The headmaster approaches the corner where the boys are fighting and stops to watch, still smiling his cold smile.

After a moment, the boys sense the headmaster and quickly untangle themselves, standing straight, expressions fearful.

It's a little creepy how all this is done in near silence, but I suppose at least the headmaster can keep order. Tom's last school was chaos. Too many pupils and no control.

I kneel down to Tom and whisper, 'Have a good day at school. I love you so much. Don't think about Dad.' I stroke Tom's chin-length blond hair, left loose around his ears today. More conventional, I thought. Less like his father. 'How are you feeling?'

'I'm scared, Mum,' says Tom. 'I don't want to leave you alone all day. What if Dad—'

I cut Tom off with a shake of my head and give him a thumbs-up. 'It's fine. We're safe now, okay? He has no idea where we are.' Then I hug him, burying my face in his fine hair.

'I love you, Mum,' says Tom.

'I love you too.' I step back, smiling encouragingly. 'Go on then. You'll be a big kid – going into class all by yourself. They'll call you Tom Kinnock in the register. Social services gave them your old name. But remember you're Riley now. Tom Riley.'

Tom wanders into the playground, a tiny figure drowned by a huge Transformers bag. He really is small for nearly nine. And thin too, with bony arms and legs.

Someone kicks a ball towards him, and Tom reacts with his feet – probably without thinking.

A minute later, he's kicking a football with a group of lads, including two of the black-haired boys who were fighting before. The ball is kicked viciously by those boys, booted at children's faces.

I'm anxious. Those kids look like trouble.

As I'm watching, the headmaster crosses the playground. Mr Cockrun. Yes. That's his name. He'd never get away with that at a secondary school. His smile fades as he approaches the gate.

'Hello there,' he says. 'You must be Mrs Kinnock.'

The way he says our old surname ... I don't feel especially welcomed.

'Riley now,' I say. 'Miss Riley. Our social worker—'

'Best not to hang around once they've gone inside,' says Mr Cockrun, giving me a full politician's smile and flashing straight, white teeth. 'It can be unsettling, especially for the younger ones. And it's also a safeguarding issue.' He pulls a large bunch of keys from his pocket. 'They're always fine when the parents are gone.'

Mr Cockrun tugs at the stiff gate. It makes a horrible screech as metal drags along a tarmac trench, orange with rust. Then he takes the bulky chain that hangs from it and wraps it around three times before securing it with a gorilla padlock. He tests the arrangement, pulling at the chain.

'Safe as houses,' he tells me through the gates.

'Why the padlock?' I ask, seeing Tom small and trapped on the other side of the railings.

Mr Cockrun's cheerful expression falters. 'I beg your pardon?'

'Why have you padlocked the gate?' I don't mean to raise my voice. Other parents are looking. But it feels sinister.

'For safeguarding. Fail to safeguard the children and we fail everything.'

'Yes, but—'

'Mrs Kinnock, this is an outstanding school. We know what we're doing.'

I pull my coat around myself, holding back a shiver. It's a very ordinary wool coat, bought while I was with Olly.

I was a shadow then, of course. Hiding behind my husband.

I'm hoping that will change here.

'It feels like I'm leaving Tom in prison,' I say, trying for a little laugh.

Mr Cockrun meets my eye, his hard, black pupils unwavering. 'There is a *very* long waiting list for this school, Mrs Kinnock. Thanks to social services, your son jumped right to the top. I'd have thought you'd be the last parent to criticise.'

'I didn't mean to—'

'We usually pick and choose who we let in.' The politician's smile returns. 'Let's make sure we're on the same page, Mrs Kinnock. Not start off on the wrong foot.'

He strolls back to the school building, and I'm left watching and wondering.

When I get back to our new Victorian house with its large, wraparound garden and elegant porch pillars, I sit on the front wall, put my head in my hands and cry.

I try not to make a sound, but sobs escape through my fingers.

Things will get better.

Of course I'm going to feel emotional on his first day.

Lizzie

I've been invited to a party, but I'm on the outside, not knowing what to do with myself. I'm not a skier or snowboarder, so I'm ... nowhere. Standing on the balcony, looking at the mountains, I feel very alone.

Morzine is one of the world's best ski resorts. I've heard it described as 'electric' after dark. Tomorrow, the slopes will be tingling with pink, white and yellow snowsuits. But tonight, they're white and calm.

It sounded so adventurous, being a chalet girl out here. But the truth is, I'm running away. Things with Mum are unbearable again. I thought they'd be better after university, but if anything they're worse. Her need to tear me down is stronger than ever.

It's not about blame.

All I know is that I needed to get away, for my own sanity.

Behind me, Olympic hopefuls talk and laugh in their day clothes, drinking sparkling water or, if they're real rebels, small bottles of beer.

Most of them aren't interested in a twenty-something chalet girl with straight, brown hair and floral-patterned Doc Marten boots.

But ... someone has come to stand beside me. He's a tall,

blond man wearing ripped jeans and a loose, light pink T-shirt. His light tan and white panda eyes tell me he's a skier or snowboarder – probably a serious one, if the other guests at this party are anything to go by.

'It's Lizzie,' the man asks. 'Isn't it?'

'How do you know my name?'

'You're still wearing your name badge.'

I glance down and see my health and safety training sticker: Lizzie Riley.

'You don't remember me?' the man challenges, raising a thick, blond eyebrow.

'I'm sorry, I don't—'

'Olly.' He holds out a large hand for me to shake. 'I'm staying in the chalet next to you. With the Olympic rabble over there.' He points to a rowdy group of young men holding beers. 'You're a chalet girl, right?' He grins. 'Nice work if you can get it.'

'Actually, it can be exhausting,' I say.

Olly laughs. 'Are you thinking about jumping off the mountain then?'

My smile disappears. 'No. Why would you ask that?'

'Just joking.'

We stare out at the peaks for a minute.

A live band strikes up behind us, playing a Beatles cover – 'Love Me Do'.

Olly's shoulders move to the music.

Mine do too.

'You like the Beatles?' Olly asks.

'Yes.' I look at him shyly, hoping this is the right answer.

'Me too! I have a massive collection of Sixties vinyl.'

'You collect vinyl?' I ask.

'No, well … not really. Most of my records are my mum's. She listens to CDs now. It feels like time-travelling when I play vinyl, you know? Like I'm part of the swinging Sixties.'

'Olly!' A tall, red-cheeked man swaggers over, holding out a beer bottle. 'Olly Kinnock. This is supposed to be a lads' night out and here you are chatting up girls again.'

Olly smiles at me, staring with blue, blue eyes. 'Not girls. A girl. A very interesting girl.'

I feel myself blushing.

'Fair enough,' announces the red-cheeked man, thrusting the beer into Olly's hand. 'We'll see you in the morning then.' He returns to his group of friends, who break into guffaws of laughter.

'Sorry about them,' says Olly, putting his elbow on the balcony and, in the process, leaning nearer to me. 'They can be morons.'

'You can go back to them if you like.'

'Actually, I've always preferred female company,' says Olly. 'Girls smell better. But you must have a boyfriend, surely? A pretty girl like you. So tell me to get lost if you want.'

I blush again and stammer, 'Um … no, I don't have a boy-friend.'

'Have a drink with me then.'

Surely he's just teasing me? Handsome snowboarders don't chat up chalet girls. And he really is handsome, with his lean, toned arms and perfect white teeth.

His eyes are serious, holding my gaze.

Maybe he isn't joking.

'Okay,' I hear myself say. 'Why not?'

'It's a date.' Olly takes my hand like he's won a prize.

I laugh, sucking in my breath as his strong fingers close around mine.

'So what are you drinking?' Olly asks.

'Um ... white wine?'

'Chardonnay?'

'Sure. Yes please.'

He winks at me. 'I love Chardonnay. Best wine ever. Just don't tell the lads. It's a bit girly. I've been noticing you for weeks, Lizzie Riley. I think we should spend lots and lots of time together. And then get married.'

I can barely believe this is happening. A nobody chalet girl like me, being chatted up by this confident, tanned athlete. I guess I should enjoy it while it lasts. When he works out what a nothing I am, he'll run a mile.

I laugh. 'Are you always so forward with your wedding plans?'

'Only with my future wife.'

'You don't even know me.'

'Yes, but I've been watching you and your purple puffer jacket for ages, wondering how you don't freeze to death in those DM boots.'

'Where have you noticed me?'

'Drinking black coffee in the café, buying a ginger cookie and giving crumbs to the birds on your way out. Always carrying a pile of books under your arm. Are you a student?'

'I'm training to be a nurse.'

'A nurse? Well, Lizzie Nightingale, you'll have to put your career aside when you have my five children.'

'Five children?'

'At least five. And I hope they all look just like you.'

Our eyes meet, and in that second I feel totally, utterly alive.

I've never been noticed like this.

It's electrifying.

And I feel myself hoping, like I've never hoped before, that this man feels the same sparks in his chest as I do.

Kate

I'm eating Kellogg's All-Bran at my desk, silently chanting my morning mantra: *Be grateful, Kate. Be grateful. This is the job you wanted.*

Apparently, social workers suffer more nervous breakdowns than any other profession.

I already have stress-related eczema, insomnia and an unhealthy relationship with the office vending machine – specifically the coils holding the KitKats and Mars bars.

Last night I got home at 9 p.m., and this morning I was called in at 7.30 a.m. I have a huge caseload and I'm fire-fighting. There isn't time to help anyone. Just prevent disaster.

Be grateful, Kate.

My computer screen displays my caseload: thirty children.

This morning, I've had to add one more. A transfer case from Hammersmith and Fulham: Tom Kinnock.

I click update and watch my screen change: thirty-one children.

Then I put my head in my hands, already exhausted by what I won't manage to do today.

Be grateful, Kate. You have a proper grown-up job. You're one of the lucky ones.

My husband Col is a qualified occupational therapist, but he's working at the Odeon cinema. It could be worse. At least he gets free popcorn.

'Well, you're bright and shiny, aren't you?' Tessa Warwick, my manager, strides into the office, clicking on her Nespresso machine – a personal cappuccino maker she won't let anyone else use.

I jolt upright and start tapping keys.

'And what's that, a new hairdo?' Tessa is a big, shouty lady with high blood pressure and red cheeks. Her brown hair is wiry and cut into a slightly wonky bob. She wears a lot of polyester.

'I've just tied it back, that's all,' I say, pulling my curly black hair tighter in its hairband. 'I'm not really a new hairdo sort of person.'

I've had the same hair since I was eight years old – long and curly, sometimes up, sometimes down. No layers. Just long.

'I might have known. Yes, you're very, very sensible, aren't you?'

This is a dig at me, but I don't mind because Tessa is absolutely right. I wear plain, functional trouser suits and no makeup. My glasses are from the twenty-pound range at Specsavers. I've never signed up for monthly contact lenses – I'd rather put money in my savings account.

'I'm glad you're in early anyway,' Tessa continues. 'There is a *lot* to do this week.'

'I know,' I say. 'Leanne Neilson is in hospital again. Gary and I were up until nine on Friday trying to get her boys into bed. I just need time to get going.'

Gary is a family support worker and absolutely should have

finished at 5 p.m. So should I, actually. But two out-of-hours team members were off sick and we were swamped.

Tessa inserts a cappuccino tablet into her Nespresso machine. 'So you were babysitting the three Neilson scallywags?' She gives a snort of laughter. 'They're like child versions of the Gallagher brothers, those boys. All that black hair, fighting all the time. You never know – maybe they'll be famous musicians. But *you* shouldn't have been putting them to bed. You should be in the pub of an evening, like a normal twenty-something.'

It's a bone of contention between us – the fact I rarely drink alcohol. Also, that I married at twenty years old and go to church twice a week.

'Jesus drank, didn't he?' Tessa continues. 'I thought it would be okay for you lot.'

'Us lot?'

'You young churchy types. You'll be drinking soon,' Tessa predicts. 'Just you wait. You're new to this, but everyone ends up on the lunchtime wine eventually. Now listen – have you done the home visit for that transfer case yet? From Hammersmith and Fulham, Tom Kinnock? The one with the angry dad.'

'No. I sent a letter on Friday. She'll get it today.'

'Get on to that one as soon as you can, Kate. The transfer was weeks late. There'll already be some catching up to do. Have they got him a school place?'

'Yes. At Steelfield School.'

'I bet the headmaster is furious,' laughs Tessa. '"More social services children thrust upon us ... we already have the Neilson boys to deal with."'

'I'm not sure a high-achieving school is the right environment for Tom Kinnock,' I say. 'Very strict and results obsessed. After what this boy has been through, maybe he needs somewhere more nurturing.'

'Don't worry about the school,' says Tessa. 'Steelfield is a godsend. They keep the kids in line. No chair throwing or teacher nervous breakdowns. Just worry about getting that case shut down ASAP. The father is a risk factor, but all the dirty work is done.'

'I'm pretty overwhelmed here, Tessa.'

'Welcome to social work.' Tessa gives her Nespresso machine a brief thump with a closed fist.

Lizzie

A brown envelope, addressed formally to Elizabeth Kinnock. The mottled paper has a muddy shoeprint from where I stepped on it.

I study the postmark. It's from the county council, i.e. social services. I know these sorts of letters from when we lived with Olly. *We'd like to meet to discuss your son …*

I should have known social services would want to meet us. Check we're settling into our new life. But we don't need any of that official stuff now. Olly is gone.

My fingers want to scrunch the brown paper into a tight ball, then push the letter deep down into the paper recycling, under the organic ready-meal sleeves and junk mail. Stuff away bad memories of an old life, now gone.

But instead I shelve the letter by the bread bin, resolving to open it after a cup of tea. There are other letters to read first.

I sit on the Chesterfield sofa-arm and slide my fingers under paper folds, tearing and pulling free replies to my many job applications. They're all rejections – I'd guessed as much, given the timing of the letters. If you get the job, they mail you straight away.

I look around the growing chaos that is our new house. There are toys everywhere, children's books, a blanket and pillow for when Tom dozes on the sofa. Really, it's hard enough keeping on top of all this, let alone finding a job too.

The house was beautiful when we moved in over the summer – varnished floorboards, cosy living room with a real fireplace, huge, light kitchen and roaming garden full of fruit trees.

But all too quickly it got messy, like my life.

I have that feeling again.

The 'I can't manage alone' feeling.

I squash it down.

I am strong. Capable. Tom and I *can* have a life without Olly. More importantly, we *must* have a life without him.

There's no way back.

A memory unzips itself – me, crying and shaking, cowering in a bathtub as Olly's knuckles pound on the door. Sharp and brutal.

Tears come. It *will* be different here.

I head up to the bathroom with its tasteful butler sink and free-standing Victorian bathtub on little wrought-iron legs. From the porcelain toothbrush holder I take hairdressing scissors – the ones I use to trim Tom's fine, blond hair.

I pick up a long strand of my mousy old life and cut. Then I take another, and another. Turning to the side, I strip strands from my crown, shearing randomly.

Before I know it, half my hair lies in the bathroom sink.

Now I have something approaching a pixie cut – short hair, clipped close to my head. I do a little shaping around the ears and find myself surprised and pleased with the result.

Maybe I should be a hairdresser instead of a nurse, I think.

I fought so hard to finish my nurse's training, but never did. Olly was jealous from the start. He hated me having any sort of identity.

Turning my head again in the mirror, I see myself smile. I really do like what I see. My hair is much more interesting than before, that mousy woman with non-descript brown hair.

I'm somebody who stands out.

Gets things done.

No more living in the shadows.

It won't be how things were with Olly, when I was meek little Lizzie, shrinking at his temper.

Things will be different.

As I start tidying the house, my phone rings its generic tone. I should change that too. Get a ring tone that represents who I am. It's time to find myself. Be someone. Not invisible, part of someone else.

My mother's name glows on the phone screen.

Ruth Riley.

Such a formal way to store a mother's number. I'm sure most people use 'Mum' or 'Mummy' or something.

I grab the phone. 'Hi, Mum.'

There's a pause, and a rickety intake of breath. 'Did you get Tom to school on time?'

'Of course.'

'Because it's important, Elizabeth. On his first day. To make a good impression.'

'I don't care what other people think,' I say. 'I care about Tom.'

'Well, you should care, Elizabeth. You've moved to a nice area. The families around there will have their eyes on you. It's not like that pokey little apartment you had in London.'

'It was a penthouse apartment and no smaller than the house we had growing up,' I point out. 'We lived in a two-bed terrace with Dad. Remember?'

'Oh, what nonsense, Elizabeth. We had a conservatory.'

Actually, it was a corrugated plastic lean-to. But my mother has never let the truth get in the way of a good story.

'I was planning to visit you again this weekend,' says Mum. 'To help out.'

I want to laugh. Mum does the opposite of help out. She demands that a meal is cooked, then criticises my organisational skills.

'You don't have to,' I say.

'I *want* to.'

'Why this sudden interest in us, Mum? You never visited when we lived with Olly.'

'Don't be silly, Elizabeth,' Mum snaps. 'You're a single parent now. You need my help.' A pause. 'I read in the *Sunday Times* that Steelfield School is one of the top fifty state schools.'

'Is it?'

'Yes. Make sure you dress smartly for pick-ups and drop-offs. I paid a personal visit to the headmaster this morning. To impress upon him what a good family we are.'

I laugh. 'You didn't think to ask me first?'

My mother ignores this comment. 'The headmaster was charming. Very presentable too. He tells me Tom is lucky to have a place there. Make sure you put a good face on.'

'Social services got us that place. I'd feel luckier not to have a social worker.'

'Elizabeth.' Mum's voice is tight. She hates it when I mention social workers. 'Don't be ungrateful.'

'You really shouldn't have visited the school, Mum,' I say. 'Teachers are busy enough.'

'Nonsense,' says Mum. 'You need to make a good impression

and for that you need my help. You never could do that on your own.'

'I appreciate you trying to help. I really do. But can you *ask* in future? Before you do things like visiting Tom's school? It feels a bit … I don't know, intrusive.'

I feel Mum's annoyance in the silence that follows. And I become that needy little girl again, doing anything to win back her favour.

'Sorry,' I say. 'Forget I said that. It's wonderful you visited Tom's headmaster. Look, come and visit whenever you like.'

When I hang up, I think about Olly.

You miss him sometimes. Admit it.

The voice comes out of nowhere and I try to squash it down.

Of course there were good times. But if I want to remember the good times, I have to remember the bad ones.

Do you remember him screaming at you? Calling you every name under the sun? And worse, so much worse … Saying things too shameful to think about.

How I could fall in love with someone who wanted to tear me apart?

Lizzie

'So why the blindfold?' I ask, as Olly leads me over crunching snow.

'Because you like surprises.'

Did I say that?

This has all been such a whirlwind. I'm insecure, certain our romance will be over when Olly finds out he's too good for me.

'This way,' says Olly, and I hear a chalet door creak. 'Welcome home.'

'Home?'

'My chalet.' Olly unties my blindfold. 'Where you'll be sleeping for the rest of the ski season.'

I laugh. 'You'll be lucky.'

As my eyes adjust to the light, I see a cosy sofa area and Chardonnay, a bowl of Pringles and glittering tealights laid on a chunky, wooden dining table.

'I'm calling this evening "Lizzie's favourites",' says Olly, plugging his phone into a speaker. 'Your favourite food. Favourite music. Favourite everything. I've got sea bass.' He goes to the fridge and slaps a wax-paper packet of fish on the kitchen counter. 'New potatoes in the oven. Lots of tomato ketchup in the fridge, because we're both philistines.' He winks. 'Sour-cream Pringles to start. And Joni Mitchell on the stereo.

Oh – and black forest gateaux for dessert. The one you like from the café.'

I smile, shaking my head in disbelief. 'You did all this for me?'

'Just for you. Right this way, madam.' He hesitates when he sees my face. 'Hey. Lizzie? Are you okay?'

'Yes. Really, I'm fine.'

'Lizzie.' Olly pulls me close. 'What's the matter? Did I do something wrong?'

I shake my head against his chest, tears pressing into his shirt. 'No. Not at all. The opposite.'

'The opposite?'

'All this for me. I don't deserve it.'

Olly laughs then, his big, cheery, confident laugh. 'You deserve this and much, much more.' He kisses my head and hugs me for a long time. 'Okay?'

I nod. 'Okay.'

'Let the evening commence!' He leads me to the table, snatching up a purple napkin. 'Your favourite colour.' He grins, opening the napkin with a flourish.

Purple isn't really my favourite colour. It's just the colour of the coat I wear. But I don't tell Olly that.

We eat Pringles, sea bass and new potatoes, drink Chardonnay and listen to Joni Mitchell. Then Olly lights a fire.

'I borrowed a Monopoly board,' says Olly, leading me to the sofa area. 'Your favourite game, right? And mine too, actually. Come on. You can thrash me.'

'Love to,' I say.

'Of course, we could play strip poker instead,' says Olly, flashing his lovely white teeth.

26

I'm hit by an uneasy feeling that this evening might be too traditional for Olly. The wine, the fire, the board game. What if he thinks I'm boring?

'I have an idea,' I say. 'How about strip Monopoly?'

'Strip Monopoly?' says Olly. 'You're on!'

We make up a few rules, deciding to lose an item of clothing every time we land on the other person's property. Then we start playing.

It doesn't take long before I'm down to my underwear.

'Are you cheating?' I accuse, taking off my bra.

Olly watches me, mesmerised. Then he says, 'You're beautiful, do you know that? Hurry up and roll again.'

'It's your turn,' I protest.

Olly struggles out of his clothes, revealing a beautiful toned body and crazy orange tan lines at his wrists and collarbone. Then he stands to remove his underwear.

'Turn taken,' he announces, standing naked. 'Now roll again.'

'That's definitely cheating,' I laugh, shy now. 'You can't take all your clothes off at once.'

'How dare you!' Olly protests. 'I am a serious rules-body. Well, if you think the game has been compromised, we'll just have to abandon it.'

He lifts me into his arms.

'But you were winning,' I laugh, as Olly carries me outside to the hot tub.

'I declare it a draw.'

Olly lowers me carefully into the bubbling water. Then he climbs into the tub himself and slides me onto his lap, arranging my legs so I'm kneeling around his hips.

'I need to learn more of your favourites,' he says, kissing me fiercely, hand moving up and down between my thighs.

Snow falls on the warm water and our bare shoulders.

I moan, but suddenly Olly pulls back.

'Wait.' He's breathless. 'I don't want to move too fast.'

'It's fine.'

'You're sure? Listen, really I can wait. I don't want this to be some quick thing. You're more than that to me.'

I must look upset, because Olly says: 'Hey. It's okay. Really. I'll get you a towel and you can have my bed, okay? I'll take the sofa.'

'No,' I insist, gripping his arms. 'I want this. Honestly, I want this. It's just ... I've never felt this way either. I've never been ... special.'

'You are special,' says Olly. 'The most special girl I've ever met.'

He kisses me again and I'm lost.

We make love in the hot tub and then again on Olly's bed. He's gentle at times, firm at others. He's considerate, but sometimes teeters on the brink of losing control.

In the morning, Olly makes me waffles covered in syrup and a sugary hot chocolate. Then we have sex again before I sneak back to my chalet to prepare breakfast for my host family.

While I'm whisking up scrambled eggs, my phone bleeps. It's a message from Olly: I miss you already.

I feel soft warmth in my chest, but also anxiety.

This is amazing. The most amazing thing that's ever happened to me. But how can something like this last? Half the things Olly thinks we both 'love', I only like a little bit. Like sea bass, tomato ketchup and syrup-covered waffles with sweet *hot chocolate. I've exaggerated so he'll think we have things in common, scared that boring little me isn't good enough.*

Oh, what does it matter?

I'm probably just a sexual conquest and Olly will forget all about me in a few days.

This can't last.

It's too good to be true.

FREE E-BOOK

WHEN YOU SIGN UP TO SUZY'S NEWSLETTER

Exclusive book download, cover reveals and launch news when you sign up for Suzy's newsletter at

WWW.SUZYKQUINN.COM/SUZYNEWS